I0729321

Chocolate Dreams
The Candy Beach Series

Interior Format

Chocolate DREAMS

Cecelia Dowdy

Praise for
Cecelia Dowdy's Writing

Dowdy writes with the right touch to keep the readers engaged and vested…
- *USA Today*

CHAPTER 1

THE LOUD BANGING at Monica Crawford's front door awakened her. She shoved the blanket away and peeked at the clock on her bedside table. Two in the morning. Who could that be?

"I'm coming!"

Still groggy, she forced herself to wake up as she trudged down the stairs toward the front door. She slipped and her foot banged against the paneled wall. Pain shot through her foot like liquid fire. Her eyes smarted with unshed tears as she peered through the peephole at her front door. She spotted her little sister Gina smiling at her.

Her heart pounded as she opened the door, gripping the knob. "What are you doing here?" Playing an internal game of tug-of-war, she wondered if she should hug her sister or slam the door in her face. Humid heat rushed into the air-conditioned living room. She stared at Gina, still awaiting her response.

"It's nice to see you too, sister." Gina pursed her full, red-painted lips and motioned at the child standing beside her. "Go on in, Scotty."

Gina had brought her seven-year-old son with her. Dark shades hid his sightless eyes. "Aunt Monica?" His little-boy voice hesitated…his tone seemed wary. That figured. Gina had probably promised him so many things since they'd been missing over the last couple of years. His poor little hopes had probably been shattered.

Her mouth quivered as she dropped to her knees and embraced him. "I'm here, Scotty." She swiped away her tears as she hugged the child. Since Gina had cut herself off from immediate family for the last two years, Monica had wondered when she would see Scotty again.

"You remember me?" Her heart continued to pound as she stared at her nephew. His light, coffee-colored skin glowed.

"Yeah, I remember you. When Mom said I was going to live here, I wanted to come so we could go to the beach in Ocean City."

Shocked, Monica stared at Gina, who was rummaging through her purse. Gina pulled out a cigarette and lighter. Seconds later she was puffing away, studying the living room. "You got an ashtray?" She wondered if her sister was actually looking for something that she could steal and pawn. She had a gold necklace that had disappeared around the same time that Gina had gone missing. *Lord, forgive me for that angry thought.*

Stop judging. She forced those words into her mind. She swallowed and continued silently praying, hoping she wouldn't lose her temper. "Gina, you know I don't allow smoking in this house."

Gina shrugged. After a bit of coaxing, she dropped the cigarette on the top step and ground it beneath the heel of her shoe. "I need to talk to you about something." Scotty slowly walked into the house.

"Scotty be careful." She said the words a bit too late as he bumped into her coffee table. The half-filled glass of water tumbled from the table onto her carpeted floor.

His breath caught. "Did I make a mess?"

She limped toward him, her foot still smarting with pain. "No big deal. It's just a glass of water. I figure it'll take a while for you to know your way around here." She took a deep breath. She figured it wouldn't take Scotty long to learn his way around her place. Since he was born blind, he was used to getting around without his sight. She recalled the red and white cane that he used to use. "What happened to your cane."

"It's in my suitcase. I only use that when I'm out in public." She eyed her laptop sitting on top of the coffee table. She turned it on and soon a Christian rap artist belted hip-hop lyrics through the room. She recalled how much Scotty loved music. Sitting on the couch, he swayed his little body to the beat.

Gina stood, staring at them. She narrowed her eyes…what was she thinking? If she didn't know better, she'd think that Gina was jealous that she was actually bonding with Scotty. Well, she didn't have time to think about why her sister suddenly seemed upset. She needed to talk to her alone, and she couldn't do that with Scotty sitting with them in the living room.

"Are you hungry?"

"I'm starving. Aunt Monica, we haven't had anything to eat since breakfast. All we had was some toast and juice." Horrified, she didn't want Scotty to know how angry she was at Gina for not feeding him all day.

She took a deep breath and left him bopping to the music in the living room. She quickly rushed to the kitchen and pulled out her iron skillet, a carton of eggs, a block of cheese. The last time she'd seen Scotty, when he was five, his favorite meal had been a hot, gooey cheese omelet, toast and orange juice. She made a mental note to get orange juice the next time she went to the store. She heard Gina quietly talking to Scotty as she cooked two omelets. She sprinkled them with salt and pepper. When toast popped out of the toaster, she slathered the toasted bread with butter. "Come on and eat Scotty." She'd made omelets, figuring Gina would be hungry too. She served glasses of ice water since she didn't have orange juice.

After they'd gobbled down their simple meal,

and Scotty was resting in her spare bedroom, she finally returned to the living room and plopped onto the couch. Man, she was tired. But, she couldn't go to bed yet. She focused on Gina, ready to hear what she had to say. "Where have you been for the past two years?"

Gina strutted around the living room in her tight jeans, her high heels making small imprints in the plush carpet. "I've been around. I was mad because Mom and Dad tried to get custody of Scotty, tried to take me to court and say I was an unfit mother."

Groaning, Monica leaned back onto the couch before holding her head in her hands. "That's why you haven't been speaking to me or Mom and Dad for two years?" When Gina sat beside her, Monica took her sister's chin in her hand and looked into her eyes. "You know you were wrong. Mom and Dad tried to find you. They were worried about Scotty."

Jerking away, Gina placed a few inches between herself and Monica. "They might have cared about Scotty, but they didn't care about me." Gina swore under her breath and dug through her purse. Removing a mint, she popped it into her mouth.

"They were worried about you and Scotty," Monica explained. "You were living with that terrible man. He didn't work, and he was high on drugs. We didn't want anything to happen to the two of you."

Gina's lips curled into a bitter smirk. "Humph. Me and Scotty are just fine." She glanced up the stairs. "You saw him. Does he look neglected to you?"

She continued to stare at Gina, still not believing she was here to visit in the middle of the night. "What do you want? What did Scotty mean when he said he was coming here to live?"

Gina frowned as she toyed with the strap of her purse. "I want you to keep Scotty for me. Will you?"

Monica jerked back. "What? Why can't you take care of your own son? Did that crackhead you were living with finally go off the deep end?"

Gina shook her head. "No, we're not even together anymore. It's just that. . ." She paused, staring at the crystal vase of red roses adorning the coffee table. "I'm getting married."

Monica's heart skipped a beat. "Married?"

Gina nodded, her long mini-braids moving with the motion of her head. "Yeah, his name is Randy, and he's outside now, waiting for me in the car."

Monica raised her eyebrows, suddenly suspicious. "Why didn't you bring him inside? Are you ashamed of him?"

Gina shook her head. "No. But we're in a hurry tonight, and I didn't want to waste time with formalities."

"You still haven't told me why you can't keep Scotty. Does your fiancé have a problem with having a blind child in his house?"

Gina scowled as she clutched her purse, her dark eyes darting around the room. "No, that's not it at all."

"Uh-huh, whatever you say." She could always sense when Gina was lying.

Her body language said it all.

"Really, it's not Scotty's blindness that bothers Randy. It's just that—he's a trapeze artist in the National African-American Circus, and they're traveling around constantly." Her dark eyes lit up as she talked about her fiancé. "This year they'll be going international. Can you imagine me traveling around the globe with Randy? We'll be going to Paris, London, Rome—all those fancy European places!" She grabbed Monica's arm. "We'd love to take Scotty, but we can't afford to hire a tutor for him to travel with us."

"You're going to marry some man and travel with a circus?" Monica shook her head, wondering when her sister would grow up. At twenty-seven, she acted as if she were still a teenager. Since Monica was ten years older, she'd always been the responsible sibling, making sure Gina behaved herself.

Gina grabbed Monica's shoulder. "But I'm in love with him!" Her eyes slid over Monica as if assessing her. "You've never been in love? I think it's odd that you're thirty-seven and you never got married."

Monica closed her eyes for a brief second as

thoughts of her single life filled her mind. Since her breakup with Kevin, her serious boyfriend two years ago, she'd accepted that God wanted her to remain single, and she spent her free time at church in various ministries.

She'd also been spending time on her career. Kevin had never been supportive of her moving forward in her career, and he'd always done a rotten job explaining why he'd felt that way.

She was working on her MBA through an online program and after that, well, she wasn't sure what she'd do after she got her degree. She was hoping to get a better job, but, she had to take things one step at a time. She was busy, her life was full of church, school and work. She filled her time praising God and serving Him, and she had no regrets for the life she led. But whenever one of the church sisters announced an engagement, she couldn't stop the pang of envy that sliced through her. After all, she was only human.

Forcing the thoughts from her mind, she focused on Gina again. "This discussion is not about me. It's about you. You can't abandon Scotty. He loves you." Gina turned away, as if ashamed of her actions. "I know he does, and I love him, too. But I really want things to work out with Randy, and it won't work with Scotty on the road with us. He needs special education since he's blind." Her heart immediately went out to Scotty. She touched Gina's shoulder.

"Scotty knows you're getting married?"

Gina nodded. "I didn't tell him how long I would be gone, but I told him I'd call and visit. Please do this for me." Her sister touched her arm, and her dark eyes pleaded with her. She opened her purse and gave Monica some papers. "I've already had the power of attorney papers signed and notarized so that you can take care of him." She pressed the papers into Monica's hand.

"How long will you be gone?"

"The power of attorney lasts for six months. Hopefully by then me and Randy will be more settled. I'm hoping after the world tour he'll leave the circus and find a regular job."

Monica frowned, still clutching the legal documents. "Please do this for me, Monica," she pleaded again.

She reluctantly nodded. If she didn't take care of Scotty, she didn't know who would.

CHAPTER 2

Two months later…

MONICA READ OVER the report she was about to present to the marketing staff of The Chocolate Dreams Candy Company, her employer. She eyed the lower right corner of the screen. Five minutes until two. She quickly printed off five copies of the report. She had a few minutes to compose herself before presenting her report to the staff. She grabbed the copies off of the printer, just as her phone buzzed from her purse.

Her breath caught. She was tempted to ignore it. The meeting was about to start and she didn't want to be late. She eyed the display of her phone. She groaned. It was the school calling….again.

She let out a deep breath. "Monica speaking."

"Monica, this is Ms. Lattimore." The principal of Scotty's school did not seem pleased. "You need to come right away because Scotty has gotten into trouble again." The soft click of the line ended the abrupt phone call.

She huffed.

"Monica, you ready?" Louis, one of the junior marketing clerks rushed into the office, smiling widely. The kid was barely twenty-one and he always had a ready smile, eager to please. Monica quickly pressed the papers into his hand. "Tell my boss that I had a family emergency. You can give everyone a copy of my presentation. I'll field questions tomorrow."

Before the clerk could respond, she rushed out of the office. She took the elevator. When the mirrored doors opened, she walked to the small store near the front of the building. The Chocolate Dreams Candy Company had a small store for employees where they could purchase chocolate candy for half price. She entered the store – the scent of homemade chocolate tickled the air with sweetness. She quickly purchased a box of the milk chocolate candies with macadamia nuts – Ms. Lattimore's favorite. Perhaps the sweet treat would soften Ms. Lattimore's prickly mood.

Oh, Lord help me. She yawned, silently chanting the prayer as she drove to Scotty's school. It'd been a rough two months since she'd taken Scotty into her care. She stayed up late at night, studying for her degree and she also had to worry about getting Scotty to school on time in the mornings.

Plus, this was the third time he'd gotten into trouble over the least two months. She pulled into the school parking lot. The American flag snapped in the breeze that was coming in from the ocean. She sighed as she entered the school, her high heels clacked against the enameled floor as she took the short, familiar route to the office.

"Scotty got into another fight." Ms. Lattimore hurled the words at her, just as she barely entered the carpeted foyer. Monica didn't even have a chance to give the woman her peace offering of rich chocolate candy. She carefully set the box on top of the desk. Hopefully, eating the candy would soften Ms. Lattimore's' mood, eventually.

"I'm sorry. You know how hard it's been—"

"Yes, I know. Actually, the fight is only one of the problems we had today."

Oh, no, there was something else? Not just the fight? Monica winced. Her head suddenly hurt. After this conversation, she'd need a few Tylenol and lots of prayer. Ms. Lattimore gestured toward a red folder. Scotty's name was emblazoned across the cover. "Scotty needs tutoring. He's way below grade level."

She sighed. Her headache was getting worse. Sparks of pain sprinkled her head like pebbles.

"Are you okay?"

She sighed. "I have a headache. A bad one."

"Would you like some Tylenol?"

Monica nodded.

"I'll go get it from the medicine cabinet." Ms. Lattimore left and returned a few minutes later with a packet of pills and a bottle of water, as well as a steaming cup of coffee. Bless this wonderful woman. Monica downed the pills and took a few drinks of water. She closed her eyes and took a few deep breaths.

She didn't realize, not in a million years, that caring for a child could be so challenging. She now had newfound respect for all of the single mothers she knew at work and church. She sipped her coffee. The hot drink had been laced with cream and sugar and it tasted good going down her throat. As she continued sipping her coffee, she digested the news. The aromatic blend slid down her parched throat. As bright sunlight, brilliant as buttercups, streamed through the window, she tried to focus on the principal's words.

Scotty's teacher, a specialist in the area of visual impairment named Mrs. Brown a petite, dark-skinned woman, breezed into the room. "Sorry I'm late." She settled into the chair next to Monica.

Monica tried to smile at Scotty's teacher, but, she just couldn't. Monica leaned back into the leather chair, gazing at both of the women. Since Gina had left Scotty at her door two months ago, Monica's life had been one hectic cyclone.

"What do you suggest?" Monica asked.

"You could hire a tutor. Scotty seems bright enough, but I just don't think his mother sent him to school very often." She pointed to a folder on the desk. "As a matter of fact, we've got the records from Scotty's old school. It says his attendance was poor, but he was bright and asked lots of questions." She removed a paper from the folder and quickly scanned it. "Ms. Crawford, he barely knows the braille alphabet. He needs help in all of his subjects."

Monica was not surprised. Gina had never been very responsible. Scotty's poor school attendance was another problem she had to solve in her nephew's life.

She'd found that Scotty wasn't used to living by rules. He had a smart mouth and he sulked, refusing to go to bed at the same time each night. Sometimes he cussed under his breath. Each time Monica said a silent prayer, asking God to give her the wisdom to deal with Scotty's negative habits.

It saddened her to learn he had no spiritual training. Hopefully he would learn to understand God's way of life from his now-regular church attendance.

"How do I find a tutor?" Monica asked.

Ms. Lattimore stood and walked to a gray file cabinet. Pulling it open, she removed a piece of paper. "I have somebody who can help you."

Monica accepted the paper and wondered how much this was going to cost. Gina had left no money to pay for Scotty's care. Another lesson Monica had learned since she was now raising her nephew: Little boys were expensive and they ate a lot of food. Having a new dependent was causing her to live on a shoe-string budget. The only reason she was able to afford the online graduate school classes she was taking was because The Chocolate Dream Candy Company had a tuition reimbursement program.

Monica read the name printed on the paper that Ms. Lattimore had given to her. "Dr. John French?" Mrs. Brown nodded, her hair swinging over her shoulders. "Yes, he's your best bet. He's licensed to teach visually impaired children. He's taught many students over the years. He knows braille, and he's familiar with the methods of teaching math to a blind child using an abacus and a talking calculator."

"Is he very expensive?" Monica asked.

Ms. Lattimore beamed. "That's what's so amazing about him. He doesn't charge for his services. He considers it his contribution to the community. If you'll read farther down on his résumé, you'll see he's a science professor at the University of Maryland at Eastern Shore."

Intrigued, Monica perused John French's list of assets. She truly sensed the Lord had given her this opportunity. After all of Scotty's expenses, she didn't think she could afford a tutor. But since it was for her nephew, she would have found a way to make ends meet. She noticed a phone number listed at the bottom of the paper.

"So, I'll need to give him a call?"

Ms. Lattimore shook her head. "No, you don't have to call him. He's here at the school now, since our volunteer tutors are having a meeting."

She checked her wristwatch. "They should be getting out shortly. I already told him he should stop by the office after the meeting is over. We've heard nothing but good things about him. He likes helping children, and I feel that he'll be more than happy to help Scotty."

Monica nodded, still praising God for this unique opportunity. Glancing around the office, she thought about Scotty's school experience here in Ocean City, Maryland. She was pleased he was able to go to a regular public school with Mrs. Brown as his visually-impaired-education teacher. She wanted to make sure he interacted with sighted people regularly.

Her thoughts were interrupted as the door opened, squeaking on rusty hinges. Her heart hammered as an attractive man strolled into the office. His skin was the color of dark coffee, and his eyes shone with kindness.

He smiled before speaking. "Hi, I'm John French." He strolled over. Monica felt as if she were the only woman in the room as he looked at her. When he shook her hand, currents of warmth traveled up her arm. She glanced at his fingers and noted he wore no wedding band. She opened her mouth to speak, but before words could tumble out, Ms. Lattimore stood, interrupting their introduction. A blush stained the principal's pale cheeks, and she laughed, placing her hand on John's arm. "John, *it is* nice to see you again." Fluttering her long lashes, she squeezed his upper arm.

Monica's mouth nearly dropped open as she watched the display of affection. She cleared her throat, wanting to get the discussion back to the matter at hand. "I'm Monica Crawford. Ms. Lattimore told me you might be able to help my nephew, Scotty."

As he nodded, she tried to make a conscious effort not to stare. Strands of gray peppered his dark hair. Releasing his hand, she leaned back into the chair, hoping her palpitating heart would slow down.

Taking a vacant chair, he continued to smile. The woodsy scent of his aftershave filled the room, making her even more aware of his presence. "I've already met Scotty."

"You did?" Monica couldn't hide her surprise.

"Yes, he's sitting right down the hallway on the bench. It was easy for me to figure out who he was."

Monica figured Scotty's teacher had brought him with her when she came to the office. She removed her phone from her purse. "So, when did you want to start?" She held the device in her hand, ready to enter the correct data into her schedule. She mentally sighed. She had so much work to do for her online classes and things were busy at the candy company right now. This would be just another thing to add to her plate.

"You look upset. Maybe you need to take a minute to calm down before we set Scotty's schedule." He softened his words with a smile.

Did this man not understand that she had a lot of things to do?

Before she could respond, Ms. Lattimore commented, "Mrs. Brown and I feel Scotty needs a tutor at least twice a week in order to bring him up to the same level as his peers."

As Ms. Lattimore and Mrs. Brown focused on John, they gave him a list of things for which Scotty needed help. John accepted the paper while Monica patiently waited with her phone… when would they get around to setting Scotty's schedule?

She eyed John while he listened to Ms. Lattimore and Mrs. Brown. While she heard what they were saying, John seemed to pick up on what they were saying more so than she. "Does Scotty interact with the other students regularly in the classroom? Sometimes a disabled child is kept separate from his classmates and it makes him feel isolated…could cause him to lash out."

Monica's heart skipped…was that why Scotty kept getting into fights? From what she'd heard, it was more or less his cursing and lashing out at students. An actual fight was hard since he couldn't really see his target.

Ms. Lattimore cleared her throat as she stood up. She squeezed her hands together as her face heated. Looked like she was nervous. "We had no choice but to isolate him. He's way below grade level and he has lots of emotional problems—"

"You created part of the problem by isolating him in the classroom. You should've known better than that."

Monica gulped. Hot shame filled her soul like a bowl of steaming soup. She'd never even thought to ask the questions that John had asked. She'd been so enmeshed in her job and Scotty's behavior problems, her online studies....she'd just assumed that Gina's bad parenting skills, as well as her abandonment of her son, were the only causes for Scotty's behavior problems. She'd never, not in a million years, figure that the school administrators were partially to blame.

John stood tall, his dark eyes sparking with anger. He didn't even *know* Scotty, yet, it almost appeared as if *he* were Scotty's father. She took a deep breath. She wanted his help, but, she didn't want to cause distress to the school administrators. She touched his arm. "John, I'm sure we can work all of this out."

He nodded. He continued his conversation with Ms. Lattimore and Mrs. Brown while Monica listened. She even typed up some notes on her phone, some of the things they were discussing she'd not thought to address before today. John asked such pointed questions so, she assumed he knew more about Scotty's situation than she. Once the discussion was finished the group stood. John had calmed down and they now had a plan of action. Ms. Lattimore rushed over to John and shook his hand. "If you have questions about any of Scotty's academic needs, you can call me."

Monica mentally groaned after seeing Ms. Lattimore flirting with John. She had to wonder if the woman flirted with every single parent that she met. Monica lifted her purse and turned toward the door, eager to get Scotty home so he could start on his homework. She also needed to speak with John regarding Scotty's tutoring schedule. They'd not yet hammered out those details. The sound of John's footsteps followed her as she exited the office.

"Wow, you sure are in a hurry." The amused tone of his voice floated around her, making her aware of how rushed she'd become since Scotty had arrived in her life.

She stopped several yards away from where her nephew sat. "I just want to get Scotty started on his homework." She glanced at the little boy. "I'm so worried about him. I know life will be hard for him since he's disabled, but the least he can do is get back on his grade level." Blinking rapidly, she turned away from Scotty's new tutor, not wanting him to see the emotional tears suddenly filling her eyes.

"Hey," John said softly, placing his hand on her shoulder. "Everything will be okay—you'll see. Wait here a second." She continued to blink away tears as John reentered the office. He appeared seconds later with a tissue. She turned and blew her nose as embarrassment filled her soul.

John took control of the situation as he led her to Scotty. "I know this may sound a little forward, but how about joining me for a bite to eat?"

Was this man asking her out in a date?

CHAPTER 3

THE LAST THING she needed right now was a date. Sure, he was easy on the eyes, but, dating was the furthest thing from her mind. After she fed Scotty and he'd done his homework, she needed to start the paper that would be due soon for her graduate-level marketing class. The itch to go further in her marketing career had been hovering in her mind over the past year. She was sure she'd thrive at a higher-level marketing job, and she was determined to make it happen any way she could.

She stopped walking. "John, I appreciate the offer, and I'm so glad that you're helping Scotty, but, I'm too busy to do dinner tonight."

He touched her arm and sparks of warmth, like tiny firecrackers, sprinkled over her skin. She pulled her arm away and stepped back, putting a little bit of distance between her and John. "I think you misunderstood me. My invite was totally about Scotty." He pointed toward the bench where Scotty patiently sat. "Before I start tutoring any student, I sit and talk to the parents and the rest of the family. I want to be sure I have their total support and I also want to get to know the child that I'll be tutoring."

She sighed. John was probably thinking that she was a selfish single mother. From his emotional outburst in the office, it should've been obvious that Scotty's needs were a top priority for him. "I'm sorry."

"I promise we won't take very long." He gestured toward the office door. "From what I've heard in there, he really needs help. But if we can buckle down, get him right to work, I can almost guarantee I'll have him on grade level by the end of the school year."

She chuckled, throwing her soiled tissue away in a nearby trash can. "We're one week into the semester. Are you sure you can have him back on his grade level by the end of the school year?"

He shook his head, still gazing at her with his warm brown eyes. "Well, yes, I think it's possible." She felt flustered under his scrutiny. "Do you mind if I call you Monica? You can call me John." She nodded as they approached Scotty. "We can go to the boardwalk and visit the beach. Scotty might enjoy walking on the beach, and we could get takeout from one of the restaurants."

He squeezed her shoulder. "Come on, Monica, I'm sure both you and Scotty will enjoy yourselves." He released her shoulder and continued walking. "Whenever I get a new student to tutor, I usually spend some time talking to the student and the parent so we all agree that we have the same goals in mind. It'll be my treat."

Monica finally nodded. "That's fine." They approached Scotty. "Scotty, you've met Mr. French. He'll be your new tutor."

"I'd prefer it if Scotty called me Mr. John," he said.

"Okay, Scotty, Mr. John will be your new tutor."

The little boy shook his head. "I don't need a tutor."

"You know you need help with your schoolwork. I don't want you to have to repeat second grade." Scotty remained silent as she continued telling him the good news. "We're going to go with Mr. John to get something to eat down at the boardwalk."

Scotty stood, reaching toward Monica as she grabbed his hand. "I sure am hungry," Scotty said.

As they walked outside, the bright sunlight gleamed on her skin, and the ocean-scented wind danced around them, beckoning them to the beach for a walk in the warm September air. John pulled his keys from his pocket. "How about I drive us down to the boardwalk? We can always come back afterward to get your car."

"Okay." Her eyes widened when she spotted his silver Lexus. He removed his key fob and unlocked the doors.

"I want to open my own door." Scotty hated it whenever she opened the door for him. He also didn't like it when she held his hand. He so desperately wanted to be independent. As she took a deep breath, she realized that Scotty's anger would only get worse unless she got him some help.

She released his hand – whenever she released his hand, that was her signal to Scotty that they'd arrived at their destination, in this case it was John's car. Scotty reached up and felt the door until he found the handle. He opened the door and got into the backseat. "Man, it smells nice in here." The happiness in his voice made her feel a bit better. John opened her door for her and she slid into the passenger seat. The car smelled new and when John started the engine, the vehicle purred like a newborn kitten.

As he rolled away from the curb, she made herself comfortable. It was kind of nice to be squired around in such a luxurious vehicle.

"Mr. John, can you turn on some music?" Scotty's request came from the backseat.

John smiled as he turned the radio onto a pop station. As the music filled the car, Scotty hummed along to the music.

"So," she paused and gathered her thoughts. "You just got a new car?"

"No, this car is five years old. I go to a car detailing place to keep it looking like new. I'm kind of anal when it comes to my car."

"Ah, I see."

During their short journey, she wondered why

a college professor would end up spending his free time tutoring a blind seven-year-old child. Well, she'd ask him about that later.

John pulled into a parking lot.

"Aunt Monica, I want chicken nuggets and fries."

After walking for a few minutes, they agreed to stop at Harrison's Harbor Watch Restaurant to get food to go. Monica noticed the unique spicy scent of Old Bay Seasoning and seafood filling the air as they stepped into the restaurant.

John spoke quietly to the server. "We're ordering food to go. Do you have a braille children's menu?"

Monica's mouth dropped open when the server gave John the braille menu. During the short time she'd had Scotty, she'd never even known that restaurants had braille menus. She'd usually read the menu to him, or, simply ordered what he'd liked.

John led Scotty to a bench in the front of the restaurant and Monica followed them. John pressed the menu into Scotty's small hands. He then placed Scotty's fingers onto the braille letters. Scotty shook his head. "I don't want to read this. I already know what I want."

"Read it anyway, sport. We need to get you up to speed with your reading so we might as well start now."

Surprisingly, Scotty obeyed him. His small brown fingers slid over the braille bumps of the children's menu. "I changed my mind. I want a cheeseburger and french fries."

"You got it, Sport."

After Monica and John had decided what they wanted, they got their food in take-out containers. They then strolled along the boardwalk, searching for an empty place to sit and eat. Tourists sauntered around enjoying the warm weather of the last few weeks of summer.

A few people flew kites on the beach, and a multitude of the colorful objects bobbed in the sky. The brisk wind moved the birdlike contraptions so they filled the expanse with a kaleidoscope of color. Monica stopped walking, lifting her head toward the sky. "That's so beautiful!" She admired the beach as the white-capped waves tumbled onto the sand.

"Why are we stopping?" Scotty squeezed Monica's hand. "I'm hungry, Aunt Monica!"

She bent toward Scotty. "I'm just looking at the pretty kites in the sky." A young man with a dog on a leash vacated a nearby bench. "Come on." She led Scotty over to the bench, John strolling close to them.

The three of them plopped onto the empty bench. John opened his Styrofoam container holding his fried shrimp and oysters. As they started to eat, Scotty said, "Aunt Monica, can we go on the merry-go-round after we eat?"

She glanced at John. "Since we came with John, it depends if he's willing to go."

"We can go, sport."

Monica bit into her softshell crab sandwich. The lettuce, sauce and sweet crabmeat made her day. She'd not had anything to eat since breakfast, so the meal was a welcome treat during this emotional day.

After they'd eaten, she took Scotty's hand and they continued walking on the boardwalk. If she'd known they'd be going out, she'd have brought his cane with him. She gestured toward The Chocolate Dreams Candy Company's boardwalk store. Their logo of a broken piece of chocolate, oozing with rich caramel, looked enticing over the storefront window. "That's where I work."

John raised his eyebrows and eyed her business suit and flat shoes. "You're dressed like you have an office job. You don't look like you've been serving candy to customers all day."

Scotty chuckled. "Aunt Monica works for The Chocolate Dreams Candy Company. She works in marketing." She'd told Scotty all about her job and that she was working on her MBA so that she could further her career.

John smiled at her. Goodness, he had the cutest dimples. Her stomach flipped with joy and she forced herself to calm down. Candy, that's what she needed. She continued to hold Scotty's hand as they entered the small candy store. The bell tinkled as they went into the shop.

"It smells good and sweet in here." Scotty's voice filled with joy.

"Yep, it sure does," John agreed.

Scotty often marveled about how good things felt or smelled. He also had a never-ending sweet tooth. She'd had to make sure she closely monitored his sweets. When he had too much sugar, he became active and jumpy. When she'd first started caring for him, he'd managed to find a box of candy in her living room.

He'd eaten the entire box of candy and had been so wired up that he was up half the night. "I want some fudge, Aunt Monica."

She grinned. Chocolate fudge sounded like a good idea. She purchased a few pieces of fudge for each of them. It was the least she could do since John had purchased their dinner. They exited the store and Monica split the fudge between the three of them. She bit into the fudge. The rich, buttery sweetness of the candy melted on her tongue.

One thing she loved about Chocolate Dreams was the taste of their candy. It was one of the few companies that mass-produced candy that tasted like homemade.

"This candy is excellent." John raised his eyebrows, obviously surprised about how good the candy tasted. "I've never had fudge that tasted so good…well, not since I was a kid. My grandma used to make a mean batch of fudge – this candy reminds me of hers."

"I'm not surprised." She explained that the mass-produced candies tasted like homemade.

They then walked toward the carnival rides on the pier. "So, Scotty, what are your favorite subjects in school? Do you like math?"

Scotty swore under his breath.

Monica's face grew warm. She pulled Scotty away from John. Holding his cheeks between her thumb and index finger, she placed her face close to his. "Scotty, what did I tell you about that language?" Her heart continued to pound with embarrassment as Scotty sulked.

"Aunt Monica, my mom said stuff like that all the time."

Sighing, she released him, still exasperated about his using the street language he'd picked up from Gina. "Well, it's wrong. Your Sunday school teacher told me she spoke to your class about expressing anger. Don't you remember anything she taught you?"

"She said it's not nice to cuss," he mumbled. Folding his small arms in front of his chest, he changed the subject. "Can I go to the merry-go-round now?" A few late summer tourists still congregated around the pier as the fake animals weaved up and down on the carnival ride.

Scotty didn't sound sorry for his actions, and she was going to make him understand it was wrong to take the Lord's name in vain. Since he'd come into her care, she'd admonished him about cursing on numerous occasions. However, he still cussed as much as the day he showed up on her doorstep. "No, I'm afraid you can't, Scotty."

Gently pulling his elbow, she sat him on a bench. "You're going to sit here and think about what you've done. When you decide to stop swearing so much, I'll let you play." His bottom lip quivered, but she left him alone on the bench, giving him time to ponder his actions.

Tears threatened to spill from her eyes as she left Scotty and returned to John. They sat on a bench close by so she could keep an eye on Scotty. John's eyes were full of kindness and understanding. Feeling like a fool, she glanced at her clasped hands. "I'm sorry about that." Shaking her head, she pressed her hands together. "I'm trying hard to teach him right from wrong, but it's just so hard to undo other people's mistakes."

Before John could respond, her cell phone rang. She glanced at the display. It was her Pierce, the Director of Marketing where she worked. She smiled. It was always nice to hear from Pierce. He was her co-worker, friend, and mentor all rolled into one. He directed the marketing department with a firm hand, and all of the marketing employees both liked and respected him. "Hi, Pierce."

"Monica. I'm so glad you answered the phone. I wanted to speak with you about something, but, it's better if I do it in person."

She raised her eyebrows as her heart skipped a beat. "Is everything okay?" She wasn't sure exactly how old Pierce was, but, she figured him to be in his sixties. Hopefully, he was in good health. How she dreaded hearing bad news.

"Everything is fine. I'm not going to be in the office for the next few days. I'm just taking a few vacation days. Is it okay if we meet next Friday for lunch? I figure we can go to The Crab Chateau."

"The Crab Chateau? Really?" How she loved that place. It was her favorite restaurant but it was so pricey that she only ate there for special occasions. "What's the occasion?"

"Oh, I'll tell you more about that when I see you. Enjoy the rest of your day."

"Bye, Pierce." She ended the call and placed the phone back into her purse.

"Who's Pierce?"

"He's…a friend."

"Must be a mighty good friend if he's taking you to The Crab Chateau. Have you been dating him for long?"

Now why did he have to go and ask her about that? The faint smell of his woodsy cologne tickled her nose with joy. He smelled good and was as handsome as could be. Yeah, she was attracted to Scotty's new tutor, but, she figured the only business they would be discussing would be Scotty's schooling. She honestly didn't think she could handle a personal relationship now. Sure, she should've been over her ex-boyfriend, but, the pain still simmered in her bones, just like an angry volcano about ready to burst.

She took a deep breath and focused on John, trying to ignore his good looks. "Pierce is the head of the marketing department at my job. He's my mentor and friend."

"So…he's your boss?"

She shook her head. "No, I don't report directly to him. The marketing department is fairly large. He's in his sixties and happily married with kids and grandkids. I've learned a lot from him over the years."

"So, Scotty mentioned you did marketing?" asked John.

She nodded. "I sure do. I help with creating ads for Chocolate Dreams. I love my job. We create ads and then book ad space in newspapers and magazines. We've even had a few commercials on local TV stations."

John nodded. "Yes, I've heard of Chocolate Dreams but had never tasted the candy before today."

"And now you're hooked, aren't you?"

He grinned and gave her a quick wink. Her stomach dipped with pleasure. She pushed the attraction she felt aside as she eyed Scotty waiting on the bench. "It's been hard since I've taken Scotty into my care." She glanced at her nephew as he sat on the bench, pouting. "Sometimes I have to leave work early because the school will call me when Scotty misbehaves, and I also have special meetings with his teachers since he has special needs." She sighed. "I just want to make sure that caring for Scotty doesn't affect my job." She took a deep breath. "I hope that doesn't sound selfish…but…" She shrugged. "I have to make a living. It's not like the sky is going to open up and money is going to pour down like manna from heaven."

He frowned when she mentioned manna. He looked away for a few minutes as they sat in silence. Her comment seemed to bother him. Well, she wouldn't ask him about that. It'd probably be best if she simply changed the subject. She'd already noticed he wasn't wearing a wedding ring, so, she assumed he was single or divorced.

"John, do you have children?"

He took a deep breath. The easy smile he'd been displaying all evening disappeared like the white-capped waves of the ocean. "No." His chilly response made her pause. Just one word and that was it?

Well, she wasn't going to probe into his personal life anymore. Better to focus on Scotty. "I just think it's odd you're a college professor, yet you volunteer your spare time helping elementary-school-aged children."

He remained silent for several seconds, not commenting on her observation. He finally checked the time on his phone before focusing on her again. "How about we set up a tutoring schedule for Scotty?"

Now why would he refuse to tell her his reasons for helping blind children. Was he simply a kind-hearted man or, was he hiding secrets?

CHAPTER 4

JOHN CHANGED THE subject, not wanting to reveal too much about his life and childless state. He eyed her reaching into her handbag to remove her phone.

He discreetly stared as she pressed a few buttons on the gadget. Her tall, chocolate brown body reminded him of a cover girl. With her short hair and cute face, she could easily win a beauty contest.

Still holding her phone, she glanced at him with her despondent dark brown eyes. "Which days of the week work best for you?" He figured she was going to put Scotty's tutoring schedule onto her calendar.

"You know I'm a professor at the University of Maryland. I have classes during the day, but I'm free all evenings."

Her eyes widened. "All evenings?"

"Yes."

A woman with a baby strolled by. The child shrieked as the mother continued to stroll down the boardwalk. John mentally blocked the disturbing sound from his mind, focusing again on Monica. Her red-painted lips enticed him, and the alluring scent of her floral perfume beckoned, competing with the clean scent of the ocean and the spicy scents of the food.

She put her phone aside. Clasping her hands together, she glanced at Scotty, who was still sitting on the nearby bench. "You know, I'm still wondering why you didn't respond to the observation I made a few minutes ago."

"You mean about tutoring children?"

She nodded. "You have to admit, it does seem strange that a college professor would tutor children—blind children at that. Ms. Lattimore told me you even know braille. You took the time to learn it just to tutor children?"

Bittersweet memories of his deceased son scattered through his mind like the tossing white-capped waves in the nearby Atlantic Ocean. Forcing himself to focus on the moment at hand, he blocked the memories. "Well, it's a long story about how I decided to get into tutoring." He leaned back on the bench. "I don't really feel like getting into that right now."

"Okay. I don't mean to be intrusive, but I can't help but wonder about it." Her eyes twinkled as she looked at him. "But I am glad you're helping us."

"I'm glad I'm helping you, too." After a few moments of silence, he asked her the question that had been burning in his mind for the last hour. "Do you think we could get together and do something this Saturday?"

She jerked back as she folded her arms in front of her chest. "Mr. French—"

"Call me John."

She gave him her full attention. "John. . .I don't think I can go out on Saturday." Her dark eyes wandered toward Scotty. "I have a child to take care of now. I don't know if I can find a babysitter. Besides, if you're asking me out, the answer is no."

"No? Why?"

She shook her head. "I can't go out with anyone right now. My life is just too complicated. I just told you how much everything has changed since Scotty's been in my care."

"I can imagine it would be hard."

"Hard doesn't begin to describe it. Scotty has a lot of problems, and right now I'm focusing on getting his life back on track. I can't have other things crowding my head right now."

"I think I have a solution for that problem. How about I come by on Saturday for one of Scotty's tutoring sessions? Afterward maybe we can go to the beach? I can talk to you about Scotty's curriculum. Maybe we can go to Phillips Seafood House for dinner afterward. I love their buffet."

"I love their buffet, too, but I can't go out afterward."

His heart skipped a beat, and he hoped there was some way to change her mind. "Why not? I guarantee you'll have a good time."

A slight flush tinged her brown cheeks, and he caught a glimpse of her pearly white teeth as she smiled. "I'm not doubting I'd have a good time. But I've been having so much trouble with Scotty lately. His behavior has been awful, and I don't want to grant him the treat of dinner at Phillips when he's been misbehaving so much." She took a deep breath. "Besides, I'll probably be studying anyway."

"Studying? Really?"

She nodded. A breeze blew and a few strands of her hair lifted in the wind. He balled his hands into fist, resisting the urge to touch her hair. "I'm in grad school right now and well…Scotty doesn't always like it when I'm studying. Believe it or not, he wants me to pay attention to him."

He nodded, understanding. "Well, we really need to get his tutoring started. How about I come over anyway? After I'm finished tutoring him, we can discuss if we can go to the beach or out to eat afterward."

"Well…of course I want you to come tutor him…not sure about going to the beach afterwards." She glanced at Scotty. "As I said, I'm not sure about going out afterwards."

"I don't want to pressure you. But I just want to point out that I usually want to spend a little time with my students and get to know them better. It's easier for me to tutor them if I can observe them outside of the lessons. I could offer to spend some time with Scotty alone, but I didn't think you'd want me to do that since Scotty doesn't know me and you don't know me very well either."

She finally nodded. "Well, since you put it that way, there's no harm I guess." She paused. "But, if I'm behind with my studies, just understand that we won't be able to socialize after the tutoring session."

He released the breath he didn't realize he'd been holding. "Understood."

"Just to let you know, I can't stay up too late. Since I've had Scotty, I've been so tired. It's hard having a kid dropped into your life." Her shoulders slumped as she toyed with the strap of her purse.

"Why are you raising your nephew so suddenly?"

She paused and stared at the ocean. She appeared to be thinking really hard, and he had to wonder what was going on in her life. She looked like she needed a friend right now. Hopefully, she wouldn't mind if he offered her his support.

"You look like you need somebody to talk to. I don't mind listening, if you want to tell me what's on your mind."

She smiled, just a little bit, and touched his hand. "Thanks." She glanced at Scotty before focusing on him again. "My sister left Scotty with me because she felt she couldn't take care of him." Her mouth hardened into a frown, and when no other details were forthcoming, he decided to let the subject drop and ask her about it again later.

"Are you all right?" he asked.

She nodded as her silence continued, so he took up the conversation about Scotty's tutoring again. The urge to help her with her recent predicament grew, and he knew he could make things better for both Monica and Scotty. "How about I come to your house on Tuesdays and Thursdays to tutor him? Would that work for you?"

"That would be fine. I do have a proposition for you, though."

"Really? What's that?"

She picked up her phone and entered the dates for Scotty's tutoring sessions onto her calendar. She put the phone away before responding to his question. "Well, I understand that you do not accept payment for your tutoring services."

He nodded, wondering why this bothered her. Thoughts of his deceased son again filled his mind, reminding him why he'd made a promise to himself to make the lives of visually impaired people better.

"Since you won't accept payment, I don't want to make it seem as if Scotty and I are taking advantage of you."

"But I want to help him. I enjoy helping others."

She nodded. "I know." Her dark eyes met his. "I can see that you're committed to helping others, and that's commendable of you. But when you come by on Saturday, and I get all of my homework completed, I'd like to make lunch for us to take on the beach. As a matter of fact, I'd like you to join us for dinner each night you tutor Scotty." Giving a small shrug, she continued, "It's the least I can do since you're helping me and you're helping him."

Thoughts of tutoring the young boy in reading and math escaped his mind like a brisk wind while thoughts of seeing Monica filled his soul with joy.

She chuckled. "But I have to warn you: Sometimes we might be eating food you're not used to."

"What do you mean?"

"Well, Scotty's diet consists of a lot of Tater Tots and chicken nuggets. I have to fight with him to eat his vegetables. I'm coaxing him into trying some other foods. I think my sister let him eat whatever he wanted."

She stood, and he touched her arm before she could go and fetch Scotty. "So, I'll see you on Saturday around noon?" She told him her address, and he suggested a few things Scotty could do to prepare for his tutoring session.

She nodded, and as he drove them back to the school so that she could get her car, he stole a few glances at her while driving. She was a dead-ringer for Hallee Berry…she was beautiful and her spirit was strong. The way she took care of her blind nephew just tugged at his heart. His heart skipped a beat as he anticipated their next appointment.

CHAPTER 5

JOHN PRESSED THE button and the overhead projected flipped to the last slide. "This is the Venus Fly Trap. It lives in North and South Carolina." The pink-tinted plant flashed on the screen. Excitement buzzed through him like lightening – just teaching this class of eager students something new filled him with liquid joy. "What's cool about this plant is that it eats bugs. Catches them and eats them. There's an entire section about this plant in the tenth chapter of your book."

He glanced around the lecture hall. Nearly one hundred students populated the room, most wearing jeans or sweats. He spotted The University of Maryland logo on a few of the sweatshirts. Thankfully, none of the students looked bored or sleepy. Some of the other science professors had often complained about some of the undergraduate students falling asleep or getting bored during lectures, sometimes whispering to one another. "Okay, that wraps up today's lesson. I'll see you next week." As the class emptied out a few students came forward with questions about next week's assignment.

He exited the building and walked to his car. He pulled his phone from his pocket and again eyed the date. September 15th. This day would forever be emblazoned on his mind. He got into his car and started the engine. Several minutes later, he pulled into the parking lot of Pete's Plant House, a local gardening center. He got out of the car and strolled to the door. He swallowed and took a deep breath. The bell above the door tinkled, announcing his entrance into the shop. He stopped and sniffed. Vivid fall foliage burst into bloom around the nursery. White, orange, yellow…flowers of different colors….so amazing. Kind of strange, how much he loved flowers. One girl he'd dated had said that she'd never met a man who loved flowers as much as he.

Well, his love of plants had always been a part of him. He loved teaching his students about plants and botany was a joy that he'd always have in his life. "Oh, Dr. French. My best and favorite customer." Pete, the plant store owner, came from the back. The bright sun shining through the nursery gleamed off the older man's salt and pepper hair. At sixty, Pete was in great shape and he ran two miles every day.

Pete offered his hand and John shook it. "Great to see you again."

"Great to see you." The man paused and

frowned. "I'm sorry…well, are you okay?"

Pete knew all about his deceased son…that was the reason for his visit that day. He barely nodded. "Thanks. I'm…well…I'm okay. You'd said the plant came in?"

"Ah, yes." The older man led him to the register. He then hoisted a box onto the counter and sliced it open with a box cutter. "I'm surprised the cemetery lets you plant in-ground plants."

John peeked into the box. The sight of the large grassy plant, tinged with white edged leaves slammed right into his mind. The memory of taking his son for a walk, when his son had been three years old, and could still see, spun into his mind. During that walk his son had seen this plant and had been mesmerized by it. "What's that?"

"That's a white edge hosta."

"A white edge hosta? That sounds funny."

After that, whenever he'd taken his son for a walk, he always wanted to stop and stare at the white edge hosta.

"You okay?" Pete clapped him on the shoulder, breaking into his thoughts.

He blinked. Thank goodness his eyes were dry. He took a deep breath. He needed to focus on what needed to be done that day. He needed to do this to honor his son's memory. "Yeah, I'm fine, Pete. Thanks for ordering the plant. How much do I owe you?"

Pete quickly shook his head as he shoved the box toward John. "Hey, it's on the house. I know how hard this day is for you and well…as many plants as you buy from me every year, this is the least I can do for you."

John opened his mouth to argue, but then stopped. No sense arguing. He then recalled Pete's question, right before he'd peeked into the box. "The cemetery said that they only allowed certain plants to be planted into the ground at the gravesite. I got special permission to do this."

John lifted the box and Pete opened the door for him. The sound of the bell above the door tinkled as he exited the nursery. He placed the box into the trunk. He'd already packed his shovel and some soil into the car that morning.

Several minutes later he took a deep breath as he pulled into the parking lot of a cemetery. He gripped the steering wheel and stared at the tombstones in the distance. He closed his eyes. Man, you'd think after three years that this visit wouldn't be so hard. His son, only twelve, lying in a hospice bed.

Dying.

No, make that dead. Died on this day three years ago.

After his son had been buried, he'd made a promise to himself to always pay his respects on the anniversary of his death. He breathed deeply and blinked. He didn't want to cry. He figured it'd been three years, he should be able to hold himself together by now, shouldn't he?

Busy…he needed to keep himself busy and

focused. He got out of the car and popped open his trunk. He lifted the box and carried it in his arms as he took the familiar walking path toward his son's gravesite. He stopped when he spotted Beverly, his ex-girlfriend, the mother of his child, sitting at the gravesite, her legs crossed Indian style. Her husband stood a several feet away from her. It appeared that he was texting. He frowned, studying both of them. Beverly always liked being alone when she was sad. He imagined she'd told her husband to give her a few moments alone.

Beverly had gotten pregnant when they'd been living together. They'd stayed together until Brian had turned four – that's when things had gotten sour.

Brian had been diagnosed with a brain tumor.

Their world had tilted.

Beverly, who'd always been okay with his agnostic beliefs, had started attending church.

Then she'd gotten saved.

Needless to say, marriage was not something he wanted to pursue…her passion for God, Jesus, that church….well, when Brian was eleven, she'd married her current husband, Aiden. She'd met Aiden at a study group at her church. Aiden had been there for Beverly…and for him…when Brian had gotten worse and had died. Even though initially he'd not been crazy about the idea of Beverly moving on with her life, finding a more suitable mate, he'd discovered that his jealousy had been wrong. Aiden had been nothing but kind and thoughtful towards him while Brian had been sick.

Some thought it strange that he considered both Beverly and Aiden friends, especially since he'd dated Beverly, heck he'd lived with her, for years. He supposed he'd always have a bittersweet bond with Beverly because of Brian.

Aiden looked up from his phone and spotted him. The tall, dark-skinned man approached him. "Hey, John."

Obviously hearing Aiden's greeting, Beverly glanced their way. She gave him a small smile. He was glad to see that her brown eyes were dry. He certainly didn't want to interrupt her if she were weeping.

"Hi Aiden."

Aiden glanced at the box, paused. Looked like he was going to ask about the plant, but, then decided not to. Beverly stood up and John came toward her. Aiden followed close behind. He placed the box beside the marker. He touched the gravestone. He then focused on Beverly. "Good to see you…both of you…again." He hugged Beverly and shook Aiden's large hand. He then gestured toward the box. "I bought a white edge hosta to plant at the gravesite. I already cleared it with the cemetery."

Beverly's mouth quivered. Oh, no, she was going to cry.

"Ah, honey." Aiden placed his arm around his wife. "Don't cry."

She sniffed. "No, I'm happy…John. I'm glad you're doing this. I remember how much he loved that plant." She then gave him a watery smile.

Aiden gestured toward the plant. "Did you need some help digging?"

John paused. Might as well tell him the truth. "Aiden, I appreciate the offer but, I'd rather do this by myself."

He nodded. "I understand."

Awkward silence. He mentally groaned. He wanted to be at the grave by himself so that he could dig into the earth and place the plant into the ground. But, he couldn't tell them to leave, after all, they had just as much a right to be there as he was. He spotted the logo on Aiden's blue tee shirt. The picture of mustard seeds blowing in the wind was eye catching. "You two still worship at Mustard Seed Faith?"

Both of them nodded. They'd stopped inviting him to church ages ago, so, he figured it was a safe topic now. "Church is having a revival tonight." Aiden checked his watch. "Honey, if we don't leave now, we'll be late."

"Okay." She kissed John's cheek and Aiden shook his hand. He eyed them as they walked back to their car, holding hands. John sighed as he got his shovel and gardening soil from the car and returned to the gravesite. He then pushed the shovel into the earth and hoisted out a huge chunk of dirt.

CHAPTER 6

MONICA PUSHED THE door open to The Crab Cheateau. She spotted Pierce standing near the hostess station, waiting for her. His bald head shone beneath the lights as he looked at her and grinned. Just seeing his wrinkled, cheerful face made her glad. Pierce was always a great older person to talk to. "Hey, Monica." He hugged her as the hostess approached.

"Pierce Morgan, your table is ready."

Walking side by side, they followed the hostess. Monica eyed the beautiful oceanic pictures on the cream-colored walls. Delicious, strong seafood smells surrounded her and her stomach rumbled. She'd gotten up early that morning to study. All she'd had to eat that day had been coffee and toast. Scotty had had a hard time waking up that morning – she'd found that out about him. He seemed to have trouble sleeping. She was unclear as to if this was a problem that had occurred because he was still adjusting to a new environment, or if he'd had this problem when he lived with Gina.

She'd tried asking him about it, but, he'd gotten upset when she'd asked him, so, she didn't pursue it. Hopefully his sleeping pattern would be back on track soon. If not, she'd have to take him to the pediatrician.

"What's wrong, Monica?" Pierce asked the question as they settled into their seats.

She opened her menu. "What makes you think that something is wrong?"

"I can tell by the look on your face."

She sighed. She didn't feel like telling him about Scotty's sleeping problem.

"You look tired," he observed.

"I am. I was up half the night studying."

After they'd ordered, he asked her another question. "How are things going with your grad school classes?"

She inwardly sighed with relief when he didn't ask about Scotty again. "Things are going pretty good."

"When will you be graduating?"

"I'll be out within the next six months."

"GPA?"

"4.0." Okay, now she really wanted to know the nature of this lunch. "Did you want to have lunch with me just to talk about my grades?"

Their server appeared with a basket of hot rolls and their bowls of cream of crab soup. They bowed their heads. "Lord, please bless this food, Amen."

Monica grinned at his short, and to the point, prayer. Her stomach rumbled again as she dipped her spoon into the bowl. The hot soup tasted heavenly with lumps of sweet succulent crab meat. She enjoyed another bite before slathering butter onto her hot yeasty roll. "This is so good."

"Sure is."

"So, Monica, I wanted you to be the first person to know that I'll be retiring in six months."

She coughed, nearly choking on her soup. He patted her back. "You okay?"

She drank some water and finally calmed down. She managed to smile. "Sorry the soup went down the wrong way." She paused. "I'm just surprised is all. For some reason, I thought you'd be working until….well, I'm not sure. You haven't told *anybody* else yet about your retiring?"

"The only other person who knows is my wife. I'll be letting the other folks at work know next week."

She took a deep breath as their entrées were served. Over fish and chips, Pierce posed a question. "How do you feel about being the director of marketing?"

She widened her eyes. "Are you kidding?"

"Of course not. You'd be perfect. You're bright and you'll be getting your masters' soon. I was going to recommend you for the position if you wish."

She put her napkin down. "Pierce, I don't know."

He patted her hand. "I know this is sudden… just think about it."

She took a deep breath, glanced around the restaurant.

"You're thinking about Kevin, aren't you?"

Boy, Pierce really knew her well. Kevin, her ex-boyfriend, had never really encouraged her to further her career. He'd scoffed at her dreams of moving forward in the marketing business. When they'd dated, he'd said that they'd not have a lot of time to spend together if she got her graduate degree. She finally managed to respond to Pierce's question with a short, curt nod.

"Don't let that one mistake make you hesitant about applying. Besides, that was three years ago…and well, it wasn't like the entire thing was your fault."

She sighed. That dark dismal time when there'd been an outbreak of the norovirus at The Chocolate Dreams Candy Company. They'd had a catered event and the food had been carrying the dreaded virus. As a result, ninety percent of the staff had taken ill and they'd had to have the building disinfected and they'd shut down for an entire week.

Surprisingly, she'd not gotten ill. So, she'd been encouraged to take the lead and coordinate the local TV commercial that was being shot during the down time. Chocolate Dreams had already paid for the set and they'd paid for the models.

It'd been awful. The models were rude and

un-cooperative. They'd acted like big-name movie stars instead of local models scrounging for work. After several takes, she'd gotten a headache and had burst into tears, right on the set.

Pierce had ironically been able to come to the set – although he'd not felt well – this was an emergency. He'd saved the day and was able to sweet-talk the models into doing the commercial. He'd worn a face mask so that he wouldn't spread his germs to others.

When she'd told Kevin, instead of sympathy, he'd laughed. He'd also stated that she wasn't cut out to be the director of the marketing department if Pierce had to step in to save her.

Whenever she spoke of moving forward in her career, he'd mention that one incident, as if it were the proof he needed to support his theory that she should remain in her current job. She took a deep breath. In spite of all that, Kevin had many good qualities. She'd honestly loved him and was upset for a long time after he'd dumped her.

She shook her head. No way was she going to ruin a good, tasty lunch appointment by speaking about that terrible incident. "It's not only that, but, I'm a mom now…well sort of. Taking care of Scotty has really been taxing me. He had some emotional problems and…well…the school's been calling me about him lately and…well…do you work a lot of late hours?"

He nodded. "Some, but, you wouldn't be in the

position, if you get the position, until after you're finished from grad school. Plus, you can work late by bringing your laptop home."

He sprinkled malt vinegar on his fish. He then speared a piece of meat with his fork and looked at her directly. "The salary starts at $138,000."

Her eyes widened. Was she even qualified? She bit her lip, hesitating, the drastic thought of the terrible TV commercial rushing to her brain.

"Just think about it. As soon as the job posting is available, I'll let you see it."

Their server returned. "Would you like dessert?"

Monica shook her head.

Pierce glanced at their waitress. "No, just bring us the check." He then focused on Monica. "Just pray about it, okay?"

She finally managed to nod. As soon as she got into her car, she pulled out her phone and made a three-way call. She phoned Anna and Karen, her two best friends. As soon as they were on the line, she made sure that they knew she needed to speak with them. "How about stopping by my house after dinner tonight for coffee and chocolate?" She'd be sure to bring a huge box of Chocolate Dreams candy for them to munch on while she picked their brains for advice.

CHAPTER 7

THAT EVENING, MONICA pulled into the driveway. She smiled as she scanned her charming white two-story house. Chrysanthemums and marigolds bloomed from her flower garden. She got out of the car and stopped, sniffing the sweet, ocean-scented air. If you stood and listened, you could hear the waves crashing on the beach that was nearby.

Scotty opened the door of the back seat and scrambled out of the car. Familiar with his surroundings, he didn't need his cane as he followed her up the driveway. "I want to unlock the door." The urgency in his young voice tugged at her heart. The previous week, she'd taught him how to unlock the door using her key. He'd been mesmerized by the lock, for some reason. She'd found that he liked learning new things as long as he wasn't in the classroom.

She pressed the key into his little hands hand he felt the lock with his fingers. He found the keyhole and mashed his mouth down – he always mashed his mouth down when he was concentrating – and shoved the key into the lock.

They breezed into the room and he slammed the door behind them. She was about to reprimand him for slamming the door, the loud echo of the door slam got on her nerves. But, she just didn't have the energy to reprimand him right now. She'd often heard her coworkers who had kids say that you needed to pick your battles. She now knew what they meant first hand.

After feasting on spaghetti and salad for dinner, she read the note Scotty's teacher had sent home with him, giving her the appropriate information on his assignment for class the following day.

She turned on her computer and hooked up the special equipment that Scotty needed to do his reading assignments. The Braille display hooked up to the computer so that Scotty could read what was on the screen. He mashed his mouth down as he struggled with the assignment. He was able to type the answers to the questions, but, it took time. His reading skills needed a lot of help. Thank God he did as she asked without swearing, and relief washed over her.

He seemed to be in a good mood the entire evening, even humming as he enjoyed his nighttime television show. She hoped that having a positive male role model in his life would help her nephew with his negative attitude.

Scotty yawned and rubbed his eyes. "Time for you to go to bed."

"Can't I stay up a little longer?"

"It's a school night, so, no." Go on upstairs and get ready for bed. He grumbled, but, thankfully, he didn't curse. When he was finally settled in for the night, she pulled out her foot massage bath machine, desperately in need of some pampering. Thoughts of relaxation entered her mind as she filled the machine with water and plugged it in. She watched the water bubble and swish in the enclosure before she retrieved a towel from the linen closet.

She plopped into her favorite living room chair. The gushing bubbles soothed her feet, and she laid her head back on the chair, basking with relief and wiggling her toes in the soothing liquid.

She forced herself to look at her Bible and study guide beside her and placed her feet into the water. She touched her Bible and study guide. Thoughts of preparing for teaching next week's lesson in her women's study group filtered through her mind; however, she found she didn't have the energy to crack her Bible open at the moment.

A contented groan filtered through her lips as she thought about all that had happened to her the previous day. She couldn't believe her nephew had such a gorgeous male tutor. Thoughts of John French continued to dance in her mind until a knock at the door interrupted her.

Reluctantly, she took her feet out of the tub and quickly wiped them with the towel before going to the door. Who could be visiting now? She wasn't expecting anybody. She glanced through the peephole and spotted her best friends. Goodness, she'd been so tired that she'd forgotten about asking them over to binge She grinned and opened the door.

"You sure do look beat!" Her friend Anna pulled her into a hug as Karen followed behind her. Karen's petite frame dwarfed next to Anna's. Monica placed her arms around Anna's wide body while Karen thoughtfully rubbed Monica's shoulder.

Anna released her and licked her lips. "So, where's the candy?"

Karen led the way into the kitchen and placed her hand on Anna's arm. "Don't you think you should cut back on your sweets? Your doctor said you're in danger of becoming a victim of diabetes or high blood pressure if you don't lose the extra weight." They placed their purses on an empty chair.

Anna plopped into a chair at the table. "I'll start cutting back tomorrow," she groaned, waving Karen's comment away.

Folding her arms in front of her chest, Karen sat across from her, shaking her head, causing her stylishly cut dark hair to bounce. "Well, I certainly hope so. Monica and I are very concerned about your health."

Anna turned away from Karen, focusing on Monica. "So, how have you been, girl?"

Monica plopped the attractive gold candy box, emblazoned with the Chocolate Dreams logo, onto the table. "Wait, before we start talking, I need a pick me up." She pulled the top off of the box and selected a piece of candy. She popped the candy into her mouth and enjoyed the sweet, delicious taste of exquisite smooth chocolate. "Mmm…I feel better already."

She started a pot of coffee. Soon all three of them had a mug of decaffeinated hazelnut coffee. Monica consumed three pieces of candy before she shared the news with her friends. "Pierce is retiring and he wants to recommend me for the director's position."

Anna raised her thick eyebrows. "Well, you're going to apply for it right?"

Karen nodded. "I think it sounds like something you'd enjoy."

"Well…." She sighed as she told them all about her lunch with Pierce. When she mentioned her doubts regarding what had happened with the commercial, and Kevin's response, Anna groaned.

"Girl, you should not be letting that man have control over what you do. You broke up two years ago, he's married with a baby now. Stop letting him take control."

Karen nodded. "Yep, she's right. Kevin smothered her passion for marketing. I know you loved the man, but….you need to see how much of a blessing it was for the two of you to break up."

Whoa, this was so much for her to digest. "It's not just Kevin's reaction, remember, I messed up when I was left in charge before."

Karen shook her head. "But, it wasn't totally your fault. Monica, you need to give yourself some grace and move on, do all that you can to make your life fulfilling."

Could she really do it? Could she find the courage to apply for the director's position after Pierce retired? Her fears and twirled through her like spoiled milk on an empty stomach. Maybe she shouldn't have eaten so much candy. She pushed thoughts of the director's position from her mind. "Let's change the subject." She then told them about Scotty's messed up sleeping pattern.

Karen sipped her coffee. "I saw a commercial about that once. I'd heard that blind people sometimes get their days and nights mixed up since they can't see. If I were you, I'd take him to the pediatrician right away. You don't want the problem to get worse."

She sighed. She hadn't even found a doctor for Scotty yet. Since she was his legal guardian for the time being, she'd been able to place him on her health insurance, which was a blessing. Now the doctor search would just be another thing to add to her to-do list. She worried about Scotty and she mentally chastised herself. As soon as Gina dropped Scotty off she should've taken him to the doctor for a checkup.

"What's wrong Monica?" Anna voiced the

question before popping a piece of candy into her mouth.

"Well…." She briefly told them her concerns about Scotty.

Karen sipped her coffee. "Monica, you're being too hard on yourself. This is the first time you've ever taken care of a child. If anyone is to blame it'd be your sister for abandoning him in the first place."

"Well, Scotty has a tutor to help him with school. I just met John recently."

Anna put her coffee cup aside. "John? You say his name almost as if you're familiar with him. How much time have you spent with Scotty's tutor?"

Good grief, she'd thought she'd keep her attraction to Monica wished she could keep her attraction to John a secret for a while longer. Under Anna's and Karen's intense scrutiny, she explained herself. "I'm attracted to Scotty's tutor."

Anna burst out laughing, the loud noise filling the small kitchen. Karen smiled, seemingly amused by this news also.

"Anna, will you be quiet! You might wake Scotty!" warned Monica. She folded her arms in front of her chest, narrowing her eyes. "I fail to see why this is so funny."

Still chuckling, Anna covered her mouth with her hand, her dark eyes shining with warmth. "You act like it's a death sentence. What's wrong with being attracted to him?"

"I agree with Anna," Karen admitted. "What's wrong with being attracted to somebody?"

"I'm happy for you," Anna said. "I just think it's hilarious that you can't be happy for yourself! Maybe now you can get Kevin off your mind!"

Rolling her eyes and pursing her lips, Monica glared at her friend. "That's the second time you all have mentioned Kevin this evening. I am over him. I barely think about him." Well, maybe that was stretching the truth a little bit. She still thought about Kevin, but, not as much as she used to.

Karen groaned. After finishing her coffee, she walked to the pot, her high-heeled pumps clattering on the tiled floor. After refilling her cup, she returned to the table. "You say that, but I saw the way you looked at him and his wife and child in church last Sunday. I think it's awful the way he dumped you two years ago and got engaged to Tamara six months later."

Turning away from her friends, she took a deep breath and wished they hadn't brought up such unpleasant memories. Since she'd gotten Scotty, she barely spent time thinking about Kevin and her nonexistent love life.

Anna squeezed her arm. "Hey, we didn't mean to make you feel bad."

"Look, I don't feel bad. It's just that since Kevin dumped me, you two always seem to mention him once in a while. I'd appreciate it if you didn't mention him again until I say I want to talk about him."

Anna put her arm around Monica. "I'm sorry. I love you like a sister, and I can tell when you see Kevin that it still hurts."

Karen nodded, placing her manicured hand on Monica's shoulder. "Yes, sometimes when you look at Kevin, you look like you're going to cry."

Monica shook her head. "No, I don't, not really. I'm glad that Kevin and his wife are happy together." When their church had held a baby shower for Kevin's pregnant wife, she discovered how hard it was to put her bitterness aside and purchase a gift for Tamara's child. A lot of the church sisters had given her looks of sympathy, and she wished the fact that she'd seriously dated Kevin for two years could be erased from the parishioners' minds forever.

"Sure, you're happy for them," stated Anna sarcastically. "You mentioned to me right before Scotty came to live with you that you couldn't believe Kevin strung you along for two years."

Monica shook her head, still wishing her friends would drop the subject. The first year Kevin had dated her, he treated her like a princess. She'd fallen in love pretty hard. At the time, her only issue with him was his discouragement of her earning her graduate degree and getting a promotion. He'd said that if a woman were to have children, they should always come first — before career.

She'd initially thought his comment was a hint – a hint that he'd be proposing sometime in the near future.

When the topic of marriage didn't come up, Monica was about to broach the subject with him when his mother suddenly died of a heart attack. He'd been so close to his mom, and their fairytale romance took a nosedive after the tragedy. When she finally did try to discuss it with him, he'd stated he wasn't in the right frame of mind to talk about marriage and he was still grieving for his mother. He gave her the same excuse for almost a year before he dumped her for another woman.

She forced the unpleasant thoughts from her brain, focusing again on Anna and Karen. "John is coming by this Saturday for Scotty's first tutoring session. He wanted us to go out, but I didn't think it was a good idea," she said, changing the subject.

Anna placed her elbow on the table, propping her chin in her hand. "Well, let me ask you this: Is he a Christian?"

Karen crossed her slim legs and nodded. "Anna brings up a good point. Is he a Christian? If he is, I don't see any harm in going out with him. The eligible bachelors at our church are practically nonexistent. If you find a good Christian man and he's interested in you and you're attracted to him, you should at least give him a chance." She sipped her coffee. "You can't blame John because Kevin was a fool."

Monica shook her head. "I can't go out with

him. Not now. Scotty has a lot of problems, and he needs me to be there for him. He needs my support, and I can't support him fully while I'm fawning over some man." She paused for a few seconds. "I'm not sure if he is a Christian. When I was speaking to him, we mostly talked about Scotty's educational needs."

"Have you even prayed about this?" Karen asked.

"No."

Karen shrugged. "Why not? I know you just met the man, but hand it over to the Lord and see what He says to you. You're always telling others to pray about things. Now I think it's time for you to heed your own advice."

Anna nodded. "Karen does make a good point. Besides, maybe God has placed John in your path for a reason. He might be the one God intended for you to spend your whole life with."

Monica was silent as she finished her snack, thinking about the advice her friends had given her. No longer wanting the conversation to focus on herself and John French, she asked Karen how the hair salon was doing.

"You know how it is, girl. It's busy in that shop. I barely had time to eat my lunch this afternoon, I was so occupied."

"How are things in the bakery and your catering business?" Monica asked Anna.

Anna chuckled. "Okay. A lot of people are preordering pies and cakes for special events.

My staff and I are going to be pretty busy filling orders next week. This Saturday we're catering an anniversary party."

"Well, after the two of you leave, I have some homework to do."

Karen grunted. "At this rate you'll be studying past midnight."

Monica shrugged. "It's not like I'm not used to it." She paused. "You know, things have been kind of hectic at work. It's hard when Scotty's school calls me about a problem in the middle of the workday. It's still hard to get used to having a child around while I'm working a full-time job."

They continued talking about their jobs for a while before Anna and Karen said they were tired. They gathered their purses and Monica hugged both of them right before they closed her front door.

She then trudged to her office and turned on her laptop. She logged onto the site where she was taking her graduate school courses. She blinked. No, how could she have missed that?

She had paper due tomorrow by eight AM. That's when the final draft needed to be uploaded. She clenched her sour stomach. She was going to be sick. She'd started the paper, but, she'd gotten distracted with Scotty's problems, then she'd gotten sidetracked by Pierce's lunch. She'd mistakenly thought she'd have another week. She took a deep breath. *Lord, help me.*

She forced herself to go back into the kitchen

to start another pot of coffee. Caffeinated this time. Looked like it was going to be a *long* night.

CHAPTER 8

JOHN OPENED HIS eyes. Weak early morning sunlight streamed into his room. He eyed the clock. Six forty-five AM. He wasn't scheduled to go to Monica's until late that morning. Good, he needed some time to work on his fall garden. After drinking coffee and consuming a light breakfast, he changed into his old clothes. He went into the garage, where he kept his gardening tools, and opened the garage door. He stepped outside.

The outside warmth was like an explosion of liquid sunshine. A light breeze teased the trees and leaves colorful leaves drifted onto the ground. Since it was September, they were bound to have several bright, sunny, hot days before the cool weather of autumn started. As he hefted the boxes of plants into his yard, he thought about his visit to Brian's grave.

Beverly and Aiden. Seeing them still seemed weird. Yeah, he was over Beverly, and he knew she deserved to be happy with someone who shared her beliefs, but…he shook his head as he took his shovel and plunged it into the earth with his foot. He then scooped the dirt from the ground and flung it to the side. He continued digging, sweat rolling down his brow.

As he planted each of the bushes, he recalled how his dad used to grow the same bushes in the family yard. He also thought about how he'd had a hobby of naming plants. Always good in science, he'd often take samples of plants home with him after taking long hikes in the woods. When he'd been a boy scout, he'd loved the nature hikes. He could name most plants in seconds and he'd been proud of his knowledge. Studying plants at the university had seemed a perfect occupation for him. He also loved teaching his students about the wonders of plants.

He patted down the soil for the last bush. He stopped and admired the leafy plants blowing in the wind. A bead of sweat slithered down his face. He swiped the moisture away. He eyed his dirty jeans and dirt-encrusted sneakers. Well, looked like he needed to clean himself up before he went to Monica's. A shower and shave were definitely on the list for that morning.

John rapped on Monica's door. Birds twittered from nearby trees and the sound of the ocean echoed in the distance. Footsteps. Light footsteps.

Hmm….sounded like Scotty coming to the door. That didn't sound right. "Who is it?" That was Scotty.

"Hey, Scotty. It's Mr. John."

He heard fumbling. A curse. Sounded like the boy was upset about not being able to open the door. The click of locks and then the door swung open. "I didn't know that Aunt Monica had locked both of the locks." He seemed to be explaining why it'd taken him a bit of time to unlock the door. He peeked into the house and saw the footstool beside the door. He figured Scotty wasn't tall enough to reach one of the locks.

Where was Monica?

He frowned. He eyed Scotty. The boy was still in his pajamas and white froth covered his upper lip. Looked like he'd been eating cereal or drinking a glass of milk. The boy wasn't wearing his dark glasses. He glanced at Scotty's unfocused eyes…his breath caught. He reminded him so much of Brian. He shoved the thought aside. He needed to figure out what to do. "Are you here by yourself, Sport?" Monica had seemed so eager and capable. He didn't imagine that she'd be callous enough to leave Scotty at home alone. He felt that the boy was still too young to be left unattended.

"Nope. Aunt Monica is asleep."

"Asleep? It's eleven o'clock in the morning."

"Yeah, I know." The boy stood taller and smiled.

His gap-toothed grin showed that he'd lost some of his baby teeth. "When I first got up I got my cereal and milk by myself. Aunt Monica showed me how to do it last week and now she doesn't have to do it for me anymore." He wanted praise, that much was obvious.

"Well, it's good that you can do that for yourself, Scotty."

The boy's smile widened as he gestured toward the living room. "Come in."

John entered the house and closed the door behind him. The blinds were closed. He spotted Monica on the couch fast asleep. The TV was on a cartoon, but, the noise didn't bother her. Her soft snores filled the living room. The unwelcome urge to kiss her cheek swept over him like a soft autumn wind. Whoa, he needed to focus. He'd not dated anybody since his break up with Beverly, so, maybe this sudden urge was a sign that he needed to start dating again. Weird, he'd not thought of dating in ages. He shook the thought away.

Should he wake her up? Maybe it'd be best if Scotty did that. "Why don't you wake her up, Sport?" He figured if she might be startled, seeing him when she first woke up. She might be so tired that she may have forgotten about their meeting.

"Aunt Monica, wake up." Scotty roughly shook her shoulder, his loud voice filling the room. "Mr. John is here."

She opened her pretty eyes and finally focused on him. Her mouth dropped open and she ran her fingers over her cheek, her eyes widening. "Oh my goodness…"

She looked embarrassed. "Monica, are you okay?"

"Oh, John…" she shook her head. "I'm sorry about this."

"What's wrong? Are you okay?"

"She's tired. She's been up all night." Scotty made his announcement as he sat facing the TV. Brian used to do that…he'd say that he was "watching" TV, although he couldn't really see it. He'd been able to decipher what was happening on a cartoon just by listening to it. He paused, the memories filling his brain like leaves tossing on an autumn wind. Whenever Brian would get bored, he'd imitate the voices of his favorite cartoon characters. He'd been pretty good at it too. Whenever he and Beverly would have company over, Brian would entertain their guests with his cartoon imitations.

He glanced at the TV screen and spotted the superhero cartoon. That cartoon character had been one of Brian's favorites. Monica yawned, interrupting his thoughts. She sat up on the couch and rubbed her eyes. "John, do you mind tutoring Scotty at the kitchen table? I'll get ready and we can go to the beach afterwards."

"We don't have to go to the beach." She still looked exhausted.

She shook her head. "I promised Scotty that we could get something to eat and go for a walk on the beach…well as long as he listened to you and did the best he could during his tutoring session."

John finally sat at the table beside Scotty and opened his briefcase. As he usually did with his new students, he tested Scotty's ability with the braille alpha- bet by using braille flash cards, giving Scotty each card and listening to him as he tried to read each word, running his small brown fingers over the bumpy white paper. The boy hesitated before reading each word aloud.

He next tested his math abilities. He pulled out an abacus and asked Scotty if he knew how to use one. The boy nodded as he counted out the white beads on the small contraption. His math skills were lousy, and John was determined to make him a more adept student before the end of the school year. He was so engrossed in helping Scotty, he didn't realize a whole hour had passed until Monica returned to the kitchen and began placing food into containers. John reached a stopping point, so he wrapped up his tutoring session with Scotty.

Footsteps sounded on the stairs and Monica came into the kitchen. She still looked tired. He'd forgotten to ask why she'd been up all night. She wore an oversized orange tee shirt and a wraparound casual beach skirt. "Scotty really worked hard during his lesson." He figured Scotty would've wanted his aunt to know that he was trying to make an improvement with his schooling.

She smiled and strolled over to Scotty. She touched the boy's cheek. "Why don't you go and wash up and then we'll head out to the beach."

"Awesome." The boy's loud voice exploded in the kitchen like fireworks before he rushed up the staircase.

CHAPTER 9

MONICA STIFLED A yawn. Well, it was a blessing that Scotty had warmed up to John during the tutoring session—which was a good sign. She again recalled what she'd told Anna and Karen the previous night. He sure was easy on the eyes and Scotty had warmed up to him. The fact that he seemed to care for Scotty made him even more appealing.

She lounged on a beach blanket. Seagulls flew overhead and the waves crashed upon the sandy beach. Fatigue rolled through her. She stifled another yawn. People dressed in swimming gear strolled on the beach. A few people flew kites, but the beach wasn't as crowded as it was during the tourist season. Folks were enjoying the last few warm days before autumn.

John had set up the beach umbrella, and they'd purchased subs, chips and drinks to eat while they sat on the beach. She'd even purchased a box of Chocolate Dreams candy to enjoy for dessert.

"Aunt Monica, I'm hungry," complained Scotty.

"Honey, we're getting ready to eat."

"Good, because I'm saying the blessing." She grinned. Since Scotty had come into her care, she'd been taking him to church and had been teaching him about Jesus. She'd encouraged him to pray before they ate, but, he always refused.

This was the first time he'd been interested. She glanced at John. He sported a tank top and his brown arms rippled with muscles. But, he was frowning. Why did he seem so upset? She then focused on Scotty. It was possible that he wanted to show off to John, let him know that he could pray, just so that John could compliment him later. She'd assumed that Gina hadn't complimented Scotty very much. The boy demanded praise and attention and she'd do whatever she could to make his life better.

She took Scotty's hand as John continued staring at them. "We usually join hands before we bless the food." She explained.

John nodded but made no effort to hold Monica's and Scotty's hands. When his hands remained limp beside him, she paused. He didn't want to pray…why?

The wind blew, fluttering the flaps of their umbrella.

Well, so be it. She didn't want to make a big fuss about this. She'd been struggling to get Scotty to pray aloud, so, looked like John's attitude might dampen her efforts. "Go ahead Scotty."

"God, thank you for this food. Amen." Well, short and to the point. She squeezed his hand.

"Thanks, Scotty. That was a wonderful prayer." Nobody said a word as they enjoyed Cokes, subs and chips. After they'd consumed the small box of candy, they removed their shoes and walked along the shore of the ocean, letting the frothy waves kiss their feet. The delicious meal made her even more tired, but, she forced herself to keep walking.

Scotty was obviously having a good time and this exercise, coupled with the sunny exciting day, were obviously what he needed. Maybe he'd get a good night's sleep that night.

The sun was a brilliant globe in the striking blue sky, and seagulls dipped toward the beach, seeking crumbs of food from beachgoers. Monica described the scenery to Scotty and reminded him about the story of creation he'd learned in his Sunday school class. "Remember God created the birds and animals."

They walked in silence for a few more minutes before Scotty asked a question. "Mr. John, do you go to church?" John held Scotty's hand as he guided him around the edge of the water.

She rubbed Scotty's shoulder. Hopefully he'd not offended John. Since John had not participated in their prayer earlier, she now wondered about his spiritual beliefs. "Scotty, remember I told you that not all people believe the same things about God."

John shook his head. "No, it's okay. I don't mind telling others about my beliefs." His warm brown eyes turned toward Scotty as they continued to walk. "Scotty, I don't go to church. I'm what people call an agnostic."

He scrunched his eyebrows, dipping his toe in the water. "What's that?" She continued rubbing Scotty's shoulder.

Looked like she needed to explain this to him. She doubted most children would know the meaning of an agnostic. "It means that he doesn't know if God exists." She looked at John. "Isn't that right?"

He nodded. "Yes, that's what it means."

She changed the subject, not wanting to discuss his agnostic views in front of Scotty. "Did you enjoy your lesson today?" she asked her nephew.

After the three of them discussed the bit of progress Scotty had made on his first lesson and what they needed to focus on later, they returned to their umbrella. The sun began to dip on the horizon, spilling rays of warmth onto the water.

"I think it's time for us to head home," Monica said. "Soon, it'll be bedtime for you."

John cleared his throat. "Mind if I stay after Scotty goes to bed? I wanted to talk to you about something." He spoke in a low voice so that Scotty wouldn't hear him.

She nodded. "That's fine."

Once they had arrived back at her house, Scotty took his bath and Monica helped him settle into bed.

She returned to the living room after Scotty was in bed.

"I think Scotty had a good day," commented John.

Monica nodded as she invited him into the kitchen. She'd make some coffee. Yes, that's what she'd do. She really wanted to talk to John about what he'd revealed to her that day. After measuring grounds into the filter, she added water and turned on the pot. Soon the aromatic scent of coffee filled the kitchen. She poured two mugs. "How do you take your coffee?"

"Milk and sugar, please."

Focus, stay focused on making the coffee, that's what she had to do. It'd been years, literally, since an attractive man had been inside her home. But, goodness, it was hard to ignore the strong, masculine scent of his cologne. As she placed the cup in front of him, she admired the way his shirt hugged his broad shoulders. He took a sip. "Perfect." His dark eyes gleamed as he looked at her, and her face grew warm.

She gestured toward the living room "Do you mind if we go into the living roowm?"

"Not at all."

He followed her into the living room, and they sat on her couch. The urge to turn on her praise and worship music tugged at her. However, she didn't think John would appreciate her musical tastes. She was about to ask him about his agnostic views, but before John placed his coffee cup on the table and looked directly at her. "You look tired and you were sleeping when I first arrived this morning. Are you alright? I know Scotty mentioned you'd been up all night?"

"Yes. I'm in grad school and well…" she took a deep breath. "Things have really changed in my life since I've taken care of Scotty. I forgot about the due date for my paper and it had to be uploaded onto the professor's site by eight this morning. So, yes, I was up all night."

"You should've put it onto your calendar."

She shrugged. "I forgot. I have more to remember since I've had Scotty."

He nodded. "I can understand that. You mentioned your sister left Scotty with you because she couldn't care for him. I was wondering if she was having trouble finding a job."

She shook her head and sipped her coffee. She placed her mug on a coaster. "I don't think Gina wants to work. My sister left Scotty with me, but I felt she could have cared for him if she wanted to."

His eyes widened. "Excuse me?"

She shrugged, folding her hands on her lap, and told him about the night two months ago when Gina had shown up with Scotty and left him in her care so she could travel with Randy in the circus.

"What about Scotty's father? Can't Gina ask him to take care of their son?"

She shook her head. "No, she can't. Gina has a history of unhealthy relationships with men. Scotty's father, William, was into some illegal activities involving drugs. Scotty was a few days old when his father was killed as he tried to attack an armed police officer."

John's eyes were full of sadness as he looked at her. "Doesn't anybody in William's family care about Scotty? Aren't there other relatives on his father's side who can help take care of him?"

Monica sighed. "The little bit about his family that Gina told me sounded awful. Scotty's father was white. His family never accepted Gina because of her race, and they weren't happy about her being pregnant. William and Gina weren't even married. She said he kept promising to buy her an engagement ring, but it never happened." Monica toyed with her coffee cup. "Gina has always wanted to travel around the world and now that she's met Randy, she has her chance to make her dream come true. I just wish she'd given her decision more thought."

She didn't realize a bitter tone had crept into her voice until he placed his hand over hers.

"Hey, are you all right?"

She shook her head. "No, I'm not okay. Just like when we were younger, I'm trying to fix Gina's mistakes." She turned toward him, enjoying the warmth of his hand as she released her burden.

"She disappeared for two years, and we couldn't find her. My parents were worried because they thought she might be strung out on drugs or dead." Tears came to her eyes as she recalled those dark two years when both she and her parents were filled with worry and dread. "We wondered how Scotty was getting along, since Gina is not very responsible. This wasn't the first time she'd disappeared, but it was the longest she'd been gone. The other times she only disappeared for a few months, before Scotty was even born."

"Did you call the police and file a missing person report?"

"We did better than that. My parents took out a loan and hired an investigator. Gina moved around a lot, and she didn't work very much. When we managed to track down where she was living, she moved right before we could confront her." Monica shook her head. "We let the investigator go when we couldn't afford him anymore, but we did have evidence that she was alive for the time being."

She pulled her hand away, ashamed to show her vulnerability. He handed her a tissue, and she wiped her eyes. "I'm sorry. I've been such an emotional wreck since we found out Gina is still alive and that Scotty is all right. . .well, all right physically, that is." She turned toward him, gazing into his brown eyes. "Do you really think you can help him get back on his grade level?"

He nodded. "I think I can. You know there are

no guarantees, but if he works hard and studies, I think he'll do fine. I've already spoken to his teacher a few times this week, and she's given me his list of reading assignments for the year. He should be receiving more of his braille books shortly."

She was pleased he showed such faith in her nephew.

"Have you talked to Gina since she left for the circus?"

"No, she never calls."

"What about your parents? Can they help?"

She recalled how pleased her parents were when they saw Scotty for the first time in two years. "Yes, they've been a big help. They live near Baltimore, so they don't see him as much as they'd like, but they do call and talk to him a lot. Also, I discovered having Scotty in my care was placing a real dent in my savings. I hesitated going to my parents for money because they're retired."

"Were they able to help you financially?"

She nodded. "I wanted to care for Scotty on my own. I'm kind of stubborn like that. I recently asked my parents if they could give me some funds to help out while I'm raising Scotty, and they were happy to help me. My dad even scolded me for waiting so long to ask for their assistance." She tilted her head. "As a matter of fact, they're coming up early next Saturday morning to get Scotty and keep him for the next few days since school is out for teachers' workdays the following

Monday and Tuesday. A lot of members of their church go on field trips to some attractions in Baltimore, so they promised to take Scotty to some fun places in Baltimore City."

He leaned toward her. "Since Scotty will be gone, you'll be free to do something fun next weekend," he said. "I've got a lot of connections in town. There's a new comedy club that opened on the boardwalk recently. Since I know the owner, I can get us good seats. How about it?"

The smooth cadence of his voice beckoned her, making her want to throw caution to the wind and go out on a real date with a good-looking man. She scooted away, suddenly finding it hard to remain calm while sitting so close to him. "No."

His brow furrowed. "No?"

She shook her head. "No. I can't."

"Why not? Scotty will be gone, so you don't have to worry about him next weekend."

"I need this time to myself to get my head back on straight. Plus, remember, I have assignments due for grad school." She paused. "I'm thinking about going after a promotion at work…and… well I've got a lot on my mind. I've been a nervous wreck since he came to live with me, and I need this time alone to think and regroup and pray."

He tilted his head, seemingly confused.

"Besides, in spite of my decision not to date since I'm trying to focus on Scotty and my studies, I still couldn't go out with you after what

I found out today." Well, she'd not dated since Kevin and the desire had not been there until she'd met John. Of course, she wasn't going to tell him that.

"You're talking about my religious views?" he guessed.

She took another sip of coffee. "Yes, I can't go out with somebody who doesn't share my faith in God. My spiritual beliefs are what keep me centered. My faith in Jesus is the most important thing in my life. It has been important since I accepted Christ when I was a teenager. I rely on Jesus for everything." Her heart rate increased as she spoke about God, and her raised voice resounded in the living room.

"I just don't understand your agnostic views." She continued to look at him, grappling to understand where he was coming from. "As a matter of fact, you're the first man I've ever met who is an agnostic."

He blew air through his lips. "I'm a science professor, so I guess that partially explains my views. Also, my parents raised me this way. Both of them were scientists, and they always said there is an explanation for everything—until you could prove God's existence they would not believe in Him."

She shook her head, still startled by John's opinion. "But how can you disprove it? Look around you—the beauty of the world, all the wonderful things on this earth, God must exist! I don't see how you can doubt that," she finished in a small voice.

"I could argue with you on that one. What about death, disease, and the turmoil on this earth? Why does God let millions of people starve in foreign countries? If God does exist, why does He allow His people to suffer so much?" He gripped his coffee cup. "It's the way I feel."

"I can't give you all the answers, but I know if you believe in God and accept Him, you are guaranteed the gift of eternal life. Isn't that wonderful?"

He shrugged, seemingly unmoved by her statement.

"So, I guess your parents aren't religious at all? They don't go to church or anything?" she asked.

"Actually, my parents were what you would call 'saved' before they were killed in a car accident a couple of years ago."

Her heart skipped a beat. "Really? Didn't they try to make you understand the gospel?"

He was quiet for so long she wondered if she'd made a mistake in asking the question. She placed her hand over his. "I'm sorry. This is none of my business. You're in my home as Scotty's tutor, and it's not right for me to try and force you to change your religious views."

He squeezed her fingers. "No, it's okay." He released her hand. "It's hard for me to talk about. You see, my parents started going to church about six months before they were killed. I'm not sure what prompted them to start going or why they changed their scientific views, but a few days before they died, my dad had been calling me, saying he wanted to talk to me about something important."

"What did he want to tell you?" she asked.

John shrugged. "I never found out. But after they died, several members of their congregation contacted me, expressing their condolences and offering help with funeral arrangements. I found out about their recent church attendance and newfound faith in Christ, and I knew they would want a church service due to their faith. So, I had their funeral at their church and had their pastor speak." He took a deep breath and continued. "I figured my father may have been trying to contact me to tell me about their reformed religious views."

She shook her head. She couldn't imagine what'd it'd be like to lose both parents at the same time. "I'm so sorry for your loss. I'm kind of surprised you were so open with me about this."

He touched her shoulder. "You know, we just met and all, but. . .I'm comfortable with you."

"Thanks." Just hearing the words made her feel warm and gooey, just like the caramel centers in the chocolate candy she ate.

"You're a strong, caring woman, and it was big of you to care for Scotty."

She shrugged. "I had no choice. And I wasn't doing it for Gina. I was doing it for Scotty." She changed the subject. "Don't you ever wonder why your parents changed their minds about God and religion? Haven't you ever thought to search this out for yourself?"

He rested his elbows on his knees, placing his chin in his hands. "As a matter of fact I have. Since I found out they'd changed their minds about God, I've thought about going to church myself to try and discover what they suddenly found so appealing about organized religion."

Silently praying for the courage to continue, she told him what was on her mind. "Well, why don't you do that? There's a class at my church every Sunday before services. It's for new believers and for those who have not yet embraced Jesus as their Savior. I've heard nothing but good things about this class, and it might help you put things into perspective."

"Do you teach this class?"

She placed her hand on her chest. "Me? Oh no. I lead the women's Bible study class, and it's taught at the same time."

"I'll bet you're a good leader."

Heat rushed to her face. "I try to do the best I can. We start the study off with prayer, and I just let Jesus lead me into saying the right things."

She stifled a yawn. She didn't know if she'd be able to climb up the stairs to her bedroom. After John left, she'd sprawl on the couch and go to sleep. She yawned, picking up their empty cups. John followed her into the kitchen, and she sensed him watching her as she rinsed out the mugs and placed them in the dishwasher. "So, will you at least think about coming to the class tomorrow? That's when the new session starts. You don't have to stay for the worship service if you don't want to, but I just feel you need this class. It'll help you with your struggle."

"Who says I'm struggling?"

"You seemed upset about your parents' new belief in God, and I figure you're struggling to understand how they happened to change their minds." She placed soap into the dishwasher before starting it up. Soon the sound of swishing water filled the kitchen. "Or was it presumptuous of me to assume that about you?"

He gazed at her. "No, you're right. I've been struggling with this for the last two years."

"Well, do something about it. You know, come to think of it, God might not have placed you in my path just to teach math and reading to Scotty. Maybe He wanted me to encourage you to end your struggle."

He shook his head. "I don't know about that. But I promise I will at least think about attending the class at your church each Sunday." He paused. "Where do you worship?"

"Mustardseed Faith."

He winced.

"What's wrong?"

"There's no way I'm setting foot in that church. Mustardseed Faith has let me down once – I'm not going there to seek any answers."

CHAPTER 10

NO WAY WAS he setting foot in that church. He'd been about to lose his temper when Monica had mentioned that church. He tossed the blanket off his bed and eyed the empty candy box beside the bed. After he'd spoken to Monica, his anger at Mustardseed Faith had sprouted up, almost as if her words had sprinkled water on his wound and caused it to grow like a poisonous plant.

Poison ivy. Both Beverly and Aiden understood that inviting him to church was off-limits. But Monica didn't understand that. He blew air through his lips and again eyed the empty candy box. After he'd left Monica, he'd been tempted to stop at the liquor store to get something to drink – he needed something to remove this raw pain.

He'd given up alcohol a couple of years after Brian's death. He'd not been able to control his drinking, so he'd had to get sober. So, instead of going to the liquor store, he'd stopped by The Chocolate Dreams Candy Shoppe on the boardwalk. He'd gotten a small box of chocolate caramel candy.

He'd eaten every piece. The overdose of sugar had made his teeth hurt, and now he couldn't sleep. He figured the sugar was keeping him awake. He sighed and got out of bed. He eyed the clock. Two in the morning.

He got a glass of water and turned on the light out back and went onto is back porch. A cool breeze blew. Man, that wind felt good. The slightly nippy temperatures hinted at the autumn days which were just around the corner. He studied the fall foliage he'd planted a few weeks ago. The vivid green leaves danced in the breeze. Meanwhile a few leaves fell from a nearby tree as the wind continued blowing.

After sitting outside for a few hours, thinking, he finally took a good hard run just as the sun started to rise. Winded, he approached Pete's nursery. Pete was just opening the door. The older man glanced over and spotted John. "Out for a run?"

John took a deep breath, still tired. When he first started his run, he didn't realize he'd keep going until he'd gone all the way to Pete's. He must've run at least a good seven miles. "Yeah, I can't believe I came this far. I hadn't planned to…" He hesitated as Pete unlocked the door.

"You're welcome to come in and join me for a cup of coffee. I'm not opening up the shop for another hour."

"Thanks, Pete." He entered the nursery behind Pete. As he usually did, he scanned the rows of plants. He sniffed. The scent of the fragrant fall flowers filled the air. He followed Pete into the small kitchen in the back of the shop.

A few minutes later, Pete served him a cup of hot coffee with cream and sugar. He also placed a cold bottle of water beside the coffee. "I figure you might need some water after that long hard run. I think I have some granola bars in the cupboard if you want something to eat."

"No, I'm good, but thanks." He guzzled the water. The cool refreshing liquid soothed his parched throat. He licked his lips before he took a sip of coffee. Oh, how he loved the taste of the hot coffee.

Pete eased into the chair beside him. He sipped his coffee. "So, what's got you out running so hard so early on a Saturday morning?"

"Well, you know I exercise."

"Yeah, I know you do, but, I can also tell when you push yourself hard when something's on your mind. Are you upset about the anniversary of Brian's death?" His tone gentled, as if he were afraid to bring up a sensitive subject.

"Well…a little bit. But…" He wasn't sure how to explain it.

"Did something happen?"

"Well, yes."

"Tell me about it."

As they sipped coffee he told Pete about

meeting Monica, tutoring Scotty, and about how much Scotty reminded him of Brian. He then told him about running into Beverly and her husband Aiden at the graveyard. He told of their worshipping at Mustardseed Faith. He then told him about Monica's invite to Mustardseed Faith, for the class for new believers.

"Hold on." Pete interrupted him as he refilled their coffee cups. "Monica wants you to go to a class for new believers? Why? You're not a believer....are you?"

"No." The word tumbled from his mouth like an angry pebble. "Sorry...no. It's just that, she said that they wouldn't turn me away and they might discuss some things that would make me think about God in a different way."

Pete settled back into his chair with their refilled coffee mugs. "You got angry when I asked you that question. You're feeling something. You also got angry at Monica."

"What's your point?"

"My point is, if you're so angry then you should do something about it."

"Such as?" He threw his hands into the air. What in the world could he possibly do to lift this weight of pain and uncertainty from this shoulders? He sighed. "Pete, I've been thinking about Monica, Brian and Scotty. God. All of it is tangled in my mind like an angry storm." Chaos. The scientific word burst into his mind like gunfire.

Chaos. He recalled first learning about chaos in his high school class. Chaos was the formless matter supposed to have existed before the creation of the universe. Well, his scientific views were part of the reason why he questioned God. He supposed his thinking about the word, right now, should be no surprise.

The word had a few meanings – the double meaning applied to his life right now. Chaos meant disorder and confusion. Well, he was certainly confused alright. His mind was so confused and disordered that he couldn't sleep. He'd had to eat an entire box of candy just to get his mind off his troubles.

Curious, he took out his phone and looked up the word chaos. Another definition of the word: behavior so unpredictable as to appear random, owing to great sensitivity to small changes in conditions.

Well, he wouldn't exactly call his behavior unpredictable, was it? He'd been a bit angry and had gone on a long hard run this morning. People did different things when they were working through their problems. That's all he was doing. Coping.

"What are you looking at?"

He shoved the phone back into his pocket. "Nothing."

Pete shrugged. "Well, like I was saying. You should do something about your anger. Try going to the class, just once, and see how it goes."

Could he find the courage to set foot into a church? He'd not been in a church Brian died.

Whew, she just couldn't believe it. John's terse tone still settled in her gut like spoiled milk. It'd been a few days since their last conversation. And during Scotty's last tutoring session, she'd again broached the subject of Mustardseed Faith. John had tersely told her that'd he didn't feel like talking about it.

Well, he'd looked upset.

Upset and hurt. His dark eyes had teared up for a few seconds before he'd stormed out of the house. Thoughts about John flooded her mind so much that it was hard for her to concentrate on her grad school studies. She yawned as she rolled out of bed. She'd gone to bed at two o'clock am the previous night because she'd been doing homework. Exhausted, she wanted to go back to sleep but, she'd promised Scotty that she'd make him pancakes for breakfast that morning.

Thank goodness it was Saturday. It was only seven in the morning and Scotty still wasn't awake. Well, she shouldn't be surprised about that. He'd stayed up past midnight, refusing to go to bed because he wasn't tired. He still had trouble sleeping and she really needed to take him to the doctor. The teacher had called her once last week because Scotty had been irritable and cranky.

The child had been exhausted since he'd had trouble sleeping the night before. Well, she couldn't put this off any longer. First thing Monday morning, she was going to contact a pediatrician for Scotty. She'd initially thought that his sleeping habits would improve with time, but, it didn't look like that was going to happen.

She opened his door. Scotty's mouth was wide opened. He breathed deeply, sound asleep. She smiled. She hated waking him, but, because of the plans they had scheduled for that day, it just wasn't a good idea to let him sleep in. "Scotty." She shook his shoulder.

"Aunt Monica." His voice cracked as he yawned.

"Honey, you have to get up. Grandma and Grandpa are coming to get you for the weekend, remember?"

He magically sat up and rubbed his eyes. He threw the blankets off and hopped out of bed. He ambled over to the bedroom door and walked down the stairs. She continued to grin as she watched her nephew. He'd gotten downright comfortable in her house. He knew his way around pretty good. He was settling into her life and...she honestly didn't know what she'd do if Gina returned to reclaim him.

She shook the thought away as she pulled out the griddle and plugged it in. After she'd mixed up a batch of pancake batter, she poured the batter onto the hot griddle. The lovely vanilla aroma of the pancakes filled her kitchen. She placed sausage links into the heated skillet on the stove.

Fifteen minutes later, she placed the hot, buttery pancakes onto the table. She poured syrup over the hotcakes and gave Scotty sausage to enjoy with his meal. After she poured the orange juice and coffee, and said a short prayer, she sliced her fork into the pancakes. She popped a bite into her mouth. The light fluffy vanilla pancakes mingled nicely with the maple syrup and melted butter.

Delicious.

She then drank a glass of sweet, tangy orange juice. She glanced at Scotty's empty plate. Without even asking, she slid two more pancakes onto his plate as well as more sausage. "Did you need help packing your stuff for your visit to Grandma and Grandpa's?"

He shook his head as he shoved a bite of pancakes into his mouth. "Nope. I have everything packed already." His voice sounded muffled since his mouth was full of food.

"Don't talk with your mouth full."

He didn't say anything as he continued eating. She fingered his kinky, tangled mass of hair. "Your grandfather is taking you to get a haircut on the way to their house today."

A knock interrupted their meal. Grinning, Scotty pushed his empty plate away. "Grandpa and Grandma are here!" He ran toward the door, almost tripping over a chair.

"Be careful, Scotty." A few times he'd run into the table and her dishes had toppled to the floor, broken. She didn't feel like cleaning up a mess this morning.

Her parents entered the kitchen, Scotty holding his grandmother's hand. Her dad's shiny bald head was covered with a Baltimore Orioles baseball cap. "Is that pancakes and sausage I smell, Miss Monica?" Her father's teasing voice filled the room as he kissed her cheek.

Her mother's dark eyes were shadowed with concern as she pulled Monica's hands into hers. As usual, she wore her short, salt and pepper hair in a chic bob-like style. "Baby, you sure do look thin." She pulled Monica closer and whispered in her ear. "Don't let Scotty run you ragged. Gina makes me so angry!"

"Mom—"

"I just don't understand how Gina could turn out so messed up and you turned out so well. We raised you both the same. . . ." She looked away as if still trying to find answers to her questions.

"Grandpa, when are we leaving?" Scotty demanded, pulling on the old man's hand.

He chuckled. "We'll be leaving soon." He placed his hand on Scotty's shoulder. "Why don't you run upstairs and get your suitcase. We want to talk to Monica for a second."

Scotty rushed up the stairs, almost knocking over the glass of water that Monica had accidentally left on the coffee table the previous night.

Her father hugged her. "Monica, you're so thin! Don't you ever eat a decent meal?"

Her mother grunted. "That's what I was trying to tell her. She needs to take better care of herself. She can't allow Scotty's behavior to put her own health at risk."

Monica gritted her teeth, not wanting to hear their reprimands. "I promise I'll try to take better care of myself. The two of you are helping me out a lot just by taking him for the next few days."

Her father grunted. "That's what we wanted to talk to you about. Is keeping Scotty too much for you? Did you want us to start keeping him all the time? Since we're both retired, we have more time to devote to his needs."

Her mom nodded. "Yes, we were talking about it on the way up here. We're just concerned that once we take him in, we'll find that we can't handle him as well as we thought we could."

Monica shook her head. "No, Scotty has to stay with me. Besides, he's learning to adjust to his new school, he's making new friends, and I've gotten him involved at the Sunday school at church. He even has a new tutor who can help him with his math and reading." She took a deep breath, thinking of another way they could help her out. "He's been having trouble sleeping." She quickly explained how his sleeping pattern had been messed up. "I need to take him to the pediatrician." She took a deep breath. "Since he didn't seem physically sick, I didn't think it was a big deal. He seems healthy and he certainly eats enough. But…he hasn't gotten any better and frankly, I'm worried about him." She took a deep breath. "Maybe you could talk to him, find out if he had this problem when he was staying with Gina. Whenever I talk to him about his sleeping problem, he gets mad."

Her dad put his arm around her. "Don't you worry about a thing. We've got this under control."

She blinked and looked at her dad. "What do you mean?"

"Well, I can take him to Dr. Mack. I'm sure he could see him over the weekend."

Dr. Mack was her father's best friend and he was also the family pediatrician when she and Gina were children. A tiny seed of joy slid through her heart like a peek of sunshine. "But, dad, he's not local…"

He shrugged. "So. You can still find a local pediatrician. We can always get the paperwork from his visit to Dr. Mack transferred over."

She sighed…a sigh of joy. It was almost as if a heavy weight had been lifted from her shoulders. She'd been taking off from work so much because of Scotty, and she'd also been stressed about her grad school class. Just having somebody else to figure out his sleeping problem was a blessing indeed. *Thank you, Jesus.* She mentally whispered the prayer straight from her heart to God.

She hugged her dad. "Thanks, Daddy."

Scotty came down the stairs again, interrupting their tender moment, struggling with a heavy suitcase. Monica hurried toward him, prying the suitcase from his hand. "Scotty, you're only going to be gone for a few nights. You don't need this much clothing."

"Why don't you let him take all the clothes he wants?" her father said. "It would be easier for Scotty to visit us more often if he had a few changes of clothes at the house."

Now, that was a nice idea. It would be good for Scotty to spend some weekends with his grandparents – it would give them a chance to bond. She nodded. "Okay."

Her mother took her aside into the kitchen as Scotty continued to chat with his grandfather in the living room. "Your father and I also wanted to talk about keeping Scotty for a week during Christmas break. I think he might enjoy that. We can talk about it later in the year, though."

Monica nodded. It was nice that they were going to start keeping Scotty. Sure, he'd visited them a few times since he'd been under her care, but, it'd never been discussed about their keeping him occasionally until that morning.

Before they left, she pulled Scotty into her arms, fingering his dusty-colored kinky hair. "You take care of yourself and mind Grandma and Grandpa. And remember, no cussing." She pulled his chin between her fingers and looked into his unseeing eyes. "Understood?"

"Yes," he grumbled, squirming out of her tight embrace. She waved at them from the doorway until they were out of sight.

They had not been gone for five minutes before she started to miss Scotty. "Oh Lord, what in the world is wrong with me," she mumbled to herself.

She entered the kitchen and cleaned up the breakfast dishes. Afterward she got dressed and drove to Karen's hair shop.

A few hours later, she left the salon enjoying her freshly permed hair. She'd had a chance to speak with Karen about John's agnostic views and about his strong reaction regarding Mustardseed Faith church. She'd also mentioned how her parents were taking Scotty to see Dr. Mack over the weekend. "That's a blessing." Karen commented while spraying hairspray on Monica's freshly-permed hair.

When Monica returned to her house, she was surprised to see that she'd left her phone on the kitchen table. She'd been so preoccupied that she'd not missed it when she was out running errands for the day. A voicemail message – John's phone number appeared on her recently-called list on her phone. Heaven help her, her heart skipped as soon as she noticed it was him. She accessed her voicemail. "Monica…." He paused. His deep voice, rich and smooth…reminded her of the famous candy made at The Chocolate

Dreams Candy Company. She grinned and plopped into a chair. She figured she looked like a love-sick teenager right now. She squeezed her eyes shut. Control. She needed to control these budding feelings toward this agnostic, handsome, charming man. "I just wanted to let you know that I'm coming to Mustardseed Faith tomorrow morning."

CHAPTER 11

MONICA CLICKED THE "submit" icon submitting her quiz for her online marketing class. She closed her eyes. *Lord, please let me get an A.* This class proved brutal and she wanted to do all she could to keep her grades up. The quiz was immediately graded by the school's online website. She opened her eyes. Ninety percent! Yes! Only one question wrong. She scanned the question and made sure she understood what she'd done wrong.

She needed to be sure she didn't make the same mistake when she took the final. She yawned and eyed the clock. One thirty AM. Whew, what a night. As she slid into bed, she again thought about her class and about her aspirations to be the marketing director.

Hey, wait a minute. She hadn't actually taken the plunge and accepted Pierce's offer of being referred for his job. Of course, there was no guarantee she'd get the position, but, deep in her soul, she knew she had to try. She closed her eyes, breathing deeply.

So, John was coming to church tomorrow. Imagine that. Well, she'd believe it when she saw it. That man was so indecisive. *Lord, please work on John's soul, Amen.*

Gospel music blared from her alarm clock, waking her up the following morning. She could really use a few more hours of sleep, but she needed to get to church this morning. She trudged to the kitchen and made a cup of tea. As she sipped the brew, she turned on her favorite Christian radio station and sat in her living room, listening to the music.

She was tempted to call Scotty and see how he was doing, but she resisted, knowing he might still be asleep. She needed to speak to her father to make sure that he was able to take Scotty to the pediatrician.

Unable to resist, she listened to John's voicemail message again. Oh, how she loved hearing his deep voice.

As she prepared for church butterflies danced in her stomach. Whenever she was nervous, her stomach would feel upset. Now, seeing John should *not* be such a big deal. She needed to calm herself down and not be so anxious. She scanned her wardrobe wondering what to wear.

Her eyes settled on a black skirt and a white silk blouse. The light-colored garment was adorned with tiny black flowers. After she dressed, she took special care in curling her short hair and applying her makeup.

Joy and nervousness tumbled within her like a thunderstorm as she drove to church.

Man, what a night. After he'd left that message for Monica, he'd doubted his decision to come to church. He glanced up at the cross sitting on the top of the small white church. The class would start shortly, and he figured he didn't want to be late. He grabbed his Bible from the passenger seat.

He stopped and glanced at the black book in his hands. He just could not believe that he, a scientist, an agnostic scientist, actually stepping into a church. Oh, my goodness. The gravel crunched beneath his feet as he approached the whitewashed building. He opened the door and spotted an elderly woman wearing a business suit with high-heeled shoes. "Welcome to Mustard Seed Faith. How can I help you?"

He offered his hand, but, she shook her head and pulled him into a hug. He sniffed…the familiar perfume, reminded him of his mom's perfume. Warmth enveloped him and his eyes teared. Whoa, he needed to get a grip. He missed his parents, he missed his son, so many things that disappointed him. Death. He shook the unwelcome though away. He quickly blinked away his sudden tears, glad that they didn't spill onto his face. No way did he want to be caught crying in front of this elderly woman.

The lady looked at him, her dark eyes wise and kind. "You look like you got a lot on your mind son. Did you want me to pray for you right now?"

No way. But, he didn't want to offend the woman. Looked like he just needed to tell her why he was there. "There's a class for new believers." Should he even mention that he wasn't a believer? Might as well. "I'm still well, not a believer, but, I was told that it was okay for me to sit in on this class."

The woman grabbed his hand and led him down the stairs. The stairs creaked as they walked down – sounded like this building was pretty old. "Let me tell you something young man, you're not a believer *yet*. You just remember that." She then gave him a short, curt nod before gesturing toward the partially open door. "Go on in there. Class will be starting in a few minutes. I've got to get back upstairs to do my duties as a greeter."

John opened the door and spotted Aiden standing in front of the wipe board. He was setting his Bible on the desk right before he looked up and spotted John. "John? What in the world are you doing here?" The shock in his voice rippled through the classroom like thunder, and a few of the people in the class giggled.

"I uh…well…" How could he explain his struggle in front of all these people? Well, he didn't have to. Aiden knew about his struggle.

Aiden shook his head. "No need to explain, man." He offered his hand. "Welcome to the class."

As John shook Aiden's hand, he thought about something. This could get interesting, taking a class that was being taught by his ex-girlfriend's husband.

After Monica led her women's Bible study class, she desperately tried to pay attention as the ladies discussed women's roles within the traditional Christian church, but she found her mind wandering a lot. John kept popping into her mind like a ray of sunshine. A few times, one of her pupils had caught her daydreaming. How embarrassing was that? Maybe she could catch up with John before the service started.

After they ended their study with a prayer, she rushed from the room, going down the hallway to where she hoped John was also being dismissed from his class. She eagerly watched people filing from the room. A few people greeted her, some stopping for short conversations. The last person to exit the room was Aiden.

Confused, she approached him.

He greeted her with a warm hug. "How's my favorite women's Bible study teacher?"

"Fine." She still wondered what had happened to John. "Aiden, I'm anxious to know if my friend John made it to your class."

They made their way back up the stairs. "I'm sorry, Monica. He came, but right before class started, he left."

"What?"

Disappointment washed over her, just like the waves crashing on the sands of Ocean City. "But he called me yesterday and said he was coming. I wonder why he left."

"Monica, John's been through a lot. He's struggling and—"

"Hold on, Aiden. You talk about John as if you know him."

He squeezed her shoulder and hesitated. He opened his mouth, then closed it. "I know him... but..." He looked at her. "Are you..."

Aiden wants to know if I like John. No way was she telling him that she had a small crush on John French. "He's Scotty's tutor. How do you know him?"

He glanced at the people mingling in the hallway. His adam's apple bobbed as he swallowed. In all the time she'd known Aiden, he'd never been at a loss for words. The man stated what was on his mind, as diplomatically as possible. "Aiden, what's wrong?" Did Aiden want to warn her that John was some kind of lunatic? Her imagination was going into overdrive. "Aiden, if you want to tell me something then just do it."

He sighed. "He used to be with Beverly. That's how I know him."

"Your *wife*? Do you mean to tell me that John was married to Beverly?" This was shocking news indeed.

Aiden quickly shook his head. The choir hummed from the pulpit as praise and worship music floated throughout the church. "No, they were never married."

"Okay….so, what's the big deal?" So, John had dated Beverly and they'd broken up. Beverly had then married Aiden. She knew firsthand that breakups could be hard. Could John still have feelings for Beverly and that's why Aiden was acting so strange.

Beverly breezed into the sanctuary. "Aiden, what's taking you so long? I was waiting for you."

"Sorry honey." He kissed her cheek.

Beverly focused on Monica. "Hey Monica."

"Hi, Beverly." The women hugged.

Aiden cleared his throat. "We'll talk later." He smiled as he gestured toward the sanctuary. "Church is about to start."

Beverly frowned as she glanced at both of them. She was probably wondering what they were talking about. Beverly and Aiden held hands as they walked into the sanctuary.

Aiden said that church was about to start. Well, she had a feeling that Aiden was just using the service as an escape from answering her questions. John had a secret, and she had to wonder what he was hiding.

CHAPTER 12

TWO WEEKS LATER, John pulled into the parking lot of Mustardseed Faith. Maybe he wouldn't chicken out this time and he'd stay for the class. He didn't feel like walking into the church right now. He needed to just sit out here and think. He opened his window and the sun warmed his face. He glanced at the church and noticed the large bunch of chrysanthemums planted near the entrance.

He saw other fall foliage near the church and spotted a few dry leaves littering the graveled path. After he'd seen Aiden the last time he'd visited MustardSeed faith, he'd felt a bit uncomfortable. It wasn't the fact that Aiden was now married to Beverly that made him uneasy…it was just that….well…he'd gotten scared.

Scared of what, he wasn't sure. The emotions he'd had when that woman, that elderly lady, the greeter, the one who'd smelled just like his late mother, had hugged him.

He'd been about to cry. Then when he saw

Aiden…after he sat in his chair in the class, he'd thought about how kind, considerate and caring Aiden had been towards Brian. He just didn't want to stay for class.

He wanted to be alone. His emotions were all over the place and he had no idea as to why. Granted, he figured that his emotional turmoil may have been linked to the anniversary of Brian's death. But, he sensed it was more than that.

He'd even visited his pal Pete and talked to him again. His friend had again encouraged him to return to church, so, he'd obviously obliged.

He clutched his Bible as got out of the car and approached the building. He again thought about the phone call he'd made to Monica a couple of weeks ago and wished he hadn't broken his promise to attend the class. Well he was too late to attend class that day, so, he'd go to service. For some reason, he didn't feel like going to class yet – he wanted to see the church and service before making the decision, again, to attend Aiden's class.

As he'd tutored Scotty over the last couple of weeks and enjoyed Monica's home cooking, she had said little about his agnostic views, but her disappointment in his cancellation of their church date was evident. Her dark, pretty eyes were full of unasked questions. She'd been polite, but a bit standoffish…downright moody. She seemed to be a bit upset about something and when he'd asked her about it, she'd brushed off his concern.

He climbed up the steps of the building. He

entered the vestibule and the same elderly lady approached him. "Hi, I knew you'd be back. Remember, you're not a believer *yet*." She chuckled as she hugged him. He was again reminded of his mom and her floral perfume and big warm hugs. He took a deep breath. At least he held himself together and didn't get emotional right now.

"John!" Monica approached him, her dark eyes sparkling. "You didn't tell me you were coming today." As she reached toward him, he took her hand. The scent of her perfume enveloped him, and he longed to kiss her, right here in the church foyer. She stepped back, and he released her hand.

He didn't realize he was staring until a warm blush covered her brown cheeks. "I didn't decide to come until this morning. I hope it's all right."

She chuckled. "Of course it's all right. I'm glad you're here."

"I know I was supposed to stay for class a couple of weeks ago, but at the last minute, I just didn't have the courage." He gazed into her eyes. "I'm surprised you didn't ask why I never showed up when you saw me during Scotty's tutoring sessions."

"John, I have a lot of questions to ask you, but…well…" She shook her head. "I figured it was a personal matter for you, and I didn't want to bring it up until you did. I didn't want to be too nosy and ask questions that…well…that you might feel uncomfortable with my asking. Anna,

Karen, and I have been praying for you to come here."

"You told Anna and Karen about. . .about what I told you?" He'd never met her best friends, but she'd mentioned them often.

Her grin faded as he dropped her hands. "Yes, I hope that was okay." People continued to bustle around them in the foyer while children scampered upstairs to the Sunday school classes. "I just finished teaching my women's Bible study class."

"Really? What did you study today?"

She brightened as she spoke of her class. "We read the book of Ruth aloud and discussed it."

"Did you enjoy the discussion?" he asked.

"Oh, so much. You know, it's a powerful love story." She pointed to his Bible. "You should read it sometime. I have a study guide to use with my class, but sometimes things go off on a tangent and we get into a deep biblical discussion. It's so refreshing." She raised her voice as she clutched her Bible, obviously excited.

Her dark eyes shined with warmth. "There're still a few minutes before service begins. If you want, I'll explain why I told Anna and Karen about you."

"Okay." As they entered the sanctuary, a few people looked at them with curiosity and some waved at Monica. Aiden and Beverly glanced their way and waved. Monica waved back at the twosome, but she frowned as she sat in her seat.

He glanced at Aiden and Beverly and then at Monica.

Good grief, he'd not thought about the fact that Monica worshipped here. She didn't know anything about his history with Aiden and Beverly. Or, maybe she did? He glanced at Aiden and Beverly. Nah, they wouldn't tell Monica much. Aiden was discreet and Beverly wasn't one to talk about their past relationship. He figured Aiden may have mentioned something to Monica, but he didn't fill out all the details.

Monica didn't know about Brian.

This was a lot for him to digest. He didn't just confide to anyone about one of the darkest, most personal and emotional times in his life. He then thought about something….was Monica at Mustardseed when Brian had died? When… well…when he got mad at the church…well… for…he just couldn't think about that now. He needed to appease his curiosity. "How long have you been going to church here?"

"About two years."

Okay, that made sense. Monica joined this church a few years after Brian's death, so, she probably didn't know anything about it. That is, unless Aiden or Beverly said something to her about it, and he doubted the did.

They understood that he'd probably want to tell Monica about that himself when the time was right. He leaned back into the pew and tried to relax. Parishioners spoke in hushed tones as the small band tuned their instruments. Sunlight streamed through the stained-glass windows, illuminating the place of worship with warmth.

She leaned toward him. "I told Anna and Karen about you because when we became friends we made a pact."

"What kind of a pact?"

"Well, all three of us are sisters in Christ—"

"Sisters in Christ?"

She sighed. "Yes, all three of us are Christians, we share a deep faith in the Lord, and I'm close to them since our faith binds us together. So, if something is bothering one of us, we promised to tell each other so we can pray about it together until God works everything out."

"Really?" Although he still doubted the power of prayer, he was impressed by their devotion to one another. "Does it usually work?"

She shrugged. "God always answers prayers. Sometimes it just might not be the answer we're looking for."

Well, prayer didn't always work. Prayer certainly didn't save Brian. Unsure how to comment on her last statement, he peered around the now crowded sanctuary. "Where's Scotty?"

"He's in his Sunday school class. We won't be seeing him until the end of the service."

As if on cue, the band started playing. Sweet notes filled the air as people stood and sang praises to God. John glanced around the sanctuary as people's voices lifted in harmony. Some were stoic, seeming to merely mouth the words to the popular Christian song. However, others like Monica swayed to the music, raising their hands toward the ceiling as they sang with emotion. A few of the parishioners had tears slipping from their eyes as they praised their God. After a half hour of worship music, the preacher approached the pulpit. John barely listened to the sermon about forgiveness—he was still so awed by the emotion showed by the parishioners as they praised the Lord.

During the service, John noticed Monica glance to the pew a few rows away near the exit. Her eyes became sad as she watched a man and woman with a small baby, obviously a married couple. The woman glanced at Monica. When their eyes locked, Monica hurriedly looked away, as if ashamed to be caught staring.

After the service was over, Monica led him back into the foyer as she waited for her nephew. Scotty entered the foyer, led by the Sunday school teacher. "Aunt Monica?"

"Hey, Scotty. Guess who's here?"

"Hey, sport." John rubbed Scotty's shoulder.

Scotty giggled. "Mr. John, I'm surprised you're here since you don't know if you believe in God."

The startled expression on Monica's face spoke volumes as she pulled Scotty aside, gently reprimanding him in a corner.

"You must be John."

John stopped staring at Monica and Scotty, still

huddled in a corner, and focused on the woman who'd just approached. She easily weighed over two hundred pounds and her dark eyes sparkled with warmth. "Yes, I'm John and you are. . . ?"

Another woman approached. She was petite, thin, and wore a dark suit. Her hair was swept up into an elegant style. "Hi, John, I'm Karen and this is Anna. Monica told us you were Scotty's new tutor."

Monica approached, holding Scotty's hand. "Hi, you two. I see you've already met John."

John watched the two friends with amusement. "Well, I'm glad to have met both of you."

He wasn't ready for the day to end but didn't want to invite himself to Monica's house.

Karen saved the day. "We sometimes go to the Bayside Skillet for brunch after church. Did you want to go with us?"

He wondered what Monica thought about the invitation. Did she want him to come?

Monica hesitated. "Yes, John, why don't you come with us?"

After some discussion, Anna decided that everybody should ride with her to the restaurant in her minivan. Monica climbed into the large vehicle, following Karen, Scotty, and John. "Anna, what's a single woman like you doing with a minivan?" he asked.

She placed a gospel CD into her player, chuckling as she revved the engine. "I guess Monica told you I'm a baker, but I'm also a cook." She continued to grin as she pulled out of the parking lot. "I purchased this van because sometimes I do some catering events on the side, and I can remove the seats and store all my food and equipment in here."

Anna dominated the conversation on the ride to the restaurant, telling John how she'd started her own business while Monica stared silently out the window.

"Are you okay?" he asked Monica.

She nodded. "I'm just a little tired. I had a little bit of trouble falling asleep last night." He figured she'd been up studying for her class. He knew first hand how brutal graduate school could be.

They pulled into a parking space. As he exited the car, the wind from the ocean blew toward them. The sun warmed the air, and they commented on the nice weather as they walked into the restaurant.

A server approached, wearing a black-and-white uniform. His muscles bulged as he removed menus from a receptacle. "Where would you like to sit?"

Karen spoke up. "Can you give us a large table with a view of the ocean?" He nodded, beckoning them to the table, then left them with their menus.

John showed Scotty his seat before he held out Monica's chair for her.

Anna stared at the waiter, whistling softly. "Isn't he the finest chocolate-brown man I've seen in months? Mm, mm, mmm."

Karen leaned in her seat, whispering to Anna. "You know your voice carries. He might hear you."

"I don't care if he does hear me!" Her boisterous laugh rang throughout the room, and Karen playfully swatted Anna's arm.

Anna chuckled as they opened their menus while admiring the view of the ocean. The picture window gave a relaxing view of the large white waves as they tumbled over the beach. A few people ran along the edge of the shore, but the ocean was devoid of swimmers.

Monica quietly read Scotty the options from the children's menu.

The server returned minutes later. "What would you all like to order?" He spoke to all of them, but his warm brown eyes remained fixed on Anna.

Anna batted her eyelashes, staring at the waiter. "What do you recommend?" He chuckled, winking at her. "The seafood frittata and the banana royale crepes are good. Our cook is a local, and he makes the best breakfast you've ever tasted."

Anna laughed. "Don't you need a pad and pen to write it down? I wouldn't want you to forget our orders."

"Oh, you don't have to worry about that. . .uh . . .what's your name?"

Anna put her menu aside, her complete

attention focused on the waiter. "My name is Anna Gray."

"I'm Dean Love."

"Your last name is not Love."

He chuckled. "It sure is. Maybe later I'll prove it to you."

"What?"

He shrugged his broad shoulders. "I was talking about showing you my driver's license."

"Oh, okay." She glanced at her menu. "I'll have the banana royale crepes and the seafood omelet, an order of bacon, and a coffee and an orange juice." She closed her menu and gave it back to the waiter.

Karen ordered a seafood frittata. Monica ordered a sausage-and-cheddar omelet with bacon for herself, John ordered a southwestern omelet, and Scotty ordered an American cheese omelet.

While Karen and Anna were having a conversation, John touched Monica's hand. "Are you sure you're okay? Are you just tired like you said earlier?"

"Yes, why do you ask?"

He shrugged, unsure of how to answer. "You look a little sad. Did something happen recently?"

She shook her head, leaning toward him. "Just worried about Scotty, that's all."

He looked at her, sensing there was more going on with her than Scotty's behavior problems. He recalled her mentioning that Scotty had been having trouble sleeping. Brian had had the same problem once he'd lost his sight. She'd also said that her dad would be taking Scotty to the pediatrician. He'd forgotten to ask if Scotty were sleeping better now.

Before he could question her further, their server arrived, and scents of seafood and eggs filled the table. As he prepared to dig into his food, the others bowed their heads while Monica led the blessing. He watched her as she thanked the Lord for their food. Her long lashes fluttered as she opened her eyes and looked at him. He returned her warm gaze before enjoying his meal.

After the meal was over, Anna left the table, and John noticed her in the corner, flirting with the waiter. They were laughing and talking, typing into their phones, so he assumed they were exchanging phone numbers. Anna returned, announcing she was ready to head back. She drove everybody back to their respective cars at the church parking lot.

John watched Monica as she led Scotty to her car. "Monica." "Yes?" She unlocked her door.

"How about another cup of coffee?"

"Huh?"

He chuckled. "Do you mind if I come by and visit for a while?" Her hand rested on the door handle.

"Well, I don't know. . . ."

"If you have plans, I understand."

"Why did you want to come by?"

He decided to be honest with her. "I wanted to talk to you about something."

"Really? What?" Her voice was full of intrigue as she awaited his response. "I'll let you know as soon as we get to your house."

"Okay."

Grinning with anticipation, he headed to his car.

CHAPTER 13

SO, JOHN WANTED to talk to her? About what? She scurried to her car, holding Scotty's hand. As she drove home she went as fast as she dared.

"Aunt Monica, you're driving awfully fast. Just like a race car." Scotty made a vrooming sound like a race car before laughing. Well, at least he was having a good time. She couldn't recall the last time she'd heard him laugh.

Well, maybe she needed to slow down. The last thing she needed was for the cops to stop her and give her a speeding ticket.

"Why are you driving so fast?"

"John's coming over." She pulled into their driveway.

"Oh." The boy cursed under his breath.

"Excuse me?" She raised her eyebrows. "What'd I tell you about that cursing?"

"Sorry." He opened the car door and slammed it shut after exiting the vehicle. "I didn't know I had a lesson today."

Looked like her news about John's visit had ruined his good mood. Maybe in due time, Scotty would learn to like school. Speaking of school, she had a ton of homework to do that evening. Man, she'd sure be glad when grad school was over. She needed to collaborate with some of her classmates about a group project via Skype.

Scotty scurried up the paved walkway with surety. It still amazed her as to how fast he could move around when he was in a familiar surrounding. She followed him to the front door. Her hand shook as she removed the keys from her purse. She dropped them and they clattered onto the ground. She lifted the keys.

She really needed to get a grip and calm down. She didn't want John to know just how nervous she was. "You don't have a lesson."

Scotty's frown melted into an easy smile. "Really? Then why's he coming over?"

Gee, Scotty could be nosy sometimes. "He has to talk to me about something."

Her keys jiggled as she tried to unlock the door. "I want to do it."

She sighed. Well, she wasn't going to argue with him about that. She was so nervous that she'd forgotten her routine of allowing Scotty to unlock the door. She pressed the key into his hand and his mouth mashed down as he unlocked the door.

She smiled. "Thank you, Scotty."

"Can I have some cookies and milk and watch some TV?"

After eating that huge breakfast, she was surprised that he even wanted something to eat. "You can have two cookies and a glass of milk." She didn't want him eating too many sweets.

Surprisingly, he didn't argue. Whenever she limited his intake of sugar, he usually tried to ask for more. She supposed he was getting used to her rules, which was a good thing.

As soon as Scotty was settled in front of the TV, a knock sounded from the door. "I want to get it." Scotty scurried to the door and opened it. "Hi, Mr. John. Aunt Monica told me you were coming."

"Hey, Sport."

Monica eyed John as he entered her home. Scotty locked the door before taking his seat near the television. He munched on his cookies and gulped his milk, not paying either of them any attention. He looked…wonderful. He still wore his suit and she loved the way the suit fit his large muscular body. Liquid heat simmered in his chocolate brown eyes and she realized she was standing there, staring at him like a lovesick teenager. *Monica get a grip.*

"Hi, John." She finally managed to speak.

"Hi, Monica." He came toward her, and, for the life of her, she felt that he was aiming to kiss her. But, he simply touched her shoulder.

She turned and went into the kitchen. John's

heavy footsteps sounded behind her. After brewing the coffee, she tried to calm her racing heart as she poured two cups of coffee before joining him at the table. Monica sipped the coffee. "Before you tell me why you wanted to talk to me, I just wanted to thank you."

"Thank me for what?"

"For helping Scotty. I know he still has a long way to go, but since you've been tutoring him, his schoolwork has improved a little bit during the last few weeks. His teacher called and told me about it. She said if he keeps his improvement level up, he'll probably be on grade level by the end of the school year."

He shook his head as if he didn't want to accept her praise. "I enjoy doing this. I sense it's my mission to help kids who have trouble in school, especially blind kids." He seemed thoughtful as he sipped from his coffee cup, gazing at her marigolds in the flower garden outside the kitchen window.

The sun had disappeared more than an hour ago, and the day was now as gray as if it were about to rain. "Why do you feel that way?" She couldn't resist asking the question.

"Excuse me?" He stopped looking out the window, focusing on her again.

"Why do you want to help blind children so much?"

"Is there anything wrong with wanting to do that? You said you've seen a difference in Scotty."

Uh oh, looked like she'd offended him. She touched his hand. "I don't mean anything negative. I think it's nice you spend time helping others." She paused. "I just sense that. . . well, that there's some reason why you're so passionate about what you do. You talk about your volunteer work more than your job at the university."

He focused on their joined hands. "You know, I really like you, Monica." She tried to pull her hand away, but his grip remained tight. "I really do. I know you don't want to date, but I'm glad we can spend time together since I tutor Scotty. I might check out that class at Mustardseed Faith and try to get an answer to some of those questions I have about God. I've been wanting to come, but I've been hesitating, changing my mind at the last minute. I think I just need to push my apprehensions aside and come next Sunday."

"The class started two weeks ago, so you're already behind."

He shrugged. "So? I'm a professor—I learn quickly. If I do find that I can believe in God, do you think we could spend some time together—dating?"

She pulled her hand away. "I'm not sure. I don't want to make it seem like I'm trying to sway your beliefs just so we can date."

"I'd never think that about you." His voice had turned husky, and he leaned toward her, running his hand over her cheek. His touch felt delicious, and she wondered if he was going to kiss her.

"Aunt Monica!"

She jumped up as if she'd been burned by fire. "Yes, Scotty!" She ran into the living room, and Scotty held his empty milk glass toward her. "Can I have some more milk?" She knew he'd prefer pouring his own milk but, the last time he'd tried pouring milk out of that gallon jug, without asking her, he'd spilled it. He still needed help with some things, so, she'd made him promise that he'd ask before doing it himself.

"Sure." She quickly poured him another glass of milk.

"Can I have some more cookies?"

"No. You've had enough sweets today."

He grumbled under his breath, and she was relieved when no curse words tumbled from his mouth. She gave him a glass of ice water and returned to the kitchen.

"Now, where were we?"

She cleared her throat. It was probably good that Scotty had interrupted them. "I was asking you why you were so passionate about your volunteer work." He paused, as if hesitant about answering her question. "What's wrong?"

"Well, I guess you could say my passion for volunteer work ties a little with my agnostic views."

"What do you mean?"

John leaned back into his chair, took a deep breath.

"Before we talk about that, I wanted to make sure you were okay."

Now why in the world was he asking her that now? "Of course I am."

"Well, you seemed kind of sad at breakfast and…well…"

She sighed. No use hiding it from him. "I wanted to know more about your connection to Beverly and Aiden." She paused. How could she explain? "Well, Aiden seemed uncomfortable giving me many details, but, he said that you and Beverly were a couple at one time?"

He nodded. "How well do you know Beverly and Aiden?"

She shrugged. "I'm acquainted with them, but, I haven't really spent any time with them outside of church. They seem like a nice, solid couple, and they're respected within the church."

He nodded. So, over the next hour, he told her all about his relationship with Beverly, their living together, her pregnancy and the birth of Brian. He then told of Brian's illness and their breakup. He then told of Beverly's salvation and her marriage to Aiden. He then spoke of Brian's death.

Monica wiped the tears from her eyes. "You're mad at God because your son died?" Her voice wavered as she wiped her wet eyes with a tissue.

He sighed and nodded. "Yeah, I guess you could say that. But, I haven't told you everything that happened. The fact that I even attended Mustardseed Faith today is a miracle."

Her eyes widened. "I'd never think that an agnostic would use the word miracle."

He shook his head. "I misspoke. That's not what I meant."

She couldn't help smiling, just a little bit. Maybe John's faith was there, but it was buried deep inside him, he just needed some time to make it flourish and grow. "So, why did you say that? What happened?" Her curiosity about him intensified. She just had to know what he had to say.

He sighed and ran his hand over his head. He looked directly at her with his chocolate brown eyes. He took a deep breath. "After Beverly was saved and had married Aiden, well, Brian got worse." He took another deep breath. "I'm kind of surprised that Aiden married her, I mean, she had a lot on her plate with Brian's illness and all. But, you know, Aiden's a good man. He was kind and caring toward both me and Brian and I appreciate that. He told me that he loved Brian as if he were his own son…he wasn't trying to take my place, Brian knew who his dad was."

She nodded. "Aiden has a good reputation at Mustardseed Faith. He's always seemed kind and caring. He's also good at settling disputes between some of the church members."

"Yeah, I can imagine his doing that. Anyway, when Brian was days away from dying, Beverly convinced me to go to church with her and Aiden. They had an all-night prayer session, people made it a priority to pray for Brian. If they couldn't make it to the church, then they spent the entire night praying at home. I'd never seen anything like that. Monica, it was amazing."

Surprised at the awe in his voice, Monica couldn't comment. John was scared to have faith in Jesus. She'd not been at Mustardseed faith when all of this had occurred, she'd been at another church. It would've been really something for her to see.

"But, Monica, as amazing as it was, Brian died. He died anyway. Where does that leave me?" The sad, broken tone in his voice made her pause.

"John, I'm so, so sorry."

He nodded toward her. "Like Scotty, Brian was blind. He became blind because of his brain tumor. I guess that's why I have a soft spot in my heart for people who suffer from blindness. And after he died, I was determined to help others like my son. I learned braille, just so I could help visually impaired people. I've been doing it for few years now, and I feel like this is something I have to do."

She carefully thought of what she should say. "So, you don't accept Jesus because you felt He let you down when Brian died."

He nodded. "I just don't understand Him, and

that's why I find it hard to believe in Him. Brian was a Christian. He accepted Christ. What kind of God allows His saved children to die?" His voice dripped with bitterness.

"John, please come to the class at my church. I think talking to Aiden will help you." Another thought occurred to her. "Do you feel strange talking to Aiden since he's married to Beverly?" Maybe John still had romantic feelings towards his ex-girlfriend. If Brian had never gotten sick and died, would Beverly and John still be together? She shook the thought away. No need to think about that. She just needed to focus on getting John to see how Jesus really was.

"No, this may sound surprising but, I'm comfortable with Aiden."

"Well, tell him what's on your mind. That's what you need to do. None of us understands God. Not even those of us, like me, who do accept Him as our Savior. We just have to believe even when we don't understand."

"Okay," he grumbled.

"So, you'll talk to Aiden? Maybe try to attend his class? Just give it a try for a while and see how it goes."

He nodded, and she hoped the class would help him find his way to Jesus.

CHAPTER 14

THOUGHTS OF JOHN crowded Monica's mind as she pushed open the glass door of the Chocolate Dreams Candy Company. After sharing coffee with John the previous day, she'd had a hard time concentrating on her school work. While she'd been online with her classmates, brainstorming about their group project, she'd had a hard time focusing on what they were saying. They'd had to repeat themselves to her a few times. She needed to stop daydreaming, but, honestly, she was worried about John.

Well, maybe worried was too strong a word, more like concerned. As she strolled into her office, she again thought about telling Aiden about her conversation with John – letting him know that he'd referred to something as a 'miracle.' She again shook the thought away. She'd be overstepping her bounds by going to Aiden without John knowing about it. Besides, their conversation had been so personal – sure, she knew that Aiden knew about John's deceased son and all, but, the fact that they'd been so open and honest with each other. Holding hands…

"What're you grinning about?" Louis, the junior marketing clerk, looked at her, smiling.

Monica returned the smile. Louis was as friendly as he could be and he was so helpful to the department. "Oh, just thinking about my weekend."

"I haven't seen you smile like that since I've been working here."

Louis had started right after she'd taken Scotty into her care, so, his observation wasn't surprising.

She entered her office and spotted the box of candy on the desk. She peeked out the office. "Louis, did you leave the box of candy on my desk?"

The young clerk came over to her. "Pierce left that for you. It's the new flavor that's being released next week, Mocha Fudge. He wants to you try it and then come to his office." He leaned toward her. "It sounded like he wanted to talk to you about something important." The young clerk lowered his voice.

Monica nodded. "Thanks, Louis."

She dropped her purse into her drawer before opening the candy box. She popped a piece of candy into her mouth. The delicious, sugary chocolate, with a hint of coffee, exploded into her mouth with decadent sweetness. "Oh, my goodness." She couldn't resist. She ate another piece before giving the rest of the box to Louis so that he could eat some and share with the rest of the staff.

She just had to tell Pierce how much she enjoyed their new flavor of candy. She walked as quickly as she could in her three-inch heels. Pierce's admin sat at her desk. She greeted Monica with a warm smile. "Hi Monica."

"Hi, is Pierce in? He wanted to speak with me."

"He'll be back in a few minutes. Why don't you go in there and wait for him? I know he wants to talk to you."

She entered Pierce's office. His large picture window had an amazing view of the beach in the distance. She'd always admired this view from his window. She then turned and glanced around the huge corner office. Marketing books from Pierce's undergraduate days dotted the shelves. His large oak desk was dominated with paperweights from his various business trips as well as pictures of his family.

She closed her eyes…what would it be like to *be* in this office as director of marketing? Man, she'd had doubts, but, now, she felt it, right in her bones. Still smiling, she glanced toward the door. Pierce wasn't back yet. Feeling a bit naughty, she sat in his desk chair. She imagined assisting the law department as they drafted contracts with high-level ad agencies. She'd have her own, personal admin, and she'd be able to stretch her wings by using the depth of the knowledge which she was learning in grad school.

No, she would no longer let her fear of what Kevin had said to her, the fear of what had happened long ago with the botched advertisement to haunt her. She was determined to move forward.

"Daydreaming, Monica?"

Her mouth dropped open as Pierce walked into the office. Oh, no, now she'd done it. "Oh, Pierce, I'm so, so sorry." She quickly got up and looked at him.

His dark eyes sparkled with happiness as he chuckled. "No worries."

"How long were you standing there?"

He laughed, the loud sound rippling through the large office. "Long enough to know that I think I know the answer to my question."

"About the director position?"

He nodded.

"Yes, Pierce. I'd like for you to recommend me for the job when you announce your retirement." She knew that Pierce's recommendation would carry a lot of weight at the Chocolate Dreams Candy Company.

John pulled his car into the parking lot of Mustard Seed Faith to attend the class. The cool October temperature felt nice. As leaves tossed from nearby trees, he strolled into the church. An announcement posted on the bulletin board about a harvest festival. As he went downstairs toward the classroom, he thought about the last two weeks since he'd attended church.

When he'd given Scotty his tutoring lessons over the last couple of weeks, he could tell that Monica wanted to continue their conversation – the conversation they'd had over coffee, when he'd told her about Brian. He sensed that she wasn't going to ask since his reasons for his views were linked to his deceased son.

She'd made dinner for him after Scotty's lessons. The last meal he'd shared with her was spaghetti and meatballs. It was the best spaghetti he'd ever eaten. Scotty gobbled down two plates. Monica had told him that she prepared the sauce using fresh tomatoes. She'd even told him that she gardened, but the past year, she'd not planted a vegetable garden since she'd been too busy with her graduate studies, plus taking care of her nephew took up a lot of her free time.

Aiden peeked out of the classroom. "John, nice to see you."

He nodded toward him. "Hey, Aiden." They shook hands.

"So, did you want to talk or anything before class starts?"

"Honestly? No. I'm still leery about this, and I realize most folks in this class are believers. But, I just want to hear what you have to say during class."

Aiden nodded and beckoned him into the

room. He gave him a piece of paper. "All of the lessons are outlined on this handout. You can go to those websites for the study materials." The tall man paused for a few seconds. "Oh, and John, I'm glad that you're here."

Before John could respond, the rest of the students came into the room. He took a seat at one of the tables in the back. He then paid attention to Aiden as he called class to order and opened with prayer.

Later, after Aiden dismissed the group, John headed out of the room. He needed to digest everything, think about it, before he spoke to Aiden about it another time. He headed to the sanctuary. He scanned the parishioners sitting in the pews. Where was Monica?

He spotted her sitting in a pew with Scotty, and his heart skipped. She looked beautiful in a gray suit. He strolled to the pew, ignoring the curious glances from the other church members. He plopped into the seat beside her. She barely noticed him as she whispered something to Scotty, obviously fussing with him about something.

Unable to resist, he touched the small mole above her mouth. "Hi, beautiful," he whispered.

"Mr. John!" Scotty beamed, recognizing John's voice. "Are you going to start coming to church with us now? Do you believe in God?"

"Don't talk so loud in church, Scotty."

The worship band started playing, and the choir filtered onto the stage, their long scarlet-

and-white robes swaying. He squeezed her hand. "I'm so glad to see you."

She squeezed his hand back. "I'm glad to see you, too."

Even though he'd seen her during the week when he tutored Scotty, he still found a small thrill in seeing her at church dressed in her Sunday best, worshipping her God.

The choir began to sing "Amazing Grace," and for once John listened to the lyrics, really listened, and found himself a little moved by the music. Monica stood with most of the congregation and closed her eyes as she swayed to the music. A tear escaped from her eye, and he stood beside her and wiped it away. She opened her eyes, giving him a gentle smile as she continued to sway, singing the inspiring words.

When the preaching began, John made more of an effort to listen but found that being near Monica was distracting. The scent of her perfume unnerved him. Well, hopefully he could spend some time with her after the service. Again, he noticed that she covertly stared at the couple who sat near the exit of the church with their infant. When the woman happened to look back, Monica hurriedly focused on the pulpit again.

Recalling that something similar had happened the last time he'd attended church with her, he made a mental note to ask her about it later. When the service finished, he followed her into the foyer. "I noticed Scotty didn't go to Sunday school today."

"The teacher was sick, and they couldn't find a substitute."

"I was good today, wasn't I, Aunt Monica?"

She chuckled, stroking his face. "Yes, you were."

"You said if I was good during the service we could go to Phillips for lunch."

Anna rushed into the foyer before Monica could answer. She greeted Monica, Scotty, and John before exiting so fast the floor vibrated. "Where is she going? I thought the three of you had lunch together every Sunday."

"Humph. Where do you think she's going? She's got a brunch date with Dean Love."

"Dean Love? You're talking about the waiter at the Bayside Skillet?"

Monica nodded. "Yes, when Anna sees a man she likes, she pursues him with a vengeance. She barely gives the man a chance to ask her out properly. She'll do the asking, and then we'll listen to her complain when things don't work out." She continued to talk about Anna's new love interest as they walked toward the door. "Dean told Anna he's a Christian, but I haven't been around him enough to see if it's really true."

John frowned. "What do you mean? Do you think he's lying?"

Monica shrugged. "It's hard to say. One man that Anna used to date claimed to be a Christian just so Anna would go out with him. After she spent some time with the man, it was obvious he didn't take her faith seriously. She stopped seeing him after that, and she told me the next time she dated somebody, she would proceed slowly to make sure he expressed his faith through his actions."

"Mmm." He didn't know what to say about Anna's dating habits. "Where's Karen?"

"She's sick with a stomach virus, so she couldn't make it to church today." Scotty tugged Monica's hand.

"Aunt Monica, can we go to Phillips now?"

"Be patient. I'm talking to Mr. John."

John chuckled, running his hand over Scotty's head. "How about I treat you and your aunt to lunch, sport?"

The little boy did a small jump with excitement. "Can he come with us, Aunt Monica?"

Monica hesitated. Oh, no, looked like she didn't want him to come. Then she smiled, just a little bit. "If he wants to come with us, he can."

Thank goodness she agreed. His heart sped up as his eyes locked with hers. He could get used to this, spending time each Sunday afternoon on an outing with Monica and her nephew.

She took Scotty's hand. The boy shook his head. "No, I want to walk to the car by myself."

"Honey, you can't. You didn't bring your cane with you and there's a lot of people leaving church. I don't want you to bump into anybody."

"Hey, sport. When we get to my car, you can open the door yourself."

"Okay." He didn't seem excited, but, at least he didn't appear to be so upset.

"You wanted to drive?"

He nodded. "Yes, I figure we can pick up your car later if you don't mind?"

"That's fine."

In the parking lot, he opened the passenger door for her.

Scotty opened his own door and jumped into the car, buckling his seat belt. He bounced on the leather seat. "I can't wait to eat at Phillips!"

CHAPTER 15

AFTER THEY'D EATEN their lunch Scotty tugged on her hand. "Aunt Monica, can we get some candy from that place where you work?" Sounded like he wanted some Chocolate Dreams Candy. She wasn't sure if they should stop at the Chocolate Dreams Candy Company store on the boardwalk. She was trying to watch Scotty's sugar intake.

He tugged her hand again. "You promised we could go last week!"

"Scotty, stop whining." She touched the boy's shoulder. "We can go sometime this week." She wasn't sure if John needed to leave. She didn't want to hold him up, especially since he drove them.

John came to the rescue. "We can go now. I could use some candy if it's okay with your Aunt."

A short time later, they entered the spacious shop. Scents of sugar and chocolate surrounded them, and workers stood behind the counter selling boxes of chocolates to eager customers.

John purchase chocolate fudge candy for Scotty and he got the new mocha chocolate flavored candy for them to enjoy.

They stopped at a small playground near the candy shop. They sat at one of the small round tables to savor their snack.

Scotty gobbled his candy. "Don't eat so fast," she admonished.

Scotty chuckled as he drained the last of the water from the plastic bottle. "Can I go and play in the playground now?"

"Okay, but be careful." She led him to the abandoned outdoor play area. When she returned to the table, instead of sitting across from John, she sat in the seat beside him because it had a better view of the play area.

"Did you enjoy the class today?" she asked.

He sipped his water. "Well, it was interesting. Aiden's a good teacher. He gave me some things to think about, and I'm looking forward to attending next week."

"You are?" Shocking that he'd attend again. "Do most of the other students know that you aren't a Christian?"

He shrugged. "I didn't tell them. I know Aiden didn't mention it. Pete, my friend, said that he was surprised that I'd be attending a class with other Christians. Even though the class is geared to new believers, Aiden still thinks it's a good idea for me to learn about Christianity."

He figured a lot of his questions about God and

salvation might be answered through the lessons. "I noticed today and last week that you were staring at that couple with the baby sitting near the exit of the sanctuary."

She picked up her water bottle and took a sip, tapping her foot. She remained silent, so he continued. "You looked upset when you were watching them, and when the woman looked toward you, you looked away. Are they friends of yours?"

"I'd rather not discuss them." The unfamiliar stony edge to her voice was like a shock of frigid water.

"I didn't mean to make you feel bad. I just wondered, that's all. You don't have to talk about it if you don't want to."

She watched the play area. "Well, I guess I have to say they're friends of mine." Her voice remained hard, and she certainly didn't sound like the Monica Crawford he had been spending time with during the last month. Her jaw tensed, and he encouraged her to continue, hoping she would calm down.

"They have to be my friends since they're members of my church, and they're good Christian people." Her voice was no longer hard, but sad and resigned.

He rubbed her shoulder, offering her his comfort. "He was your old boyfriend, wasn't he?"

"What makes you think that? Did Karen or Anna tell you?"

He shook his head, raising his hands into the air. "I wouldn't talk to Karen or Anna behind your back about your love life. I'm not that underhanded."

She touched his shoulder. "I'm sorry," she muttered. "I wasn't thinking. Please forgive me."

He nodded, still wondering if Monica trusted him after that comment. "Tell me about this guy. Who is he?" He touched her hand. "Why does he make you look so sad? Are you in love with him?"

She blinked rapidly, and for a minute, he thought she was going to cry. But her eyes remained dry as she fiddled with her empty water bottle. "Not really."

"Not really? Sounds to me like you still love him."

She shook her head. "No, that's not true. I dated him for a long time."

"How long?"

"Two years."

"What happened? Wasn't it possible for the two of you to work through your problems and make your relationship work?"

She laughed harshly, shaking her head. "You know, I wish it were that simple, where we had issues we needed to work through and then we could have made it work."

"But it wasn't that simple?"

She shook her head. "No, it wasn't."

He squeezed her hand. "Be honest with me.

What's up with this man at your church and his wife and baby?"

"I was in love with Kevin. We dated for two years." She briefly told him about the norovirus outbreak at her job and about the fiasco with the commercial, and about how Pierce had come to the set, sick, just so they could get the commercial done. She told of Kevin's snide comments whenever she wanted to move forward with her career.

"Sounds like he was jealous. He probably figured you'd be a success and he didn't want a woman who could be more successful than he."

"Do you really think so? Anna and Karen had said the same thing as you."

He nodded.

"If I were still with him, he'd probably discourage me from applying for the director position at my job. I'm going to apply after Pierce retires."

"Good for you. I know you can do it. Kevin shouldn't have made you feel bad about what had happened on the commercial set. He should've been supportive." He shrugged. "Monica everybody makes mistakes and you learn from that." He paused for a few minutes. "So, what else happened between the two of you?"

"Well, I was ready to settle down and get married."

"And he wasn't?"

"No, actually he was."

He shook his head. "I don't understand."

"You will understand when I finish telling you." The hard edge returned to her voice as she told him about her old boyfriend. "After we'd been dating for a year, I wanted to know where things stood between us. Before I could ask Kevin what his intentions were, his mother died."

"So, you never talked about marriage after his mother died?"

"I waited for a while, since he grieved pretty hard after his mother's death. They were really close and I could tell it was a difficult time for him. He was sad and kind of moody after she died, which is understandable, but things changed between us after that."

He frowned. "How did things change?"

"Our relationship shifted. Kevin was obviously going through a difficult time, but he didn't want to talk to me about it. We continued to date, but I could tell something heavy was on his mind. He refused to open up to me and that bothered me. When I finally asked him about marriage, he put me off by saying he was still dealing with his mother's death and he wasn't in the right state of mind to make a marriage commitment."

"You believed him?"

She sighed. "At first, I did, but when our two-year dating anniversary crept up, I figured I was kidding myself. I was about to give him an ultimatum when he took me to a fancy restaurant. It was my favorite place to eat, and I figured he was taking me there to propose."

He squeezed her hand. "And he didn't?"

She shook her head. "He told me we would always be brother and sister in Christ and that he would always care for me as a member of the church. But he said he couldn't continue to date me because he didn't love me."

He gasped. "Really?"

She again nodded.

"Hold on, I don't understand something. You were going to Mustard Seed Faith when this happened?"

She shook her head. "I switched churches — I switched to Mustard Seed Faith. My breakup with Kevin was why I switched churches. I just couldn't face him." She paused for a few seconds. "I joined Anna's and Karen's church. I'd enjoyed the few times I'd visited over the years, and I was ready for a change. But then, something weird happened…"

He leaned toward her. "What happened?"

"To make matters worse, he started dating a woman at Mustard Seed Faith not long after I joined. I hadn't been a member for long when this happened. He showed up at Mustard Seed about a month after we broke up, with the woman he ended up marrying."

"So, he was dating both of you at the same time?"

"I'm not sure. He probably knew her while he knew me, but I never knew if they were dating.

Perhaps he wanted to break up with me before he pursued her."

He whistled softly. "That's rough. So, was that the woman he was with at church today?"

"Yes. They got engaged six months after he broke up with me and married two months later."

"Six months?"

"Yes."

"He probably was seeing her while he was dating you. Did you ever ask him about it?"

"No."

"Why not? You dated the man for two years, so he at least owed you some sort of explanation."

She shook her head, and he gave her a hug. "He didn't love me. That's reason enough to break up. I had my dignity to consider. I didn't want to call him and demand to know if he was two-timing me like that. It would have made me look like a lovesick fool who couldn't let go of a man who obviously didn't love me."

He released her. "Well, Kevin is the king of all fools. If you'd let me date you, I promise I wouldn't treat you like that. I wouldn't date another woman behind your back. Do you still think about Kevin often?"

"Not really. When I see him with his wife and child, it's like a cold splash of water in my face, a reminder of what I imagined for myself if things had worked out with us."

"I think you still have feelings for him. You need to get him out of your mind and not be sad when you see him with his family. How long ago did you two break up?"

"Two years."

"You should have moved on by now. Don't let his negative treatment of you make you doubt all men."

"I'm not doing that."

"Yes, you are. You should see the sad look in your eyes when you see Kevin with his wife and baby."

"So, you never told him you loved him?"

She shook her head. "I started asking what his intentions were after we'd been dating for a year, but I never told him I loved him, and my mother always says if a man loves you, he'll let you know." She shrugged. "I guess Kevin finally let me know his feelings. It just wasn't what I wanted to hear."

Scotty yelled for her. "Aunt Monica!"

She hurried over to her nephew, who complained about being thirsty. She purchased him another bottle of water, and after he drank it, he tried to return to the play area.

"Scotty it's time for us to go home."

"Aww, Aunt Monica. I like playing on the swing. Can't we stay for just five more minutes?"

"No, we can't." She led him back to their table. "John, thanks for treating us to candy, but I think it's time for us to get home. Scotty has some homework to do this weekend, and he hasn't even started."

He stood, hugged her before he squeezed

Scotty's small shoulder. "Hey, sport. Your teacher told me you've been assigned some books to read. I'll be by this Tuesday, and you can read to me."

"Okay, Mr. John," he grumbled as she led him to the car.

The three of them were silent as he drove back to the church so Monica could get her car. The parking lot was deserted. Monica opened her door and helped Scotty out of the car. She turned toward John. "Thanks again for lunch. I'll be seeing you this Tuesday."

"I'm looking forward to it." Their eyes locked like two pieces of a puzzle, and he wished their time together that day did not have to end. He watched them drive away.

When he returned to his house, he changed out of his dress clothes into a sweat suit. He drove to nearby Assateague Island. After getting out of the car, he stretched and admired the wild ponies frolicking in the woods nearby. A beautiful chestnut-and-white horse galloped past, heading toward a car with an open window. The car's occupants closed their windows, adhering to the island's rules of not petting or feeding the wild horses.

He broke into a slow jog before going into a full-blown run on the sandy shore. He breathed deeply, enjoying the cool wind that surrounded him, glad that the mosquitoes around Assateague Island were now gone since it was already October. He saw a few more ponies and a wild deer in the bushes. He continued running. When he could run no farther, he stopped and walked along the shore. He breathed deeply as he watched the golden rays of the sun splash upon the cloudy water. Thoughts of Monica's breakup filled his mind, and he wondered if they could ever find a way to be together. He thought about Jesus, and His claim of being the Messiah while He walked on the earth. Monica and Jesus filled his mind. As the sun sank onto the horizon, he said a little prayer.

God, Jesus Christ, if You are really my Savior, could You show me a sign to let me know these things are true?

CHAPTER 16

MONICA KEPT THINKING about John over the following month. He'd pop into her mind for no reason and she eagerly looked forward to seeing him when he came to tutor Scotty. Amidst daydreaming about John, she continued working on her graduate school studies while Pierce gave her a few pointers about the director position. He was honest, emphasizing that his endorsement was no guarantee that she'd get the job.

She totally understood. She knew that although his endorsement carried some weight within Chocolate Dreams, there were no promises that she'd get the esteemed position. She'd been visiting Pierce's office quite frequently and her daydreams about obtaining his job had spilled over into her night dreams.

While sleeping, she found herself dreaming John as well as the director position. She'd been praising God as her prayers were answered about Scotty. He continued adjusting to his studies and to his school. Scotty had gotten used to John's twice-weekly tutoring sessions, and he was growing fond of having a male role model in his life.

As she drove to Scotty's school after work, she recalled that the busy time of year for her job was approaching, and she would need to work some overtime hours. Pierce had been doing a lot of extra advertisements for their special festive chocolates that would be released this coming Christmas. When she had spare time during the workday, she'd been helping Pierce with the extra work and he was glad to have her help. Christmas was still weeks away, but, with advertising, it was always best to start early. She knew the upcoming holiday season would keep her busy at work, and she wondered if Anna or Karen would be able to babysit on the nights she might have to work late.

She pulled into the parking lot of Scotty's school. The wind blew, and the American flag and the banner bearing the school's crescent logo snapped in the strong November breeze. Escaping the frigid air, she entered and found Scotty chatting with his friends who also stayed for the after-school care program. "Hey Scotty."

She longed to give him a hug and a kiss, but realized that he wouldn't appreciate that affection in front of his friends.

"Oh hi, Aunt Monica."

She helped him fetch his coat and backpack.

After their short commute she pulled into the

driveway of here house. As usual, she allowed Scotty to unlocked the door. As soon as they were inside, she enjoyed the delicious scent of cooked meat and vegetables. She swallowed as her mouth watered. She'd been so busy working with Pierce earlier on a new holiday ad campaign that she'd skipped lunch. Scotty sniffed, pulling his coat off and throwing it on the floor. "You cooked already?"

"Put your jacket in the closet." She ignored this question. She must've told him a million times not to throw his jacket onto the floor.

He grumbled, and when a curse word slipped from his mouth, she pulled him to a nearby chair. "You haven't cursed in a long time. I thought we already talked about this."

His eyes filled with tears. "Why doesn't my mother call or visit? Does she hate me?"

She often wondered the same things herself. Why didn't Gina at least call to see how her son was doing? "What happened today? Why are you suddenly asking about your mother?"

His lip quivered. "We're making paper turkeys for Thanksgiving. My teacher is helping me make mine."

She hugged him. Thanksgiving was eight days away, and she had been so busy working on the Christmas campaign at work that she hadn't given the holiday much thought. "What's the matter?" She kissed his forehead.

He moved out of her arms. "People talked

about where they would spend Thanksgiving. Since it's Family Week at school, my teacher told everybody to tell about their parents and their brothers and sisters." He shook his head. "I don't have a daddy, and my mother is gone. Where is she?"

She rubbed his shoulder. "Your mother didn't tell you where she was going?"

He shook his head. "No. She told me about some circus but didn't tell me where they were going. Is the circus coming to Ocean City? Can we go and see her if it comes here?" His voice was so full of hope that she didn't know what to say. Surprising that it'd taken him this long to say anything about Gina. Since he seemed to be adjusting to living with her and his behavior had improved, she'd not wanted to rock the boat by mentioning her wayward sister.

Instead of answering him, she pulled him into her arms again. "Jesus, please help Scotty during this difficult time. Please keep Gina safe and please place it upon her heart to call us to let us know she's okay. Please make Scotty strong during this period of adjustment in his life. In Jesus' name, amen."

"Amen." He sighed. "So, does that mean Mom will call me since you asked God about it?"

She pulled his chin between her two fingers. "I want you to always remember this: God hears all prayers. He might not answer them as we want Him to, but God just heard us, and He has the power to make you feel better. Now I can promise you that."

He still didn't seem to believe her as he put his coat in the closet. She studied him as he pulled out his braille reading material and began his homework. She shook her head, ashamed that her sister could abandon her child for a man.

She didn't think it was wise to let Scotty know she'd been trying to track down Gina for the last two weeks. She'd called the National African-American Circus information line, trying to find a way to contact Randy, the trapeze artist, so she could get a message to Gina. She had managed to get a few messages through, but she wasn't sure if those messages were passed to her sister.

An hour later she served the dinner that had been cooking all day in the slow cooker. The cubed steak, vegetable, and potato stew was tasty, but she was so upset about Scotty's questions about his mother that she'd lost her appetite. Her stomach felt sour and she could barely eat. She sipped on a glass of soda, her stomach in turmoil. Closing her eyes, she said another silent prayer for Gina's safety and for Scotty's peace of mind. She also prayed for her own health—if she worried incessantly about something, it always brought on a stomachache.

After she whispered her amen, the phone rang. The sound pealed throughout the house, so she walked into the living room. She glanced at the Caller ID. The display read 'number unknown'.

She sighed. It was probably a sales call. She was just too tired to speak to a sales person right now. Maybe she should ignore it. *Answer it.* She paused. Her gut was telling her not to ignore the call. Her stomach again rumbled with upset. She swallowed and picked up the receiver. "Hello?"

"Monica?" Gina's slurred voice carried over the line.

"Gina!"

Scotty ran from the kitchen table so quickly that he bumped the table and his bowl of stew toppled onto the floor. The bowl shattered into pieces, and seconds later he'd found her and was pulling on her leg. "I want to talk to Mom!"

"Is that my baby?" Gina asked.

She turned away from Scotty, whispering into the phone. "You're drunk! How can you call here like that?"

"Aunt Monica, I want to talk to my mom!" He was crying and grabbing at her like a madman, so she handed him the phone, hoping he was so excited about hearing from his mother that he wouldn't notice she was inebriated.

"Mom! Why haven't you called me before now?" Scotty clutched the phone as he spoke to his mother. "Uh-huh. Yeah."

Monica hovered, listening to his side of the phone call, wondering what Gina was telling him. She wanted to get the phone back so she could give her sister a piece of her mind. The dialogue continued for five minutes before Scotty said good-bye. As he attempted to hang up the phone, Monica grabbed the receiver. "No, I have to talk to her, Scotty."

He shrugged. "She's gone."

She held the receiver to her ear and heard silence. She slammed the phone back into the cradle, trying to control her anger. "What did your mother tell you?"

"Nothing much. She says the circus isn't that much fun, and maybe I can come and live with her again. I'm glad she doesn't hate me. If she wants me to live with her again, she must not hate me."

She picked up the receiver as her heart pounded. She had to find Gina. She honestly couldn't remember the last time she'd dialed the operator, but, she was so desperate that she'd try anything just to find her sister. She called the operator who informed her the call was made from an international location and she couldn't track the number for her. Frustrated, she banged the phone down, muttering under her breath.

"What's wrong, Aunt Monica?"

"I needed to speak with your mother, and she hung up." She gazed at the mess in the kitchen. "Did you want some more stew?"

He shook his head. "Can I go to my room?"

"Yes, you can go to your room." She was glad to have a few minutes alone after the disturbing phone call. As she cleaned up the mess on the kitchen floor, she couldn't stop her tears from falling.

CHAPTER 17

THE FOLLOWING DAY after the last student had taken their exit from his college classroom, John gathered his papers and his briefcase and headed to his car, eager to get to Monica's house.

Later, he pulled into her driveway. Scotty tugged on John's hand as he met him at the door. "Hey, Mr. John!"

He chuckled. "Hey, sport! How did you know it was me at the door?"

"I heard your car drive up, and Aunt Monica told me to come and let you in."

John entered the house, disappointed when he didn't smell one of Monica's tasty meals cooking. "Mr. John, my mother called me last night."

Intrigued, he looked at Scotty. "Did she? What did she say?"

"I might go and live with her again. Wouldn't that be great?"

Confused, he glanced into the empty kitchen. It was spotless and again he wondered where

Monica was. "Where's your aunt?"

"She's upstairs." He pulled John into the kitchen. "Come and hear me read. I got these Dr. Seuss books in braille a couple of days ago!"

John sat at the table but could barely listen to Scotty read the rhyming words in the braille book. When he struggled with a certain word, John forced himself to pay attention and help him out. They continued their reading exercises for an hour. He was tempted to go upstairs and get Monica himself when he heard soft footsteps plodding down the stairs.

She entered the kitchen. Her eyes were sad, and there were circles beneath them. He stood, sensing she needed a hug. He pulled her into his arms. "What's the matter?"

She shook her head, motioning toward Scotty. "I'll tell you later," she whispered in his ear, obviously not wanting her nephew to hear their conversation.

"Aunt Monica, I'm hungry."

She eyed John. "I'm sorry. I'm not feeling well and didn't make dinner tonight."

He squeezed her shoulder, noticing how the bone protruded beneath her skin. "You need to eat something. You're getting too thin."

"My parents say the same thing."

"How about I take us out to dinner at Phillips?"

"Yeah, let's go to Phillips!" Scotty jumped from his seat, excited.

She shook her head as she sat at the table. "No,

I don't have the energy to go out."

"Aw, Aunt Monica."

Scotty was obviously disappointed. John sat beside her, taking her hand. "How about I have the food delivered? Why don't we order some pizza? What would you like, Scotty?"

"Pizza is awesome, Mr. John. My favorite is cheese pizza."

He touched her shoulder. "What would you like?"

She shrugged. "I'm not very hungry. Whatever you get is fine."

"Aunt Monica likes pepperoni pizza with olives and mushrooms."

John placed the order over the phone, and he added an order of sodas. "They said it'll be here in thirty minutes."

When the food arrived, he answered the door and paid for their meal. He entered the kitchen and opened the boxes. Steam floated from the hot pizzas, and the scents of tomatoes and olives filled the air. He set the box in front of her and opened it. "Here, you need to eat something."

She shook her head. "John, I can't." She held her stomach.

Concerned, he sat beside her, rubbing her shoulder. "Are you sick? Did you catch that stomach virus that was going around awhile ago?"

She glanced at Scotty, who was already gobbling his food and guzzling soda. "My stomach gets upset when I'm worried."

He coaxed her to eat a slice of pizza. "Don't get that upset. It can't be that bad. Is it life or death?" He whispered to her so Scotty wouldn't hear them.

She shook her head. "No, but it is serious."

"Well, it won't help if you don't eat something." He took a paper plate and plopped some of her food on it. "Eat that and drink some soda. I'm sure you'll feel better when you're done."

He sat beside her with his plate of pizza. He remained next to her until she ate. She tasted the food and drank her soda. He was even more pleased when she reached for seconds.

After dinner he placed the leftovers into the refrigerator and threw away the paper plates and napkins. Scotty asked if he could watch TV until bedtime, and she told him it was all right. After Scotty took his exit, John sat beside her, taking her hand. "Now, what's the matter?"

Tears spilled down her cheeks. "Gina wants Scotty again. I can't give him back." She glanced into the living room. "His life was a mess when he came here, and I've done so much work on teaching him about the Lord and about how important it is to do well in school." She shrugged. "If Gina takes him back, he'll revert to the way he was. She never instilled good values in him."

He rubbed her shoulder. "I'm sorry. Did you pray about it?"

She raised her eyebrows, giving him an intense stare. "Yes. I did. You believe in the power of prayer?" Her voice sounded hopeful.

He wiped away her tears. "No, but I know that you do. I'm still unsure what to believe about God and prayer, but I do know that it can't hurt to pray." She turned away as he continued to hold her hand, offering comfort. "Besides, how do you know Gina hasn't changed in the last few months?"

She laughed. The sound was loud and grating. "My sister will need longer than a few months to change. It'll take an utter miracle to change her."

"Well, don't you believe in miracles? God is capable of anything. I read it myself in my Bible."

For a brief moment, her sadness seemed to disappear. "You've been reading your Bible?"

"Of course, I have. That's why I've been taking that class you recommended and going to church. I'm still trying to figure out this whole God thing." He paused. "I've been talking to Aiden. I even went to Aiden's and Beverly's house for dinner the other night."

She frowned. "Isn't that awkward, considering you used to live with Beverly…and you had Brian together?"

He shrugged. "We'd broken up years before… before Brian passed, so, it's not like our relationship is recent. After we had dinner, I spent a long time talking to Aiden. He's a good teacher and I respect him."

She nodded. "Well, good. I'm glad that Aiden is helping you. I think you'll figure out this 'God thing' in due time. Your salvation depends upon it."

Not wanting to talk about his journey in finding out the truth about Jesus Christ, he changed the subject. "So where are you and Scotty going to spend Thanksgiving? Will you be cooking dinner?"

"No, I don't see the need since it's just the two of us. I usually go down to my parents' house for Thanksgiving. What are you going to do?"

He shrugged. "I'm not sure. Since my parents passed, I can't go and see them anymore for the holiday. Sometimes I'll spend it with a college friend of mine who lives down in Baltimore. But this year he and his family are traveling to Florida for Thanksgiving." He was disappointed Monica and Scotty were going away for the holiday. "I'll probably eat at a restaurant."

"Why don't you come with us?"

"Come with you? Why?" He tried not to sound too startled at her invite.

"I just don't like the idea of your spending a holiday alone."

Touched by her concern, he hoped this gesture was an indication that she would soon change her mind and allow him to date her the way he really wanted to. "Are you sure your parents wouldn't mind?"

"Of course not. My parents would welcome you."

"But...don't you think we'd be giving them the

wrong impression? You said we aren't seeing each other. Wouldn't they think I'm your boyfriend?"

She shook her head. "I've already told them you're Scotty's tutor. They know how grateful I am for all you've done for Scotty."

"Okay." He hesitated, still unsure of accepting her invite but intrigued by her gesture. His feelings for her during the last few months had done nothing but grow deeper, and if he spent the holiday with her, he suspected it would make his affections go over the top and make him imagine them as a couple even more.

"Hello?" She waved her hand in front of his face. "What are you thinking about?"

"About your invite. Yes, I accept."

"Good!"

"So, what time should I get here?"

"My parents live about two and a half hours away—"

"Two and a half hours? You're going to go only for the day?"

"Yes. I don't think you'd want to spend the night at my parents' house, let alone the whole Thanksgiving weekend."

"I don't want you to change your plans just because of me."

She shook her head. "You're coming, and it's settled. My parents eat dinner around two o'clock. Scotty and I leave in the morning since I do help my mother a bit in the kitchen. Can you be here around eight o'clock?"

"I'll be here. Did you want me to bring anything?"

"No, my parents will have plenty of food. Sometimes people from their church drop by during the day to eat their leftovers." She leaned back into her chair, her dark eyes sparkling with curiosity.

He checked his watch. "Well, I see it's getting late, so I'm going to head home." He was pleased she had cheered up. "Try not to worry about Gina. I'm sure she was just bluffing." Her frown returned as they stood. "I didn't mean to make you feel bad by mentioning your sister."

"It's okay. She would have popped into my mind as soon as you left anyway." She walked him to the door. After they'd said good-bye and he was driving home, he smiled. It'd be nice to spend Thanksgiving with Monica and her family. He grinned as he turned a corner. What were her parents like? What kind of home did she grow up in? Well, he was anxious about meeting her family. As he pulled into his driveway, he thought of something wonderful that he could do for Monica's family. He grinned as he strolled into his house. Yes, they'd be impressed when he met them…well, at least her mom would be impressed. Well, Thanksgiving was less than couple of weeks away, so, he had some time to scout out the perfect gift for Monica's parents.

CHAPTER 18

THE FOLLOWING SUNDAY, after John was finished with Aiden's Bible class, he entered the crowded sanctuary and scanned the pews.

Monica sat in the middle pew alone. He didn't see Karen, but he spotted Anna sitting in the back with Dean Love. They were holding hands and she grinned, her hair bouncing as she focused on the pulpit.

Monica looked great, as usual, in her church clothes, and he noticed she again stared at the couple who sat near the back with their infant. He wondered if she was still in love with her ex-boyfriend. Her mouth drooped with sadness, and he wanted to sit beside her but at the last minute decided not to. Her charming presence would distract him during the service. He found a seat in the back, intent upon looking up the scriptures Aiden had recommended during class. While people sang and swayed in the church praising God, he pulled out his Bible, wanting to find answers to the questions he so desperately sought.

After the service was over, Monica spotted him in the foyer. Her dark eyes were curious, and he sensed she wondered why he hadn't sat with her during the service. Before he could speak, Scotty entered the foyer, led by his Sunday school teacher. "Hi, Aunt Monica."

"Hi, Scotty." She assisted her nephew with his jacket.

John approached. "Hey."

"Hi, John. Until a few minutes ago, I didn't realize you were here today."

"I sat in the back."

"So, you didn't go to Aiden's class?"

He shook his head. "No, I was here on time. I just needed to be alone for a while."

She frowned, pulling her coat from a hanger. He helped her put it on. "I'm making sandwiches for Scotty's lunch when we get home. Why don't you join us?"

"I have a lot on my mind, so I think I'll be heading home."

"Mr. John, why don't you come with us?" Scotty reached toward him until he found his hand. "Please?"

He squeezed Scotty's shoulder. "I'll see you later this week, sport. Didn't your aunt tell you we're spending Thanksgiving at your grandparents' house? I'm coming with you."

"You are?" Scotty turned toward Monica.

"Will my mom be there? Is the circus coming to Grandpa's town for Thanksgiving?"

Sadness etched her face as she took his hand. "I don't think so. Maybe she'll call you soon."

"She'll call me on Thanksgiving?"

She placed a hat on her head. "We'll have to wait and see. I never know when your mother is planning to call."

John rescued Monica and changed the subject. "I noticed Anna was with her friend Dean Love."

"They were here? They didn't say hello."

"I saw them leave right after service. They were sitting in the back." He glanced around the foyer. "Where's Karen? I wanted to say hi to her."

"She's out of town at a beauticians' convention in Baltimore. She's supposed to come back tonight. Both Karen and Anna said they would drop by tomorrow evening for a visit."

As Kevin and his family walked by, John touched her arm. "Well, you have a nice day, and I'll see you later this week."

He heard her mumble a good-bye as he exited the foyer.

After her conversation with John at church, Monica returned home with Scotty and they had corn chowder and grilled cheese sandwiches for lunch. Scotty had been making some friends at school and she was thankful for that.

He'd been invited to a birthday party late that afternoon. The party was at an indoor place where the kids could jump on huge inflatable bounce contraptions while wearing special socks. The place was like a giant moon bounce. She couldn't recall the exact name of the place, but she knew the location. She knew Scotty would have a blast since he wouldn't need his vision to enjoy himself. Plus, he loved cake and ice cream and pizza. The mom hosting the party lived in her neighborhood and she promised to bring Scotty home later.

She did school work until one in the morning. It was hard for her to concentrate on her schoolwork since she kept thinking about John. She was also still worried about Gina. She wasn't sure what her sister was planning to do regarding Scotty. She was exhausted the next day at work. As she lunched with Pierce in the employee break room at work, her mind kept wandering. Pierce was telling her about his job, giving her pointers, as he'd been doing over the last several weeks. Yes, she realized she needed to pay attention but, John French kept popping into her mind like an unwanted cloud of dust.

She struggled to understand why John had refused to sit with her in the sanctuary the previous day. His standoffish behavior was very puzzling, and she wondered if he were interested in another woman.

She was glad when it was time to go home. She

picked up Scotty from school, and she prepared his favorite meal when they arrived home. She pulled the pan of chicken fingers and fries from the oven. "Come and eat, Scotty!"

He hurried into the kitchen, using the wall to guide himself. "You made chicken fingers and french fries?" He plopped onto a chair. "Do we have any ketchup?"

"Yes, we do." She removed a serving of broccoli from the boiling water and added butter and salt. She placed the food in front of him.

He sniffed. "Do I have to eat the broccoli?"

"Yes, you do." She fixed a plate of food for herself, even though she didn't care for chicken fingers and fries. She hoped that by fixing Scotty's favorite meal, she might cheer him up and help him forget that his mother still had not called him back. He'd told her that he'd had a great time at the birthday party the previous day, and she'd been thankful that he'd enjoyed himself.

After they said grace, they enjoyed their meal in silence. After he swiped his last french fry into the puddle of ketchup on his plate, he pushed his plate toward her. "Can I have some more?" She could barely hear him, his mouth was so full of food.

"What did I tell you about talking with your mouth full?"

He finished chewing the food in his mouth. "Can I have some more?"

"No, You'll get more after you eat your broccoli."

"Aw, Aunt Monica!" He sulked but eventually ate his vegetable. She served him another helping of food and added more ketchup to his plate. He chewed happily, humming as he munched his chicken and fries.

She finished her food and rinsed her plate, placing it in the dishwasher. When Scotty was finished, he left the table and returned to the living room. He paced the floor as if he were bored. "Can I go outside?" Since he didn't have any homework, she figured it was fine for him to go outside.

She opened the blinds. Dusk was falling, and the temperature had dropped. "You can go into the backyard." She pulled a ball from the closet and gave it to him. "You can play with this out there. But be sure to come inside when you get too cold." He ran to the closet and got his coat, hat, and gloves, then went into the backyard, bouncing his ball.

She was about to use the time to go through her devotional since she'd overslept that morning, but before she could start, her doorbell rang. "I forgot about Karen and Anna stopping by," she mumbled as she answered the door. They entered, bringing in a cold gust of air. They hugged her before removing their coats and laying them on the couch. She invited them to sit in the living room.

"So, how was your conference, Karen?" Monica asked.

Anna folded her thick arms. "After Karen tells you about her conference, remind me to tell you how things are progressing between Dean and me."

Karen fingered her hair. "It's only been a few weeks. Things couldn't have progressed that much between you two."

Anna chuckled. "You'd be surprised. When God allows you to find the right man, you are on His timetable, and maybe He's telling me that Dean Love is the right man for me." She looked at Monica. "Last time I saw, it looked like John was really smitten with you. Is he still tutoring Scotty?"

Surprised at the question, she nodded. "John and I are not in a relationship, though."

"But you like him, that counts for something," Anna commented.

"Of course, I like him. I think I'm falling in love with him, and that's the problem."

Their mouths dropped open as they stared at their best friend. "You're serious?" Karen whispered.

Monica nodded. "I can't wait to see him again. He still hasn't accepted Christ, which is why I won't date him." She recalled his cool attitude.

"What's wrong?" asked Anna.

Monica explained his frosty attitude toward her at church the previous day.

"Well I don't blame him. He's probably falling for you, too, but knows it can't lead to anything right now." Anna's opinion didn't make her feel any better.

Now, she wasn't so sure she should've invited them over. She needed some more alone time to process her thoughts. "Both of you are Christians. You know it's wrong to be unequally yoked with nonbelievers."

Anna leaned back into the couch. "I'm not knocking what you're doing, because I'd be doing the same thing if I were you. I'm just saying look at it from John's point of view. You're falling in love with him, and he might realize that." She flung her braided hair behind her back. "He might love you, too. And being around you is hard, knowing you two can't be together. Instead of acting loving and affectionate toward you, he decides to act cool and calm, hoping these emotions between the two of you will dwindle a little until he decides what he wants to do about God."

Karen gazed at Anna. "I'm assuming Dean is a Christian?"

Anna nodded. "He sure is. He was born and raised in the church. I wouldn't be going out with him otherwise."

Karen placed her hand on Monica's arm. "Are you sure you're over Kevin? I see the way you stare at him and his wife at church. Sometimes..."

"What?" Monica narrowed her eyes.

Anna cleared her throat. "Sometimes you act like you haven't gotten over him. You don't talk to him unless he speaks to you first, and you're not exactly friendly toward his wife."

"It's hard for me to get over things. When I see him, it's a reminder of what I lost. Kevin is a charming, good-looking man, and he's godly. You don't know how much I used to fantasize about marrying him."

Karen arched her eyebrow. "Well, he's not very supportive of your goals. Remember how he kept reminding you about the commercial fiasco at your job."

Monica winced. "Yes, that's true."

Karen folded her arms in front of her chest. "You don't still fantasize about him, do you?"

Monica shook her head. "Not anymore. But it's still hard seeing him."

Anna touched her shoulder. "Will you ever get over him? Two years is long enough to grieve over a lost love."

Karen nodded. "I agree with Anna. You've told John about Kevin?"

"Yes."

"I'm sure he's seen you looking at Kevin in church. Maybe John thinks you're still in love with him. You need to let him know that Kevin is part of your past and you're over him for good. And stop being so obvious about your pain. Stop looking at him during service. I'm sure John finds it unnerving," Karen offered.

Anna offered to pray, and the three of them stood in a circle and joined hands as Anna's loud, strong voice filled the living room asking God for guidance during this difficult time.

When their prayer was over, Monica gave her friends the details about recent events in her life. She told them about Gina's phone call and John's acceptance of her Thanksgiving invite.

Anna threw her head back, her long hair hitting the back of the couch. "Which one of these things do you want to talk about first?"

Karen focused on Monica. "Do you really think Gina will take Scotty back?"

Monica shrugged. "Who knows? Gina lies so much, it's hard to tell when she's telling the truth."

"Your sister has always been jealous of you," Anna offered. "Perhaps she's just trying to get you upset, knowing you've probably bonded with Scotty. I wouldn't put it past her to do that." She seemed to think about it. "And you know if it was her intent to upset you, she's succeeded. I can tell her phone call really bothers you."

Karen looked at Anna. "Monica can't help being upset. She loves Scotty, and she only wants what's best for him. I'll be sure to keep the matter on my prayer list."

How nice to have friends like Anna and Karen. They didn't always agree but, their support did wonders for her. "Thanks so much for your support. If she does take Scotty away and disappear again, I don't know how I'll handle it.

I'll be a basket case worrying about him."

"Can't you get a lawyer or something? Try to prove she's an unfit mother?" asked Anna.

"I'm not sure. Right now, my hands are tied. Gina is still legally his mother, but I'm leery of taking her to court to prove her as an unfit parent. The last time my parents tried this, Gina disappeared for two years. Right now, I have power of attorney, but it's only for six months. When that time frame is over, Gina has to decide if she wants to continue giving me power of attorney or if she wants to take Scotty back."

Karen pursed her lips. "Well, if you had to, you can prove Gina as unfit. She dumped Scotty on your doorstep."

God didn't want her to take Gina to court to get custody of Scotty. Deep within her soul, she just knew it. "Like I said, I can't risk doing that. Scotty loves his mother, and he misses her."

Anna changed the subject. "Why did you invite John to your parents' house for Thanksgiving?"

"John has done a lot for Scotty over the last few months. He's been patient, kind, and caring toward my nephew, and he doesn't charge us a dime."

"But you make dinner for him every time he comes," Karen pointed out.

"I like cooking for him, but I wanted to do something more. When he told me he would be alone on Thanksgiving, I just knew I couldn't allow him to do that after he'd done so much for us. So, I invited him to my folks' house. I've already told my mother about his agnostic views, so she doesn't have the wrong idea about us being a couple."

"Speaking of your folks," Karen commented, "are they still harping on the fact that you're thirty-seven and not married?"

"They haven't been on my case about that since Kevin broke up with me. I think they were disappointed when things didn't work out between us, especially since they met him several times and they both seemed to like him."

The back door banged open, and Scotty ran into the house, dropping the ball on the kitchen floor. "Aunt Monica! I'm thirsty!"

She traipsed into the kitchen, picking up the blue ball. "Young man, put this back where it belongs." He grumbled as he dropped the ball into the closet before removing his hat, gloves, and jacket. "We have company. Don't forget to say hello."

"Hey, Scotty." Anna hugged Scotty, and Karen kissed his cheek, leaving a smear of lipstick.

"Yuck." Scotty rubbed his cheek before saying hello. Monica gave him a glass of water. When he was finished, she sent him upstairs to run his bath.

"Was he excited about talking to his mother?" asked Karen.

"He sure was. I'm at a loss. Scotty loves his mother and misses her, yet she refuses to call regularly to check on her own son. She doesn't even leave a phone number where she can be reached. I'm so worried. What if an emergency happens? How will I even be able to contact Gina?"

After Anna and Karen had left, Monica checked on Scotty before pulling out her laptop to do schoolwork. But she couldn't concentrate. How could she contact Gina if an emergency happened with Scotty? Did Gina even love her son?

CHAPTER 19

D URING THE NEXT couple of days, the college campus bustled with activity as the young people looked forward to the upcoming Thanksgiving break. John wondered what it would be like to spend the holiday with Monica's family.

As he continued to go through his week, he thought about Aiden's class at Mustard Seed Faith. He'd been thinking about his pain over losing Brian, as well as his anger about his loss. Aiden suggested that he openly talk to people at Mustard Seed's grieve counseling group.

He'd refused. Over the last few years, he'd openly spoken with Pete at the nursery about his grief and he was glad that he had the older man to talk to. He'd also been telling Pete about his conversations with Aiden, and he'd found his whole outlook on life was changing.

What if Brian really *was* alive, right now, in heaven? What if he could really see and was happy? Could that possibly be? The belief went against all that he knew, and made no logical sense, but, Aiden had quietly pointed out to him that God didn't always make sense. One just had to step out on faith and trust and believe.

John continued to think about his recent conversations with Aiden and Pete as he woke up early on Thanksgiving morning. He still could not believe that he'd be spending the holiday with Monica and her family. As he spent more time with her, his feelings grew deeper, so deep that he didn't know what to do with himself.

He appeared on Monica's doorstep an hour later. The wind howled through the trees, and snow flurried and fluttered to the ground. He buried his hands in his pockets, wondering if the temperature would rise before the end of the day. Monica answered the door, looking as lovely as ever. Recalling how she pined after her ex, he held back and simply touched her arm. "You look pretty."

He noticed the dark circles beneath her eyes.

She invited him in, and the scents that filled the house made his mouth water. He sniffed the air. "What are you cooking?"

Giggling, she led him into the kitchen. Scotty was finishing his breakfast. "Hi, Mr. John. Did you want to taste Aunt Monica's blueberry muffins?"

John sniffed again. The scent of blueberry muffins and apple pie filled the air. He saw an apple pie and a sweet-potato pie on the stove. A carton of eggs and a plate of bacon sat on the counter. Monica removed two of the eggs from the carton. "How did you want your eggs?" She held the white oval globes, patiently awaiting his response. He grinned. He certainly could get used to seeing her like this, in his own kitchen, each day, making breakfast for him.

"Mr. John…Aunt Monica wants to know how you like your eggs."

He shook his head, dispelling the pleasant daydream. "I like my eggs scrambled."

She broke the eggs into a bowl and whipped them before pouring them into the hot skillet. After she finished cooking, she served him his eggs along with two warm blueberry muffins and bacon. John savored his meal. He'd been so engrossed in his thoughts earlier that morning that he'd forgotten to eat breakfast. She served him coffee and orange juice. When he was finished, he pushed his empty plate aside. "Monica, that is the best breakfast I've had in a long time."

After John finished his coffee, they traipsed to her car. As she started to open her door, he took her hand. "Do you mind if I drive?"

"Are you sure?"

"I don't mind driving." He touched her cheek. "You look a little tired. You can give me the address and I'll use the GPS on my phone to drive to your parents' house."

"Thanks. I appreciate it. Come on, Scotty." She pulled her nephew's hand. "Mr. John is driving us to Grandma and Grandpa's house."

The boy climbed into the backseat and buckled his seat belt.

John opened her door for her and gestured toward the back seat. "I got your mom a poinsettia. I have a good friend who owns a plant nursery and these were just shipped in for Christmas." He paused. "I'm not sure if I ever told you this, but, I like plants. I teach botany at the college."

She peeked into the backseat. He noticed her bright smile as soon as she spotted the huge red and green leafed plant. He'd gotten an extra-large plant for her mom. "John, it's beautiful. My mom will love it. She loves plants and has them growing in almost every room in her house."

As they got into the car, Scotty placed his music headphones on his ears and listened to the music app that Monica had set up for him on her phone. Apparently, he was ready to tune out the adults.

Once they were on the highway, John was about to comment on the weather when a soft snore wafted through the car. He glanced at Monica as she dozed.

She slept for an hour before her eyes opened, and she looked confused as they raced down the interstate, pine trees passing by in a blur. She blinked. "Why didn't you wake me up?"

"Because you needed some sleep. I figured you've been awake the last few nights worrying about your sister."

She glanced into the backseat and saw Scotty was still occupied with his music.

He squeezed her hand. "Although I don't consider myself to be a Christian, I do have one Christian quality. I'm honest. I haven't been totally honest with you about everything, but I want to rectify that now."

"What are you talking about?"

"Well, if you haven't noticed, I've been a little distant toward you over the last week."

She remained silent as she gazed out the window, looking at the passing scenery. He waited, seeing if she would comment on his recent behavior, but when her silence continued, he plunged on. "Well, one reason I've been cool toward you is because I think you still love your ex-boyfriend, and I don't think you've done anything to get over him. Until you do, I can't see you having a relationship with anybody else."

"You have no idea what I'm feeling, so I'd appreciate it if you kept your comments to yourself." She was shaking. He didn't know if she was shaking with rage or if a sudden chill from the air had crept into her side of the car. He turned the heat up. Oh, no, looked like he'd upset her pretty bad.

"Don't get mad—"

"What gives you the right to tell me how I feel about Kevin?"

Fatigue swept over him like a tidal wave, and he wondered if they should pull over to finish this conversation. He eased the car into a truck stop and turned off the engine.

Scotty pulled his earphones off. "Are we at Grandma's?" His voice was full of excitement.

"No, sport. We're not. I had to go to a rest stop for a minute. Just listen to your music." Scotty shrugged and shoved his earphones back onto his ears and tuned them out as he listened to his music.

He squeezed her hand. "Please don't be mad."

She glared at him. "How can I not be mad? It's one thing for Karen and Anna to say something like that—"

"Karen and Anna said the same thing?"

"Yes, they did, but they're my best friends. You haven't known me for very long. It's wrong of you to tell me how I feel about somebody when you can't see into my heart. Besides, you know there's no hope for us because of your religious views."

"But, I care about you a lot. I'm falling in love with you—" "John!" She looked at him as if he'd lost his mind.

"I'm just being honest with you. I'm really falling in love with you, and I know we can't be together right now. But I care about you so much that if you can't be with me, I at least want to see you with somebody that makes you happy. You've got so much going on in your life with Scotty and your sister." He stared at a family as they entered the truck stop. "I think you deserve a good man to be with you and help share your burden. If that man can't be me, I need to learn to accept that." He massaged her fingers. "But you should be able to find happiness with somebody else, and until you release your bitterness toward Kevin, then I think you'll be stuck being single."

Her eyes flared with sparks of anger as she jerked her hand away. "What makes you think being single means being stuck?"

The question surprised him, and he wondered if he'd jumped the gun on his advice. He just wanted her to be happy, and he knew that with her present situation, if she had a good, kind husband to lean on, she wouldn't worry so much and would take better care of herself. "I'm not sure why I said that." Maybe he should've just kept his big mouth shut. He eyed a soda machine at the rest stop. Maybe he needed to buy her a cool drink to appease her heated temper. The last thing he wanted was for Monica to be mad at him right now, and she sure was mad. Now, he just needed to fix that.

"I said the wrong thing. I'm sorry." He truly was sorry. Monica had a lot going on in her life right now. She was obviously losing sleep worrying about Gina and Scotty. She was taking graduate classes in addition to pursuing the marketing director position while working with Pierce.

Well, he really needed to do all that he could to rectify this situation. He didn't want her to think that he wasn't sincere about his apology. "Look, Monica, like I said, I'm sorry I said you were stuck. I didn't mean that in a bad way. But you have this sad look when you see your ex, and it seems like you two really had something special. I think you can find that with somebody else, and until you put the past behind you, you'll be stuck with fantasies of your life with Kevin. . .fantasies that more than likely will never come true."

She looked out her window at a trucker running to his vehicle while yelling to one of his driving buddies before getting into his rig.

"Are you all right?" He wasn't sure if he even had the right to ask her that, considering that she was probably still mad at him.

She turned toward him. "Look, you might have a point about Kevin. Both Anna and Karen have mentioned the same thing to me, and I just need to let those memories go and not focus on him so much during church."

He nodded. "Yeah, but..." He hesitated. He didn't want to make her even madder by suggesting she do something to rectify her situation with Kevin. She was already upset and if he made her angrier, well...he wasn't sure if he could fix that situation on such short notice. It was Thanksgiving and he'd be seeing her parents soon and if they picked up on her anger...well... he didn't want Monica's dad mad at him for upsetting his daughter. He had no idea as to what her parents were like, but, figured he couldn't rock the boat.

Yes, it'd be best if Monica was happy, in good spirits, when she saw her folks. So, he needed to just say what was on his mind and then try to think of something to cheer her up. "Look Monica, I think you need to do *something* about Kevin. I'm sure you're making both Kevin and his wife uncomfortable, staring at them like that during the service."

Surprisingly, she didn't get upset. She looked away, out the window for a few seconds. She then bit her lower lip and stared down at her feet. It appeared she was thinking about his advice. Well, good, maybe she was finally noticing how her actions may have been affecting others. Kevin was a total loser. He didn't support Monica or her dreams. She needed to understand that Kevin would've never been a good match for her, at least he didn't think so. "Do you really think they notice? It's not like I sit there and blatantly stare at them."

"Well, you look over there enough. I think they know what you're doing. I see you talking to other church members after the service, but I've never seen you speak to them."

She huffed. "Well, maybe I just don't have anything to say to them."

"Uh-huh," he said. "Aren't Christians supposed to forgive? If you're a true Christian as you claim, shouldn't you forgive him for what happened?"

She rolled her eyes, staring out the windshield. She checked her watch. "Can we continue this conversation another time? My parents will be expecting us shortly, and they'll worry when we don't show up on time."

He started the ignition. The rest of the drive was made in silence.

As John drove through Baltimore, she told him about some of the nostalgic places she used to visit while growing up. She pointed to the Inner Harbor and mentioned the fun she had shopping in the many stores built around the waterfront. A few boats bobbed in the frigid water, and the squiggly wave decorating the Baltimore Aquarium shone in the distance. As they passed the Maryland Science Center, he reminisced about the field trips he'd taken while he was in elementary and junior high school. When he turned a corner, he hoped Monica's mood lifted as they made their way to her house.

CHAPTER 20

WHAT A WONDERFUL Thanksgiving… well, somewhat wonderful. After Thanksgiving Monica kept thinking about how much fun she had spending the holiday with John. In spite of their argument, they did have a good time with her parents. When John gifted her mom with the poinsettia, she'd been flattered. He'd had a long conversation with her mom about plants. Over dinner, he told her about the different plants he'd grown over the years.

Their conversation had shifted to springtime gardening and before the day was over, John had pulled out his phone and was telling her mom all about some interesting plants she could plant in the spring. He'd recommended both edible plants, like herbs and veggies, as week as some vibrant flowers. Her mom had even recommended some shrubs that John could plant around his home.

The only sad part of the holiday was when Gina unexpectedly showed up on her parents' doorstep with a black eye and wearing a tight dress and high heels. She was drunk, and Monica's father had to pay the taxi driver for Gina since she had no money. Scotty had been so ecstatic to see his mother that he refused to accompany Monica back home.

Monica wondered what had happened to Randy, the trapeze artist Gina was supposed to marry. When Monica's mother questioned Gina about her marriage, Gina shouted that she didn't want to talk about it. Her parents said they'd drop Scotty off during the weekend, so she hoped they were able to convince Scotty to come back to live with her in Ocean City.

Her thoughts returned to John. Having John with her at her parents' house made it seem as if they were really a couple.

These thoughts shifted through her mind as she cleaned her house and pulled a box of Christmas decorations from the attic. She came across a box of mementos she'd collected with Kevin. She opened the box, scanning the pictures of her and Kevin at social events. She even found a printed copy of an old e-mail he'd written to her when he was away on an extended business trip. He claimed how much he'd missed her and that his strong affection for her kept him awake at night. She opened a heart-shaped box next. It had been filled with expensive chocolates. She sniffed the interior, still detecting the faint scent of cocoa.

She stuffed the items back into the box, again recalling how much she had loved Kevin. Since her breakup with him had been so sudden and painful, she wanted to be cautious about loving another man. John had said he was falling in love with her, and she knew her emotions were just as strong.

But what would happen between them if he never accepted Christ?

She knew if he never accepted Him as his Savior, she could never have a relationship with him. As she threw her memorabilia into the garbage and removed Christmas decorations from the cardboard box, she wondered if she would be strong enough to survive another breakup as devastating as the one she'd had with Kevin. Should she continue to spend free time with John, falling in love with him, when he was unsure about his salvation?

She stared at the Christmas decoration in her hand. Her heart was telling her to keep seeing John, but her mind was telling her to be cautious. "Oh Lord," she prayed, "I don't think I'm strong enough to continue seeing John until I know for sure that he's accepted You. Please guide me in saying the right words when I see him at church on Sunday." Tears stained her cheeks as she finished her short prayer. Yes, she was sure she'd made the right decision.

Where in the world was Monica? Thanksgiving was only a few days ago and he'd been thinking about Monica non-stop for most of the weekend. He figured she'd be in church. John searched the sanctuary for Monica. He saw Anna and Dean before spotting Karen and Monica in the middle pew. Monica looked toward him, and their eyes met. As he took a seat beside her, he noticed her dark eyes looked troubled.

"Hi, Karen."

Karen grinned. "Hey, John."

He took Monica's hand. "I hope you don't mind my sitting next to you during the service."

She pulled her hand away, gazing toward the podium. "I don't mind at all." Goodness, her attitude was so frigid that he could imagine if she touched water it'd turn into ice. Well, maybe she was still upset about Gina and Scotty. Yes, that's was it. Scotty was her pride and joy and she was worried that Gina would ruin everything by taking him away.

During the praise and worship time, she lifted her hands toward the ceiling, praising God. But her shoulders slumped and she checked her watch often while the preacher spoke. He knew he needed to do something to cheer her up.

After service was over, he touched Monica's arm. "What's the matter?"

"My mother called this morning. Gina's been acting up all weekend. She's broke, and she's mad at my parents because they won't buy her alcohol."

He shook his head, helping her with her coat. "They're still bringing Scotty back today?"

"They're supposed to, but they said he's been upset all weekend, crying, not understanding why his mother is so irrational." He opened the door for her, and they stepped into the brisk morning air. The fierce, cold wind blew with a vengeance, and the sky was bright blue and dotted with large clouds. Puffs of white air escaped their mouths as they spoke.

"But they said they were going to bring him?" he asked again as they walked among the crowd to her car.

She nodded as she unlocked her door. "Yes, they said they will. But. . .my sister is so vengeful that she might have something up her sleeve."

"What do you mean?"

She stepped into her car. "Well, if she's determined, she'll think of a way to get her way. Do you know what I mean?"

He nodded. "I think so. But how can she stop your parents from bringing Scotty?"

She closed her eyes as if fighting bad memories. "Gina will stop at nothing to get what she wants."

He touched her shoulder. "Don't get so upset."

He continued to stand next to her open car door, wondering how he could comfort her. "What did your sister do in the past to upset you so much?"

"One time, when she didn't get her way, she threatened to harm herself."

He inhaled quickly, widening his eyes. "Would she have done something so drastic?"

She shrugged. "I'm not sure. She could have been bluffing but...I don't know. I've been trying to get my sister to give God a chance, but she won't listen to me, and she certainly won't listen to my parents about Christianity or religion. They raised us as Christians, but Gina never wanted to embrace their beliefs."

He rubbed her shoulder. "Did you want me to come home with you? Did you need my support for whatever happens later?"

As she shook her head, the sunlight glinted off her dark hair. "No, it's sweet of you to offer, but. . ." She looked at him with her brown eyes. "To be honest with you, I'm wondering if this whole thing is a mistake."

"What thing?" Was she thinking about taking care of Scotty? She couldn't think that taking him into her home was a mistake, could she? He shook his head, trying to make sense as to what she was referring.

"Come on inside the car." She gestured inside her vehicle. He got into her car. She turned the motor on, letting the heat warm up her vehicle.

"I'm talking about us. I know we're not dating or anything."

"We're not officially. But…." He watched a young couple walk to their car. "I'm falling in love with you—"

"John—"

He touched her arm. "Let me finish. Sometimes I do feel like we're a couple, especially when we spent the day at your parents' house for Thanksgiving."

She gripped her steering wheel, gazing out the windshield. She turned and looked at him. "I feel the same way, and that's what bothers me so much. You've been so nice and supportive, and I understand how you feel about me because I feel the same way."

"You do?" She'd never admitted her feelings to him before.

She nodded. "That's why I think we should put the brakes on our relationship for a while. I can't let myself get carried away, falling for somebody, only to have him exit my life the way Kevin did."

He shook his head. "But I'm not like Kevin. I would never abandon you like that. I like you too much to treat you so poorly."

"It's more than that. I should never have invited you to my parents' house at Thanksgiving. I should never have invited you to spend time with me and my friends for meals after church." She gripped her steering wheel again. "I was looking for you this morning in the sanctuary, and when

I saw you, I was so happy."

He touched her hand. "I was happy to see you, too."

"Don't you understand? My cooking for you and your spending time with me outside of tutoring my nephew have allowed things to escalate too soon. We need to just stop this."

His heart skipped a beat. "Stop what?"

She took a deep breath. "Stop spending time together outside of tutoring Scotty. When you come to my house, you can tutor my nephew, but that's all there is to it."

He gritted his teeth. "So, you're saying that when I come to your house on Tuesdays and Thursdays that I'm just supposed to tutor Scotty and that's it? No more talks, social time, or dinners?"

Tears shimmered from her eyes and fell down her cheeks. "I don't want to do this—"

"Then don't!" He tried to put his arms around her, but she pushed him away. "Don't push me away. You're going through a lot right now, and I need to support you."

She shook her head. "We can't keep spending time together. It reminds me too much—" She stopped speaking and looked out the window. Her ex-boyfriend approached his car a few feet away. He placed the baby into the car seat and helped his wife into the vehicle before he got behind the wheel and drove away. "It reminds me too much about how I felt with Kevin. You know how much he hurt me, and if I keep spending time with you, it'll just get worse."

"Don't say that." He tried to touch her again, but she pushed him away.

"But it's true." Her voice resonated in the car. She wiped her eyes and reached in her purse for a tissue to blow her nose. "I appreciate all you've done for my nephew, and I hope my decision for us to stop spending time together won't make you want to stop tutoring him."

He flattened his mouth, hurt she would make that assumption. "I told you about my son Brian and why I like to help blind kids. I would never punish Scotty just because I don't agree with your actions. I don't operate like that, Monica."

As her tears continued to fall, his heart crumbled. "Is there anything I can say or do to change your mind?"

She shook her head and continued wiping her tears. "I'll just make sure I make myself scarce when you come and tutor Scotty. I can't keep sharing dinner with you because it's getting too personal. I fell for Kevin so hard, and it took me over two years to finally get over him." She ran her fingers over her hair. "I don't want to take my chances on another man unless I know for sure that he is a Christian."

"Kevin was a Christian, and look at how much he hurt you. Being with a Christian man won't guarantee you happiness."

She gasped and stared out the window, as if gathering her thoughts. Before she could speak, he got out of the car and slammed the door.

CHAPTER 21

THAT EVENING MONICA was so upset that she didn't know what to do with herself. She could barely concentrate on her homework as she waited for her parents to bring Scotty back home. Her cell phone buzzed. She glanced at the display, surprised to see Pierce's number.

"Pierce?" He hardly ever called her on her cell phone. "Is everything okay?"

"Are you okay? Your voice sounds funny. Sounds hoarse or something."

Yeah, she probably sounded funny since she'd been crying. "Something happened today and well…"

"Did you want to talk about it?"

She sighed. She needed to get her mind off of John for a few minutes. "Not right now. Why'd you call?"

"Well, I know I've been giving you pointers about the director's position, I wanted to warn you that something has come up."

"Really? What do you mean?" This didn't sound

good at all. Pierce actually sounded worried, and it usually took a lot to rattle Pierce. She'd been enjoying spending time with him during the work day, when she was able. She was learning a lot from Pierce and she was grateful for that.

"Well, the CEO'S nephew is going to apply for the marketing director position. He has an MBA from Yale and he's also got a few years' experience working for the largest computer company in the country." When he named the company, her eyes widened. "You're kidding."

"I wish I were."

She took a deep breath. This news did not sit well with her at all. Just hearing this made her feel worse. He cleared his throat. "Our CEO told him that the job wouldn't be open for months, not until after I officially retire. But, I guess he knew his nephew was on a job search, so, he mentioned it to him. He's very interested."

"Why does he want to work at Chocolate Dreams? Seems like it's a far cry from a large, well-known computer company."

"Monica, I heard he's burned out. He says he works sixty-hour work weeks and he wants a marketing job with a less stress."

"How old is he?" Maybe if he were really young, that'd work against him while being considered for the job.

"He's about your age. He's married with kids and eager to make a fresh start at a new job." He paused. "Just keep it in your prayers. I'll continue to show you pointers and give advice that may help you land the position, but, I just thought I'd have to let you know about that."

"Thanks, Pierce." She ended the call and dropped onto the couch. Amidst taking care of Scotty and falling in love with John, she'd fantasized about Pierce's job. She pushed the thought away. She couldn't dwell on that right now. Her phone buzzed.

Anna. She told Anna what had happened between her and John. Sympathetic, Anna stopped by later that night, after her parents had dropped off Scotty. Anna offered to keep Scotty overnight and take him to school the following morning. "I think you just need an evening to yourself to think and pray about this whole situation with John, as well as what Pierce told you about that job. You know you can find a marketing director position at another company if you don't get this one."

"Yes, I know, but, from my research, just finding a marketing director position, and then getting hired for it, well…it's a highly competitive position. I could probably find a similar position elsewhere, but, it'd take time, like a few years, I'd imagine."

"Well, hang in there." Anna hugged her right before leaving with Scotty.

As the hour grew late, Monica continued to worry about her situation with John. She wished her feelings for him weren't so strong. She dreaded going to bed, knowing she'd have a hard time falling asleep. She had some schoolwork to do, but she knew she wouldn't be able to concentrate. Feeling like a caged animal, she decided to go to Wal-Mart. She needed to get some beauty items. A short time later, she breezed into the huge store, anxious to get her shopping done. Not paying attention, she collided into somebody walking in the opposite direction. "I'm sorry," she said as she looked up into Kevin's familiar dark eyes. She jerked back, shocked.

"No, I'm sorry, Monica. I wasn't paying attention." The familiar scent of his cologne reminded her of the time they used to spend together. She glanced at the square package he clutched. "Tamara sent me out to get diapers for Tyler." He held the package up. "My life's really changed since he's been born."

She nodded. "I can imagine."

He continued to look at her, his dark eyes full of curiosity. "Are you sure you're okay? You've got that worried look about you."

Monica smiled. Kevin could always tell when something heavy was on her mind. "I'll be okay."

He checked his watch. "Are you sure? I've got a few minutes if you need somebody to talk to."

The urge to tell Kevin about her problems with John came upon her; however, the feeling disappeared. "No, it isn't something I want to talk to you about."

"Well, I want to talk to you about something."

Monica widened her eyes. "You do?" She wondered what in the world Kevin had to talk to her about.

He nodded and pointed to the soda machine inside the Wal-Mart. "Will you join me for a quick soda?"

Still curious, Monica nodded. After they were seated on a bench with their Cokes, Kevin started the conversation. "I noticed since we. . .since we stopped seeing each other that you've been staring at me and my family at church sometimes."

Monica's skin heated with embarrassment. She sipped her soda. *Lord, please make so that Kevin can't tell that his sudden breakup still makes me bitter.* Before she could respond, he stretched his legs out and leaned back against the bench, and gave her a direct look. "I was wondering if you were okay with everything. I know I broke things off suddenly."

Monica sighed, setting her can of soda on the floor. "Tamara also noticed that you keep staring at us in church. At first, she just ignored it, but she said it's starting to bother her, and she wondered why you haven't gotten over me in two years."

Monica jerked back. "Gotten over you?"

"It's obvious you're still upset about our breakup."

"Upset about our breakup? Kevin, you told me you didn't want to see me again after we'd been dating for two years. I know your mom died and everything, and you told me you weren't in the right frame of mind to make a marriage commitment. Yet not long after our breakup you show up with Miss Tamara the following Sunday at church." Her raised voice caused some of the Walmart customers to look their way. She closed her eyes and tried to calm down. After she took a few deep breaths, she figured she needed finish telling Kevin everything that was on her mind. "How do you think that made me feel? Were you dating both of us at the same time? Or did you just happen to meet Tamara not long after our breakup and decide to proudly parade her around our church, introducing her to half the congregation?" The whole ordeal had been so painful that she'd not told John about Kevin bringing Tamara to their old church right after the breakup. She sighed. When she'd switched to Mustard Seed Faith, she'd discovered a short time later that's where Tamara worshipped and, of course, Kevin migrated there, too.

She shook her head, her heart still full of shame. "Everybody knew we were a couple, but the way you abruptly brought Tamara around made people wonder, and I could tell they pitied me. You should have seen some of the looks I got when I left church that day. You could have at least respectfully waited a few weeks before bringing her to church with you. You could have let me know what you were going to do. It was like a splash of cold water in my face when you did that."

His dark eyes widened. "You are still angry."

Her heart pounded, and Monica realized Kevin was correct. "Yes, I am still angry. I know it's wrong for me to feel this way, and I've been praying about it, but I still don't understand what happened between us. I felt that we were dating one minute, then the next you tell me you want to break up, and then you show up with Tamara. Were you seeing both of us at the same time? You at least owe me that explanation."

He sighed. "Not really."

"Not really? What does that mean?"

"I met Tamara at the men's retreat—"

"You met her at a men's retreat? How is that possible?"

"She was one of the volunteers at the host church to provide the food. I started talking to her, and I asked her for her phone number."

Monica sighed, wondering why she even wanted to hear this. "When was the men's retreat?"

"Remember, I went to the men's retreat a couple of months before we broke up."

"So, you were dating her while you were dating me." How despicable was that?

"I didn't see her again until the Sunday I brought her to church. I talked to her on the phone a few times, but I wasn't dating her." He threw his hands up in the air as if he needed to protect himself from her tirade.

"Okay, I have a few questions. Why did it take

you two months to tell me what was going on, and why did you show up at church with her right after you'd broken up with me? Did Tamara know what you were doing?"

"What do you mean?"

"Did she know you broke up with me days before you brought her to church?"

He shook his head. "No, she didn't know. I'm sorry about the way I handled things. I guess I should have been more sensitive."

"More sensitive? You shouldn't have been leading me on for two years!"

"Look, I liked you, but I knew after we'd been dating for about a year and a half that we weren't going to get married."

Monica jerked back. "Then why did you keep going out with me?"

"I enjoyed your company, and I didn't want to hurt your feelings. But it was wrong of me to treat you that way, and I'm sorry. Initially, when you asked about marriage, I really was pretty messed up because my mom had died. But months later, I knew you weren't the right woman for me." He paused, staring at his soda can as if in deep thought. "You know, before my mother died, she always told me I didn't have much common sense when it came to women, but I didn't mean to hurt you," he repeated.

"Well, I agree with your mom." She sighed. "You know, I hated it when you always belittled me when I told you that I wanted to be a marketing director. I know that the commercial in which I assisted was a fiasco, but, I'd had no training and it was a last-minute thing. Why did you always put me down whenever I spoke about my professional aspirations?"

"Honestly?"

Honestly? What kind of question was that? "Of course, I want you to be honest, Kevin."

"It hurt my ego. A lot of men hate it when their wife or girlfriend is more successful than they are. I didn't want you to be some big wig corporate woman making more money than I was. You know what I mean?"

She couldn't resist rolling her eyes. "That sounds awful." In a rush, she told him about the Pierce's retirement later that year and her dream of getting the marketing director position. She also told him about taking care of Scotty.

"Monica, I think you'll get that director's job. I'm sorry about all the hurtful things that I said to you in the past. I'm learning from my mistakes." He paused for a few seconds. "And I think it's great you're bonding with your nephew. I hope Gina gets better."

She gave him a short, curt nod. At least that was out of her system. "Apology accepted."

"I know we left a lot of things unsaid, and I just want to clear the air before we move."

"Move?"

He nodded. "Yes, Tamara and I are relocating to Hawaii."

"Hawaii?"

"Yes. Tamara's company is transferring her there, and they offered her a position in the new office. I've been searching on the Internet lately, and I was able to find a job there, too. We leave in a couple of weeks. They'll be announcing our departure plans at church on Sunday. We think it'll be a nice place to raise Tyler."

Stunned. That's how she felt. Such surprising news to hear. Kevin checked his watch again. "I've got to get going because Tamara will start worrying if I don't show up at home soon." They stood, and he pulled her into a clumsy embrace. "I feel bad about the way things ended between us, and I hope things work out for you and John."

Monica looked into his dark eyes. "You know about John?"

He shrugged. "Of course, I do. It's hard not to know. We're in a small church, and people talk. I know he's taking Aiden's class, so I hope he makes the decision to accept Christ. If he does, you never know what might happen between the two of you." He grinned, a teasing glint in his dark eyes.

Monica watched Kevin walk away. It wasn't her usual routine to get beauty supplies at Wal-Mart late at night. She could only imagine that God had orchestrated her running into Kevin that evening, giving her the opportunity to ask him questions she'd been wondering about for two years. Although she'd reconciled herself to the situation, a part of her was still a little glad that Kevin's family would now be a long distance away.

CHAPTER 22

DURING THE NEXT couple of weeks, John continued to be plagued with questions about salvation and Christianity. He invited Aiden over for a chat so they could discuss his questions. When he arrived, John invited him into the kitchen. He made a pot of coffee. Aiden spotted the box of Chocolate Dreams candy on the table. "Mind if I have a few of these? They're my favorite."

"Go ahead." It was the new chocolate mocha flavor. He loved the candy, but, didn't feel like indulging at the moment. Aiden tore open the box and ate three pieces of candy within a few minutes. He then helped himself to a large cup of coffee. He added a lot of cream and sugar. "Beverly keeps telling me I eat too much sugar. I try to cut back when I'm with her since it upsets her so much."

John nodded as he got his mug of coffee. "Yeah, she's always been a health fanatic."

After Aiden had sipped his coffee, he focused on

John. "So, why did you want to meet with me?"

"I have so much going through my mind that I don't want to bother you with too many details. Suffice it to say my search for the truth continues."

"Have you been getting a lot out of my class?"

"Yes, I have. I've even been talking to my friend Pete, who owns the nursery. I've been visiting him and telling him about everything on my mind." He'd even told Pete about Monica not wanting to see him anymore. Although his friend had been sympathetic, he'd said that he didn't blame Monica for what she'd decided to do. He pushed Monica out of his mind as he focused on what he needed to speak to Aiden about. "I'm still not sure what to believe."

"You know, the Lord tells us if we seek Him, we'll find Him. We're humans, and we make mistakes. We're by no means perfect, and we need somebody to guide us and protect us. Our Savior does that and nobody else. As humans we walk around the earth living our lives, but we can't be gods over our own lives. God has control over all of the universe, and in order to understand Him, you must accept Him and live according to His commands."

"But what about suffering?" John threw his hands up into the air.

"What about Christ's suffering? I know there's a lot of suffering on this earth, but you need to focus on the fact that Jesus died on the cross for us." Aiden shook his head, gazing at John with his wise, kind eyes. "God has offered us the gift of eternal life. Accept His gift, be earnest in your quest to know and understand God. Seek Him with your whole mind and heart, and He'll make Himself known to you."

"But scientifically—"

Aiden shook his head. "Forget science. Forget your agnostic views for a minute. You can't deny the evidence that there has been no man like Jesus that walked this earth. You can't deny the evidence that He did indeed exist. I'm talking evidence other than the Bible. Does it make sense that this man, living on earth as God, would suffer so much pain for nothing?" Aiden raised his voice, and stood up tall, as if preaching from the pulpit. "He gave His life for us, and we need to accept His gift."

John closed his eyes, letting Aiden's words sink into him. Aiden took John's hand, and after he said a prayer, John swallowed and took a deep breath. "Amen." The single word barely slipped from his mouth.

A few days after his meeting with Aiden, John stood on the frigid, deserted beach. He placed his hands in his pockets as he watched the angry waves tumble onto the brown, grainy sand. *God, are You trying to tell me that You're real?* As he continued to stare at nature, he recalled what he'd read in the book of Genesis. God had created all things, the birds of the sky and the creeping things and the creatures of the ocean. John sniffed the ocean-scented air as feelings of warmth and peace settled upon him.

There was no way this earth just happened to appear due to chance. God created it. As scientific theories about earth's creation, like the big bang theory, fluttered through his mind, he pushed the thoughts aside, instead focusing on God. *Lord, thank You for creating this earth. Thank You for creating me, thank You for giving Your Son for our sins. I accept You, dear Lord, I accept You as my Savior. Amen.* John wiped the tears from his cheeks as he continued to stare at the beach.

During the last few weeks since her accidental meeting with Kevin, thoughts of John had swirled through Monica's brain as she worked at Chocolate Dreams. The CEO's nephew had come in for a visit and he'd met Pierce. Both the CEO and his nephew had asked Pierce out for lunch. She figured that the CEO wanted Pierce to see his intelligent and hardworking his Ivy League nephew. The CEO probably wanted Pierce to give his nephew a good, personal description about the job he'd been doing for decades.

She sighed, still focusing on how hard it had been lately. All she'd wanted was to spend time with John. She prayed as she went through her day, asking God's help in making her strong enough to accept whatever happened with Gina and with John.

As the days passed, she had become aware of the holiday lights and festive decorations in the malls and on the city streets. Monica, Anna, Karen, and Scotty had even taken time out of their busy holiday schedules to attend the annual Ocean City Carolfest at the Music Pier. Before the free concert started, they'd placed their donated canned goods into the collection boxes for the needy.

When the concert started, Monica had swayed to the music, holding Scotty's hand. Just hearing the sweet Christmas carols warmed her heart. They'd also gone to Ocean City's Winterfest of Lights on another evening. After riding the tram and seeing the beautifully lit displays, they'd stopped for hot chocolate and Scotty had gotten to meet Santa. When Scotty begged to see Santa again, she'd taken him to the Music Pier another cold, blustery night so he could get his picture taken with Santa Claus in a lifeguard boat, as a gift for Gina.

She'd found comfort in prayer and her daily devotions, and she still prayed that Gina was okay and that she would continue to stay with their parents until she got her life back on track. So far, she'd not made any more threats to take Scotty away, and for that, Monica was grateful.

The holiday season was now in full bloom. However, since she'd not been dating John, sadness had hovered around her in spite of her moments of joy.

She missed John like crazy…oh, how she craved to see him. When he came to tutor Scotty, she'd let Scotty answer the door, and then she'd scamper upstairs. She was a coward, but when she saw his dark brown eyes and heard his deep voice, her insides turned to mush, and she knew she would be in his arms at a moment's notice. She found it easier to ignore the attraction when she was around him for only a few minutes at a time. It had gotten so bad that she'd even dreamed about him. She almost wished she'd never met him so she wouldn't be going through this emotional turmoil.

Days later, she gazed around her living room, enjoying the Christmas tree she and Scotty had decorated together. She'd decided to get a real pine tree instead of using her artificial one this year so Scotty could enjoy the scent.

Since Scotty had gone to bed, she decided to wrap his gifts. She scanned the packages, hoping she had not forgotten anything. The little guy had had a difficult year. She hoped she could make up for it, just a little bit, by indulging him with an abundant number of gifts. Her grad school class had been completed and she had only one more class left before graduation in the late spring. It was a blessing that she could enjoy the holidays without worrying about school for a few weeks.

Her gift wrapping was interrupted by a knock on her door. Figuring it was Anna or Karen, she rushed to answer, craving some adult company. She gasped when she saw John on her doorstep, carrying two large wrapped packages. His dark eyes seemed to plead with her. "Hello, Monica."

She swallowed, wondering if this visit was a good idea. "John."

"Don't say anything, just let me come in and talk to you. Please. Don't run and hide upstairs like you've been doing for the last few weeks."

She nodded, her heart pounding as he came into her home and placed the presents under the tree. The Christmas lights twinkled in the semidarkness. "That's a pretty tree." He eyed the tree while removing his coat and sitting on the couch.

She sat beside him. "I got it for Scotty. I know he enjoys the pine scent."

He noticed the presents scattered on the floor and chuckled. "Looks like your nephew hit the jackpot."

"He's had a rough year, so I thought I'd make sure he had a good Christmas." He took her hand. "Why did you come by tonight? Just to bring presents for Scotty?"

"No, the presents are not just for Scotty. One of them is for you."

She looked at the tree, embarrassed. "But I didn't buy anything for you. . . ."

He chuckled, squeezing her hand. "The best present you could give me is your company again."

She shook her head. "John—"

He pressed his finger to her lips. "Please, let me finish." He glanced around the living room, as if gathering courage to continue. "As you know, there're only a few more weeks for Aiden's class."

She nodded. "I realize that." She'd been counting the weeks of the class, paying attention to the lesson plans on the bulletin board, wondering which lesson and which words would sway John to finally accept Jesus.

"Well, I just want you to be the first to know that I've finally accepted Jesus."

Her mouth dropped open, and she couldn't find words to express her joy. He smiled. "It happened a few nights ago. I've kept it to myself, but the Christmas Eve service is only about a week away. That's when I was going to go forward at the altar call and tell the pastor about my new vow to accept Jesus into my heart." He paused and before she could speak, he continued. "A woman named Marilyn Tyndall called me the other night."

Monica furrowed her brow, confused. "Who is Marilyn Tyndall?"

"She was a good friend of my mother's. She knew my parents when they were first saved, and she was a mentor to my mother." Monica wondered where this was leading. "Anyway, she found my phone number on a piece of paper in my mother's Bible. She also found a letter that my mother had written to me and had never gotten a chance to mail."

"What did the letter say?"

He was silent, and she wondered what he was thinking. "She apologized for raising me as an agnostic, and she was telling me to give Christianity a chance." He went on to explain that she gave him a few scriptures to look up, including Jeremiah 29:13. He told her of his conversation with Aiden, and his constant thoughts and comments to God. "I found myself talking to God and praying regularly. It was so gradual over the last month, my thinking about God. But when I started praying and talking to Him all the time, it occurred to me that God is real and He hears me." He squeezed her hand. "He hears me, Monica, and you just don't know how good it feels to know that I'm no longer in disbelief and I've accepted Him as my Savior!"

"Oh, John, that's so wonderful!" she gushed, barely able to contain her joy. "I'm so glad you told me." She hugged him.

He cleared his throat as she released him. "I just want you to keep this to yourself for now. I want the other people in the congregation to know when I step forward on Christmas Eve." He took her hands. "Are you planning to go to your parents' on Christmas Eve?"

She shook her head. "I was going to go there on Christmas Day after Scotty opens his gifts. He wants to spend his holiday with his mother, so I was going to let him stay at my parents' house during his Christmas break."

"So, will you be here for the church's Christmas Eve service?" Her stomach tumbled with anticipation. "Of course, I'll be there."

"Are you off next week?"

"No, I took the week between Christmas and New Year's off."

"Well, you know the college is closed for their holiday break. So, since Scotty will be gone for the week, I figured we could spend some time together. That is, if it's okay with you."

"I wouldn't mind at all." Thoughts of spending the holidays with John— seeing Christmas lights, drinking hot cider, gazing at her Christmas tree together—gave her a warm bubbly feeling in her stomach. "I think it's a perfect idea."

He hugged her. "Okay, it's a deal then?" He whispered in her ear before they kissed.

When she pulled away, she felt breathless. "John, you have yourself a deal."

CHAPTER 23

AS CHRISTMAS EVE drew closer, Monica's health began failing. Scotty ran around the house excited about Christmas, and she could barely stand the noise. The church had their annual Christmas cantata, and Scotty participated with the rest of his Sunday school class. During the performance, she could barely enjoy the music her head hurt so much. When she went to work the following day, she had to leave early because she was sick. She felt hot and then cold before she broke out in a sweat.

She begged Anna to pick up Scotty. She had enrolled him in a child care center for a few days since he was out of school and her vacation from work had not started. She also asked Anna to get some medicine at the drugstore. John called several times, and Monica told him she'd caught the flu and didn't know when she would recuperate.

"I'm sorry to hear that. Did you need me to bring you anything?"

"No, thanks." However, she wanted to be at that church when John made his public proclamation to God. "I'll try and come to the service tomorrow night."

"No, don't do that. We can celebrate over the holidays. If you don't feel up to it, I'll just come and sit by your side until I know you're feeling better."

In spite of her illness, his words warmed her heart. She hung up the phone and snuggled beneath her blankets. She heard Karen's and Anna's voices in the kitchen as they made spaghetti for dinner. She was thankful that her best friends had been over frequently, taking care of Scotty while she was ill. Her parents had already called and said they'd pick him up on Christmas Day so he could spend his winter break with Gina.

On Christmas Day, Scotty's shrieks resonated throughout the house. Anna spent the night to help out, and Monica heard Anna join Scotty under the tree, helping him with his new toys. Monica swallowed. Her throat was still sore, and her body ached. When she came downstairs, she was surprised to see Karen. "What are you doing out of bed?" Both of them admonished her as she stood on the steps, watching her nephew open his gifts.

"I wanted to see Scotty open his presents." His euphoric mood made her shopping spree worth it.

She returned to bed after the gifts were opened.

When she awoke hours later, the sun was no longer shining and her room was semi-dark. She attempted to sit up, and John came into the room. "You're awake."

As he approached, she took his hand. She glanced at the clock and noted it was midafternoon. "It sure is dark outside."

"The weatherman is calling for snow."

He helped her sit up. The enticing aroma of chicken soup wafted through the house, and for the first time in days, her stomach growled. "That smells good."

John chuckled as he went to her door. "That's some chicken soup. I made it myself."

She swung her legs to the side of the bed. "I'll come down and eat some." "No. Don't come down to the kitchen. I'll bring up your lunch on a tray. Your parents stopped by hours ago to get Scotty, and they didn't want to wake you. They left some Christmas dinner for us if you want to eat it later or maybe tomorrow."

She shook her head. "I don't want my mom's Christmas dinner now. I want some of your soup."

"Well, you stay put, and I'll bring you a tray." He left the room. Soon he returned carrying a wooden tray with a bowl of chicken soup, a plate of crackers, a glass of orange juice, and a red rose in a vase. "Oh, this is so sweet." She patted her hair, hoping she wasn't scaring him away with her hideous appearance. The hot soup tasted good going down her sore throat, and she ate the whole bowlful. When she finished, he asked her if she wanted more, but she declined. He set the vase on her dresser and took her dishes to the kitchen. He came back with the package he'd left for her days ago under her Christmas tree.

He gave her the gift. "Merry Christmas."

Smiling, she touched the box. "I feel so bad. I didn't get you a gift."

He placed his finger over her lips. "Don't worry. I accept gifts all year round. It doesn't have to be on Christmas."

No longer able to hide her curiosity, she ripped the paper open and found a large white box. When she lifted the lid, she saw an exquisite cherry red sweater. She fingered the garment, and the knitted material was as soft as a cotton ball. She held it to her face, relishing the texture. "This is lovely."

"When I saw it at the store, I knew it would be perfect for you. That red color looks good against your brown skin."

She continued to finger the garment. "It sure does. I'm glad you bought it for me. I can't wait to wear it."

He sat in the empty chair beside her bed. "Maybe you can wear it over the holidays. If you're feeling better over the next week, we might be able to spend some time together."

She put the sweater aside and took his hand. "I'm looking forward to that. I really am." Thoughts of how she had acted filtered through her mind.

"Uh-oh. What's wrong?"

"I just wanted to apologize for the way I acted in the church parking lot a few weeks ago. That was insensitive of me."

"Don't say anything else about it. You were just trying to avoid getting hurt, and you were following your beliefs. There's nothing wrong with what you did." He looked into her eyes. "You did hurt my feelings. But I know it wasn't intentional."

"To be honest with you, I hated doing it. My feelings for you didn't go away."

"Mine didn't go away either. As a matter of fact, my feelings for you have grown deeper." He caressed her fingers.

Warmth and compassion flowed through her, making her feel loved and wanted. Being around John was making her crazy. When he released her hand, she got out of bed, and opened the curtain. "It's snowing. Look." She gestured toward the window.

He stood behind her, gazing at the white flakes as they floated from the sky. "Looks like we're having a white Christmas." He pulled her into his arms.

"It looks like we're having a wonderful Christmas." Her voice faltered with the enjoyment of being held by him as she watched the falling flakes of snow.

Monica couldn't remember the last time she'd had such a joyous Christmas away from her family. Her sore throat and stuffy nose put a slight damper on the day. However, when John showed her his loving-kindness, her illness melted away like ice during a spring thaw.

They continued to enjoy his tasty soup for the rest of the day. John lit a fire in the fireplace, and she turned on the stereo. Christmas carols boomed from the speakers, and when her favorite tune, "Silent Night," was playing, John took her into his arms and held her as they softly sang the lyrics together. Monica's voice croaked, and she thought she sounded horrible, but John's voice was smooth and mellow, blending nicely with the music. "You know, you've got a great voice." She complimented him once the song was over.

He chuckled, continuing to cradle her in his arms. "You're not the first person to tell me that."

"Since you're a member of the church now, perhaps you should get involved with one of the ministries."

He ran his fingers over her cheek. Her insides quivered like jelly, and she had to force herself to pay attention to the conversation at hand. Then he raised his thick eyebrows. "What do you suggest?"

She giggled, thoroughly enjoying their time

together. "I'm suggesting you try out for the choir. They sound good now, but I think they'd sound even better if you were up there with them."

He nodded at her suggestion. "I might do that. There're so many things I want to do now that I'm a Christian. I feel like I've wasted my whole life, and I'm ready to start anew."

She picked up on the eager tone in his voice. "What kinds of things?"

He hesitated and looked away. She sensed he was hiding something, but she didn't want to pry too much since he was a new Christian and was still searching for ways to serve the Lord. "I've been thinking about various things. My mind isn't made up yet, but when it is, you'll be the first to know."

She nodded, still pleased he was so eager to serve the Lord. "You should speak to the pastor or Aiden about that. We even have an awesome men's ministry that meets on Thursday nights, and we have several Bible studies."

They stared at the orange flames crackling from the warm fire. The curtains were open, and they watched the snowflakes as they continued to drift from the sky, creating an undisturbed blanket of whiteness around them.

Around six o'clock, Monica took a nap. When she awoke a couple hours later, she saw that the snow had stopped. She crept into the living room and found John sitting on the chair near the extinguished fire, reading his Bible. He looked so handsome reading God's Word that she could just stand there and watch him forever. "Hey, handsome."

He closed his black book. "Did you have a good nap?"

"I sure did." She pointed to the window. "Looks like you'll have to stay here. We're snowed in."

He shook his head. "I just heard the news on the radio. The back roads are bad, but the main ones aren't too bad. I'm going to shovel your driveway and go home."

Her heart skipped a beat. She wished he didn't have to leave. "Are you sure? The weather looks pretty terrible."

"Even though you're sick, you still look beautiful to me. I'll be honest and say that I don't trust myself to stay all night in this house with you."

She widened her eyes, surprised at his boldness.

"I'm a new Christian, and I'm still learning a lot, but I am familiar with what the Lord thinks about premarital sex."

So refreshing and touching to see that he was taking his Christian vows so seriously. "Are you sure you won't get stuck out there?"

He put his Bible aside and walked to where she still stood on the stairwell. "No, I'll be okay. I've got some good snow tires on my car, and I'll be sure to call you when I get home." He checked his watch. "It's almost ten o'clock, so I'll just borrow your snow shovel and clear out your driveway. Then I'll be on my way."

"Okay." She was still reluctant to let him go but knew it was best under the circumstances. She walked down the steps toward him, and he pulled her into his arms. He kissed her, and she found warmth and comfort from his strong embrace.

He cradled her face between his hands. "There's an indoor ice-skating rink not too far from here. Maybe we can go there for a while this week sometime. I don't want you out on that ice this soon after you've been sick, but if you're feeling better, we can also go to this neat café called Tea by the Sea. They serve great scones. We can go there and relax while we enjoy a hot cup of tea."

She nodded. "Yes, that sounds like a good idea."

He gathered his coat and gloves and found her snow shovel in the basement. He then headed outside. She turned on the outside light and watched him for several minutes as he shoveled the snow. After the driveway was cleared, John came into her house and placed her shovel back in the basement. He kissed her cheek and said good-bye before he took his exit.

During the next few days, Monica grew stronger as her flu vanished. John called often and came by to see her. She even convinced him she was well enough to go out on the boardwalk to see Ocean City's Winterfest of Lights. Although she had already seen the display earlier that season, she longed to see it again with John. The seashore was illuminated with close to a million Christmas lights. Many pedestrians were bedazzled by the beautiful display, and Monica's heart leaped with joy since she was able to see such an exquisite sight with John by her side. They also went to the indoor ice-skating rink another day, and Monica enjoyed the lemon-flavored tea and cinnamon scones at Tea by the Sea.

She found the energy to clean her house, and she missed Scotty. She wondered if he was enjoying his Christmas presents, so she called her parents and was glad to hear her mother answer the phone. "Hey, Monica!"

"I'm surprised you haven't called me, Mom." She figured she would've heard from her mom by now. "You know I've been sick."

Her mother laughed. "We didn't want to bother you since we knew you were spending some quality time with John. You know, your father and I were just talking about how nice it is that he's found the Lord. That's truly a miracle."

Her heart felt warmed by her mother's sincere words. "I feel the same way. You know, Mom, my prayers for John's salvation have been answered. I've been praying about this since I first found out about his agnostic views, and I'm just glad that John has accepted Christ as his Savior."

"Speaking of accepting Christ—" Her mother was interrupted by Scotty's eager voice.

"Is that Aunt Monica on the phone?"

She was thrilled to hear her nephew when

her mother handed him the phone. "Hi, Aunt Monica!" He sounded like he was out of breath.

"Have you been running?"

"Yeah! My mom and me made a snowman!"

She clutched the receiver, having a hard time picturing Gina in the snow building a snowman with her son. "That's nice. Did you have a good time?"

"Yeah! We had a carrot for the nose, and we used rocks for the eyes! My mom said it looked like a funny snowman." He chuckled, his voice filled with glee.

She was glad to hear the enthusiasm in his voice; however, she had a twinge of doubt niggling in the back of her mind. Was Gina planning on being a good mother from now on? Did she still want to take Scotty away and keep him permanently? Could Monica stand not having Scotty with her anymore if Gina did decide she wanted to be a parent again? All of these questions swirled through her mind like scattered snowflakes on the wind. She barely paid attention to Scotty's incessant chatter as she wondered what would happen to him now that Gina continued to form a bond with her son.

Her mind wandered so much that she barely noticed when her mother was back on the phone. "Monica, I've been speaking for the last two minutes, and you haven't said a word. What's wrong?"

"Mom, what's going to happen to Scotty now

that Gina is back? Is she going to take him away again and disappear?"

Her mother's voice was tinged with excitement as she relayed her news. "Well, I wanted to tell you something about Gina. You'll never guess what I saw her doing today." Intrigued, she clutched the receiver, awaiting her mother's next words. "I saw her reading her Bible."

Shock coursed through Monica's veins when she heard the news. "You're kidding. Are you sure you're not mistaken?"

"No, not about this. She doesn't realize I saw her, so I haven't mentioned it to her. I'm going to leave her alone about it now. I think she's working through some things, and I honestly think she's sorry for abandoning Scotty."

Monica sat down in the kitchen chair, still stunned by this news. When she'd accepted Christ as a young teenager, Gina was only a toddler. However, when Gina got older, her interest in church and the Bible never developed. She never participated in the youth fellowship groups as Monica had and instead remained mixed up in the wrong crowd. She had shunned the Bible and God, drowning her pain with drugs and alcohol. The first time she came home intoxicated, she'd been only fifteen years old. Monica remembered her mother had called, frantic about Gina's rebellious behavior. Since Monica was no longer living at home at the time, she didn't have to witness Gina's antics firsthand; however, she did recall her mother always saying she didn't understand how two women could turn out so differently after being raised in the same house.

She barely remembered saying good-bye to her mother as she hung up the phone. She pressed her hands together, bowed her head, and prayed for Gina, hoping she was on her way to having a permanent relationship with Jesus.

CHAPTER 24

DURING THE NEXT few weeks, Monica kept her sister in mind, saying prayers daily for her salvation. On Sunday she stayed after the church service, along with the rest of the congregation, to celebrate with the new members. It was New Member Day, and John had been one of the new members to be welcomed into the congregation.

Afterward everybody celebrated in the large mess hall in the church basement. Scotty scampered about with other children. The scent of roasted pork and barbecued beef warmed the air, and platters of fruits, vegetables, and chips adorned the serving tables. After Scotty was fed, Monica made a plate and searched for John so they could sit together. Dejection spread through her when she spotted him sitting at a table with some of the members of the men's choir. The four people he sat with were single, and he'd been spending a lot of time with them lately. He'd told her one night after Scotty's tutoring session that they talked a lot about the Bible, and he said he'd been learning a lot from them.

She continued glancing around the room until she saw Anna and Karen sitting at a table in the corner. She made her way over with her plate of food. "Hi." She sat down, still wishing she could sit with John.

Karen arched her eyebrow, giving her a sly look. "You're not eating with John?"

She shrugged as she bit into her pork sandwich. It was delicious. She enjoyed her food for a while before responding to Karen's comment. "You see him sitting over there with the choir. I didn't just want to go over there and interrupt."

Anna folded her arms in front of her chest. "Why not? He's your man, isn't he?"

She huffed, still trying to enjoy her food. "Just leave the whole subject alone, okay?"

Karen leaned back into her seat, observing her friend. "My, my, aren't you snappy today. I'd think you'd be in a good mood since John has accepted Christ."

Monica put her fork aside, not sure of how to tell her friends things weren't progressing between her and John as smoothly as she liked. She pushed her plate of half-eaten food away, suddenly changing her mind and deciding to reveal her doubts to them. "I've barely spent any time with him since Christmas." She spent a fair amount of time on her grad school class. But when she wasn't studying, focusing on Scotty, or working, she thought about John.

Anna widened her dark brown eyes. "You're kidding. None at all?"

She shrugged. "Not really. We had such a romantic Christmas holiday. He told me awhile back that he was falling in love with me."

Karen leaned closer. "Are you sure he said that?"

"Of course, I'm sure." Surprising that Karen would think she would make something like that up.

"Did you tell him you loved him?" Anna narrowed her eyes and leaned toward her. Obviously eager to hear her response.

She shook her head. "No, I didn't. Well, not really anyway. I told him that I shared the same feelings he had for me just before I told him we shouldn't spend any more time together right after Thanksgiving."

"Monica…" Karen groaned. "You've admitted to him that you're falling in love with him right before your breakup? You need to tell him how you feel now. He's worked through his issues with God, and now it's time to get your relationship with John back on track."

"I thought it was too soon to tell him my true feelings. I wanted to see if things would work out between us."

"And?" Anna raised her eyebrows.

She shook her head. "They're not working out at all. At least not for me. You'd think I'd be happy he's now a Christian, but you know, I'm jealous of the time he spends with God."

"Monica…" Karen grabbed her arm.

"He comes to tutor Scotty, but he doesn't eat dinner with us anymore. He spends time with the new friends he's made in the choir, plus he spends so much time reading the Bible, soaking up knowledge. We haven't spent any time together since Christmas, and I'm starting to wonder if I imagined the joy I felt during the holidays."

Anna sighed. "Have you talked to him about it?"

She shook her head. "How can I say I'm jealous of the time he's spending with God and the church when I was the one who spouted how important it was for him to become a Christian?"

Karen nodded. "That would sound a little weird. Why don't you ask him out? Maybe he needs to be reminded that you care about him."

She recalled the present he gave her for Christmas. "He gave me the most beautiful sweater for Christmas, but I didn't get anything for him. Maybe if I get him a thoughtful gift, he'll be reminded of my existence."

Anna shook her head. "It's a shame you sound so dismal. If the man says he's falling in love with you, then he's falling in love with you. Stop griping and just cherish the time you do get to spend with him. He's a new Christian, so he's probably zealous and eager. His getting closer to God is more important than getting closer to you."

Monica pulled her plate toward her, deciding to finish her meal after all. Anna's words were full of truth. She was going to go ahead and buy a special gift for John, but she wouldn't mention how disheartened she'd felt about his recent absence from her life. She glanced at the men's choir table. John was laughing heartily, enjoying the fellowship with his new Christian friends. He looked so handsome that it was hard not to stare. His dark suit fit his trim body nicely, and she wished they could have shared their meal together. She hoped things would work out between them.

John clutched the bouquet of fragrant roses, hesitating before he knocked on Monica's door. He'd visited Pete earlier and his friend had a shipment of roses that'd been delivered. He said he was going to expand his nursery and start selling flowers, just to see how it worked out.

John had been glad to buy the blossoms for Monica. Earlier when he'd sat with his new friends from the men's choir, he'd seen her look of disappointment after she'd gotten her plate of food. He'd been tempted to abandon his friends and go and sit with her after all. He'd glanced in her direction several times as she ate with Anna and Karen, and he could sense she was unhappy.

He hesitated, gripping the flowers in his hand. He'd found a new happiness upon accepting Christ. There was something he needed to do, and so far, he had not discussed this matter with anybody, except for Jesus. Monica wasn't going to like what he had to tell her tonight, but hopefully she would understand.

He finally found the courage to knock on her door. Her dark brown eyes widened when she opened it. "John." Her pretty voice echoed in the dark night.

He entered her house, kissing her cheek. As he handed her the bouquet of roses, he glanced around the silent house. "Where's Scotty?"

He followed her as she made her way to the kitchen and filled a vase with water. "He's spending the night with Anna. She promised they could make pizza and have popcorn afterward. She's even going to drop him off at school in the morning."

He watched the clear water tumble into the glass vase. "That was nice of her."

"Yeah, wasn't it?" She placed the vase on the kitchen table and removed the tissue paper from the fragrant buds before cutting the ends and placing the stems into the water. "Thanks for the flowers." An awkward silence followed. He still didn't know how to tell her his news.

"Remember I once told you how pretty it is walking on the boardwalk at the beach in the wintertime?"

"Yes, I remember."

"Since Scotty's not here, how about we go for a walk?"

"But it's cold outside."

He chuckled, pulling her into his arms. "So? Just bundle up. Plus, I'll be around to snuggle with to keep you warm."

Her dark eyes twinkled with pleasure. "Okay. Just give me a few minutes to get ready." He waited in the living room while she went upstairs. She returned wearing boots, corduroy pants, and an oversized gray sweatshirt. She opened the closet and removed a puffy black coat and a knitted hat. He helped her put her coat on. She pulled the hat on her head. "I should be warm enough with all of this on."

"You'll be fine." Their breath came out in frosty puffs as they walked to his car. Minutes later, he pulled into a parking space near the deserted Ocean City boardwalk. Lights illuminated the stark area as a few pedestrians walked their pets. The black sky was littered with tiny silver stars, and the moon was a full white orb. He blinked again, amazed how God created the heavens and the earth. Since his salvation, his whole outlook about the earth and the people on it had changed dramatically.

He held her gloved hand as they walked. A few restaurants were open, but most of the businesses were closed. He stopped under a bright streetlight, inviting her to sit with him on a bench. They silently watched the foamy waves crash on the deserted beach. He was still trying to decide which words he should use when he told her his news. He was silent for so long that she finally squeezed his arm. "John, what's wrong?"

The question hung in the frigid air between them, unanswered. "Why do you think something is wrong?"

She shrugged beneath her thick coat. "It's just a feeling I have. Things have been different between us since Christmas."

He still didn't answer her as he removed her glove and held her bare hand in his, kissing her fingers. Her dark eyes were laced with questions and doubts. "I really do love you, Monica."

She remained silent as he continued to hold her hand, massaging her palm. "Are you cold?"

She shook her head, her dark eyes full of fear. She tried to pull her hand away, but he kept it firmly in his grip. "I'm almost sure you're about to tell me some bad news. I can sense it."

Monica turned away, but he took her chin in his fingers and urged her to look into his eyes. He leaned toward her and kissed her on the mouth. When the kiss finally ended, he found his heart was pounding. "That was an amazing kiss."

She looked toward the foamy water before focusing on him again. Her dark eyes glistened with unshed tears, but she quickly blinked them away. "You want to end our relationship." Her voice took on a hard edge as she scooted away from him on the bench. He continued to clutch her hand as he massaged her fingers.

"No."

Her eyes widened. "No?"

"No, I don't want to end our relationship. I'd like for us to keep seeing each other."

"But. . .I thought you had something negative to tell me tonight. I can tell when something is bothering you."

He leaned back on the wooden bench. "You're right, something is bothering me."

He again sensed her shiver beneath her thick coat. "Are you sure you're not cold?"

Before she could respond, he helped her up from the bench. "Let's go to the OC Daily Grind and get something to drink. It hasn't been too long since you were sick. And I don't want to be responsible for your getting ill again by being out in this cold air. Let's stop for a cup of hot chocolate, and I'll tell you what's on my mind."

As they walked toward the establishment hand in hand, the night lost its beauty. The twinkling stars no longer seemed romantic, and the sound of the rushing water no longer enticed him. Monica's sadness surrounded them like a hot, thick blanket, suffocating their happiness.

He opened the door, and warmth rushed around them. Music played softly in the background, and a few people sat at tables drinking hot beverages and reading newspapers. He chose a secluded table with a nice view of the ocean before he left her alone to place their order. He returned minutes later with two steamy mugs of hot chocolate covered with mounds of whipped cream and sprinkled with cinnamon. He set the thick white mugs on the table. Monica lifted hers, warming her hands on the cup. She took a small sip and a spot of whipped cream clung to her upper lip. He playfully wiped it away, licking the sweet cream from his fingertip.

She tried to smile, but her eyes were still sad. "Please tell me what's wrong." He took a sip of his sweet hot chocolate, barely tasting it before it traveled down his throat. After taking a deep breath and saying a quick prayer, he decided to tell her his news. "I've decided to join a ministry."

"Oh?" She stirred the whipped cream into her chocolate. "That doesn't sound so bad. As a matter of fact, it's a good idea. I'm sure Aiden will be pleased that you're joining a ministry."

He shook his head. "I haven't spoken with Aiden about it."

Seemingly crushed, she took another sip of chocolate before asking him another question. "Why not? He would be the best person to speak with about this."

"To tell you the truth, the only other person I've spoken to about this, except you, is Jesus Himself."

She stared outside as she seemed to gather her thoughts. "Joining a ministry is a blessing, but you're acting like it's something negative. Why?"

"Because I don't want to hurt you."

"What?" Turning away from the window, she looked into his eyes.

"I would like to join a speaking ministry, one that reaches out to people who don't believe in God. Some of the people I'd be speaking to might even be agnostic, just like I used to be. I would like to take a year and just travel around the country, maybe even the world. I would give talks about how I was raised, my doubts about Jesus, my struggles, and about how I finally came to accept Him in my life. There's a group who does this, and they need volunteers."

Her mouth dropped open as she gripped her cup. "You're leaving?"

He shook his head. "Not right now. I still have to talk to some people and get things arranged. I don't have to worry about working for a year because when my parents died, they left me a large inheritance. I plan to use that to take a year off from my job and travel, telling other nonbelievers that they need Jesus in their lives."

Her bottom lip quivered, but she quickly controlled herself and clutched her mug of hot chocolate. "Why do you feel you want to do this?"

"Because I feel like I've lost so much time not being saved that I think I need to do more than the average Christian to make a difference in people's lives. Monica, I'm almost forty years old, and my life has been a waste since I haven't found

Jesus until recently."

She shook her head. "No, it hasn't. You've done many good things in your life. One of them is helping blind children."

"I know, but I didn't tell anybody about the gospel my whole life, like I should have. If I take a hiatus from my job for a year and join this ministry, I feel like I could make up for lost time."

"Oh, John. . ." She took a sip from her mug before slamming it upon the table. Hot chocolate spilled onto the surface so she quickly swiped it away with a wad of napkins. "Jesus is not concerned about your making up the time before you came to Him. People usually join ministries like yours when they feel called to do it. Do you feel called?"

He wasn't sure how to answer. He squeezed her hand, unsure of how it felt to be called. "I just know this is what I want to do. But I did want to ask you to do something for me."

"What's that?"

"When I am able to get everything into place for this ministry and I'm able to leave for a year and give my talks on my salvation, I wanted to ask you to wait for me."

"Wait for you?" She pulled her hand away, folding her arms in front of her chest.

He nodded. "I'm not sure how long it will take me to get everything arranged, but when I do, I want to know you'll be in my corner and you'll support me. I want to know when I return to

Ocean City within a year that you'll be waiting for me so we can continue our relationship." She looked away, and he wondered what she was thinking.

CHAPTER 25

AS THE CLOUD of whipped cream floated on her hot chocolate, she wasn't sure if she should laugh or cry. He wanted her to put her life on hold for a year so he could travel the country and do ministry work?

She pushed her beverage away, no longer wanting to taste the chocolate sweetness. Why did he not mention an engagement—or marriage? He'd certainly proclaimed his love for her, so what was holding him back from proposing? If he asked her to wait for a year, wouldn't it make sense to place a ring on her finger?

Also, did John really know what he was doing? He was a new Christian, and although he was zealous in his faith, she had to wonder if his reasoning for entering this ministry was skewed. "I think you need to speak with Aiden about this. Tell him about what you want to do."

"You don't think I should do this, do you?" His deep voice held a note of accusation as he folded his arms across his chest, awaiting her response.

She shook her head. "I'm not going to answer your question. This is between you and God."

"But you don't like my decision. Why?"

She rubbed her forehead, feeling a headache coming on. "I think I'm ready to go home now."

"No, I'm not taking you home."

"Excuse me?"

"I said I'm not taking you home. Not until you tell me what's wrong."

"I won't be seeing you for a year. Isn't that reason enough to be upset?" Her heart already ached for the impending time they would be apart.

"But I'm doing this for Jesus. I'd think you'd be more pleased." She remained silent as she stared into her hot chocolate.

"Oh, I know what's wrong." His deep voice broke into her thoughts. "You're upset because I didn't ask you to come with me. I didn't want to ask you because it would force you to make a decision between Scotty and me. I know you can't have Scotty moving around the world for a year, and that's why I didn't ask you to come with me."

She shook her head. "No, that's not why I'm upset."

"Oh, Monica." He tried to take her hand again, but she pulled it away. "When I finally get all the paperwork and arrangements done and leave, I'm going to miss you—a lot. We've already been through so much, and just when it seems as if things were falling into place, I get the idea to join this ministry." He watched the other patrons in the room, looking as though his thoughts ranged elsewhere. "But this is something I feel I have to do. Please, be honest with me and tell me what you think."

The pleading tone in his voice touched something deep in her heart. "I don't know a whole lot about joining ministries, so it's hard for me to tell you my opinion."

"But?"

"But since you asked for the truth, I'm going to give it to you." She took a deep breath and looked into his eyes. "I think you're making a mistake. I think you're pursuing this ministry for the wrong reasons."

His mouth hardened as he urged her to continue.

"Like I said before, Jesus wouldn't want you to join a ministry to make up for lost time. He would want you to do this if you feel like He's telling you to."

"So, you don't think I should go? You think I should abandon my vision for joining this ministry?" His hardened tone echoed in the room as he looked away from her as if he was hurt.

"Please don't misunderstand me. If you feel called to do this and you feel deep within your heart that this is what Jesus wants you to do, you'll have my blessing." She tried to gather her scattered thoughts. "But if you're merely doing this to make up for the time you weren't saved, then I think you need to reevaluate this whole thing. You're still a new Christian. Do you even know what the scriptures say about good works?"

"I'm not a child. I know what I want to do."

"Please don't be offended. But you say you love me, so you must respect my feelings. Can't you trust that I'm saying these things for your own good?"

He ignored her question. "I said I loved you, but you never told me that you loved me." He stared at her. "I wonder why that is. Are you really over your old boyfriend? I know he and his family have moved to Hawaii, but I still wonder if you're over him."

She jerked her head back, floored by his question. Thoughts of her accidental meeting with Kevin raced through her mind. She shook her head, not wanting to give him the wrong idea. "It was hard for me when Kevin and I broke up, but I'm not in love with him."

His eyes narrowed. "Are you sure about that?"

She stood, her chair scraping across the floor. "I spoke with Kevin shortly before he left."

"You called him?"

She shook her head, not wanting John to get the wrong idea. "Of course not!" She took a deep breath and calmed herself down before telling John about her accidental meeting with Kevin at Wal-Mart. John didn't comment about the conversation she'd had with her ex-boyfriend.

"I'm still not sure you're over him."

She shook her head, angry. "I think it's time to end this conversation. I'm ready to go home now."

As they exited the shop, the cold wind wrapped around her, and she shivered. Salty tears spilled down her cheeks, but she quickly wiped them away, not wanting John to see the evidence of her pain. She stuffed her fists into her pockets, not giving him the opportunity to hold her hand as he usually did when they were together.

Their brisk walk to his car was full of silence. Minutes later, he was pulling up into her driveway. He didn't say good-bye as she exited the car. She didn't close the door right away, wondering if she should say something. Her mind went blank, and she honestly had no idea what she should say. Instead, angry, sad, and flustered, she slammed the car door shut and walked into the house.

She pulled off her coat and dropped it on the couch. As she heard him drive away, she lifted the curtain and watched his taillights disappear around the corner. *Oh, Father God, why oh, why does John really want to join this ministry? I thought he was the right man for me, but now I'm not so sure. I'm falling in love with him, Lord, but I'm scared. I'm so scared that I don't know what to do with myself. But I'm going to leave this in Your hands, Lord, and I'll try not to worry about it so much.*

The following week, Monica shook her head as she pulled into her driveway. Scotty was singing a new song he'd learned on the bus trip he'd taken that day with his Sunday school class. She was glad he was preoccupied because she was still thinking about the lunch she'd had with Karen and Anna earlier that day.

Since Scotty had been on his bus trip, she had shared lunch with her two best friends. However, the conversation had focused on Anna and Dean Love. Things weren't going well between Anna and Dean, and Karen pointed out that Anna was too pushy and anxious and that's why Dean was now avoiding her. Monica had wanted to hear what they had to say about her problems with John, but they'd talked about Dean for so long that she didn't even feel like talking about John. Focusing on Anna's relationship gave her a brief reprieve from thinking about her own problems.

A few hours later, after she'd had dinner with Scotty and sent him upstairs to go to bed, her longing for John's company returned. She sat in her living room, flipping through channels on TV, trying to find something to keep her mind occupied. She yawned, wondering if she should go to bed early. Going to bed early? Who was she kidding? She still had two more chapters to study in her textbook plus she had a paper due the following week. She yawned again. She knew going to bed early wasn't going to allow her to get more rest. Thoughts of John would plague her until she fell into a fitful sleep.

She sat at her desk and started doing her school work. When somebody knocked at her door, she stopped working. Who could be coming by at such a late hour? As she opened the door, she checked the clock, noting it was almost 10:00 p.m. John stood on her doorstep clutching a sheaf of papers, his dark eyes apprehensive. "Can I come in?"

She nodded. Her heart pounded as he entered her home. He handed her the papers. "Scotty left these at the school during his last tutoring session. I figured he'd need them since some of the material will be used in his class tomorrow." John had held Scotty's tutoring sessions at Scotty's school since his argument with her.

"Thanks." She placed the papers on the coffee table. "I'll be sure he takes them to school with him."

An awkward silence followed, and before Monica knew it, John placed his strong arms around her. He muttered an apology into her ear as she returned his hug. "I'm so sorry for getting angry with you."

When he released her, she was initially speechless. It took her a few moments to gather her thoughts. "I shouldn't have spoken so negatively about something you really wanted to do."

He took her hand as they sat on the couch. "Can we talk?"

She nodded, wondering what he was about to tell her now. "I guess you want to talk about this ministry."

He toyed with her hand, listening to her words. "I'd like to."

"But?"

"But so far I haven't taken any steps into going into the ministry."

She tried to decipher his words. "That's odd. You seemed so intent upon doing this. Why don't you get the ball rolling?"

"I'm still considering it, and I'd like to do it, but I'm still giving the matter some thought and prayer."

Butterflies floated in her belly as he continued to hold her hand. She tried to focus on his words. "Talk to Aiden about it."

"I'm one step ahead of you."

"Really? How so?"

"I'm supposed to meet up with Aiden later this week." He ran his hand over his head. "Look, we had a disagreement, and couples need to learn to work through disagreements in order to make the relationship work."

"So, you do consider us in a relationship?" The thought pleased her. She hadn't been sure where she stood with John until this moment.

He scooted closer, pulling her into his arms. She found comfort in his embrace as she listened to his deep voice. "I'd like to think we are in a relationship. I know it's been years since I've felt so strongly for someone. Do you realize how much I've missed seeing you over the last week?"

"I've missed you, too. But by the way you've been acting lately, I just assumed we were finished with each other."

He grunted and encouraged her to continue.

She balled her hands into fists as she recalled the last week. "Well, for starters, you've definitely been avoiding me. You're tutoring Scotty at school now. You obviously don't want to see me, since you haven't been coming to my house." She sighed, folding her arms in front of her chest. "You also refused to acknowledge me at church. It's like I don't exist."

He held her chin between his fingers, forcing her to look at him. "I'm sorry. That was childish and immature on my part. I should have let you know that you hurt my feelings by not agreeing with my ministry idea." He kissed her, and the butterflies in her stomach exploded. "But I know we can work through this. Let's give it some time. Maybe things will work out with your sister and Scotty, and you'll be able to come on the road with me if I should decide to join the ministry."

She turned away, not at all enthused with the idea of traveling around the world. Although she loved being with John, she didn't know if she could give up her job…what if she got the marketing director position after Pierce retired? She certainly couldn't abandon her home and her security to travel for a year. However, she kept those thoughts to herself as she thought about the situation logically.

He had still not mentioned marriage, so she knew the question of her traveling with him was out unless he decided they should marry. She also wondered if God was really calling him into this ministry. Hopefully Aiden would be able to shed some light on that subject. "Well, I'm not sure what'll happen with Gina. I've been praying for her a lot lately."

"Speaking of your sister, how is Gina doing?"

In spite of the turmoil with John during the last week, Monica did see a ray of hope in her life. "Well, I'd mentioned that she's started reading her Bible."

He nodded. "Yes, you did tell me about that."

She sat up straighter, enthusiastic about Gina's progress. "And my mom said she's gone to church a couple of times, even spoke with the reverend once."

"That's wonderful. Do you think she's ready to turn her life around?"

She shrugged, not wanting to get her hopes up. "I'm not sure. Gina can be very sneaky at times. There were times when it may have appeared she was getting better, but she would backslide and go back to her old ways. I wouldn't put it past her to be attending church and reading her Bible just because she knows it's something my parents want her to do, not because she wants to."

He scratched his head, obviously puzzled. "I'm missing something here. Why would she do it just to please your parents?"

"I just said she was sneaky. She may want to ask my parents for a large sum of money and figure if it appears she's cleaning up her life, then they'll give her what she wants."

"Well if she's done that before, wouldn't your parents be aware of what she might be up to?"

She shrugged. "Not really. When Gina gets on their good side, I think they're so desperate to have their daughter back in their lives that they make the mistake of giving her the benefit of the doubt. All we can do right now is pray and hope she's making a change for the better."

"Well maybe it will be different this time. Maybe she's ready to make a positive change in her life. Scotty told me he wished his mother could live with you two."

Her heart skipped a beat. "I know he missed his mother in the beginning, but I didn't realize he still wanted her to live with us."

"I don't think he wanted to mention it to you again because he doesn't want to hurt your feelings. He loves you, too, and I'm sure he senses his mother isn't very stable right now."

She shrugged, saying the first thing that came to her mind. "Well, maybe God will work with

His Holy Spirit and make my sister stable."

He pulled her into his arms, kissing her cheek. "Yes, maybe He will."

CHAPTER 26

THE NEXT MORNING Monica woke up early. The bright sun was streaming through her window, and in spite of the winter temperatures, she heard the faint chant of birds carrying on the wind. While enjoying a few pieces of buttered toast and a fragrant cup of coffee, she read her devotional for the day, soaking up the words of wisdom like an eager sponge. She found peace and comfort in the words and hoped she could recall the timely advice as she went about her day.

She closed the book as she finished the last sip of coffee. She still could not believe John had stopped by the previous day and actually apologized for his actions. She gripped the handle of her cup, still basking in the afterglow of his kiss, still wishing she could force things to work out between them.

She bowed her head, praying God would help her and John to work everything out in their relationship. As soon as she whispered her amen, the pounding of Scotty's feet echoed down the stairs. "Aunt Monica. You didn't wake me up."

She checked her watch, astonished that so much time had passed. "Hurry up and get dressed. The bus will be here in a few minutes, so you'll have to miss it. I'll drive you to school today."

Thirty minutes later, she rushed to get Scotty to school on time. She went through the drive-through lane of a fast-food place to grab Scotty some breakfast before he got to school. She walked him into the school building, making sure he was safely in his class before she drove to work.

During her workday, she found it hard to focus. Pierce officially announced his retirement so the marketing director position was officially posted. Pierce had already given her his endorsement to the Human Resources department and Monica had already applied for the position.

Her thoughts wavered between John, his ministerial endeavors, and the future of their relationship. When she'd had lunch with Pierce, he had to keep repeating himself when he spoke to her and at one point asked if she was okay. She hurriedly told him she was fine, so she tried to remain focused on working on an advertisement with one of the new marketing interns.

When she arrived home that evening, she kicked her shoes off while Scotty ran into the kitchen. He wasn't paying attention and bumped into the table. "Ouch." Thank goodness he didn't curse. Sometimes, she forgot he was blind, especially when he moved around the house with such surety.

"Be careful."

He rubbed his arm. "What's for dinner?"

"Oh," she groaned. "I forgot to take something out of the freezer this morning."

Scotty scampered back into the living room and she joined him on the couch. He mentioned a popular restaurant that catered to children.

She groaned, not looking forward to a meal at a place that served chicken fingers and seafood to a child clientele. Before she could comment on his suggestion for a meal, her phone rang. Scotty lunged toward the sound of the phone, not giving her a chance to answer. "Hello," he piped into the receiver. "Mom! Hi!"

She listened, wondering what Gina was telling her son. He just gave a lot of yeses and nos and a few uh-huhs. Finally, he raised the phone from his ear. "Aunt Monica, my mom wants to talk to you."

She took the phone away from Scotty, plopping back on the couch. Her brain felt drained and full of fatigue, and she hoped Gina hadn't called this evening to start an argument. "Hi, Gina," she grumbled.

"Man, don't sound so enthusiastic to hear from me," Gina's voice dripped with sarcasm. Monica's shoulders tensed, wondering if she should put off this conversation for another day.

"Gina, what did you want? I'm tired, and it's

been a rough week."

"Hmm," Gina replied. Monica could imagine Gina twirling her hair through her fingers as she tried to figure out what was wrong. "Are you and that guy you brought over for Thanksgiving having problems? You always did have a hard time holding on to a man."

Monica gritted her teeth, ignoring Gina's question. "What do you want?"

Gina sighed, lowering her voice. "Look, I know we haven't always gotten along, but I love my son, and I want to live with him."

Monica's heart skipped a beat as she clutched her stomach, wondering if Scotty would be ripped away from her as soon as she'd grown to love him so much. She glanced into the kitchen and saw Scotty sitting at the table eating a banana. "You can't take Scotty away from me," she whispered, not wanting him to overhear. "I'll call you right back."

She hung up the phone, rushed up the stairs, entered her room, and closed the door behind her. Sitting on her bed, she quickly dialed her parents' phone number. When Gina answered, she closed her eyes, hoping she could find the right words to make her sister change her mind. "Look, you can't take Scotty away. He loves it here. Plus, he's doing well in school. The counselor at his school said you let him miss a lot of days, and he fell behind. Since John is tutoring him, he's been doing so well and he seems to enjoy his classes."

"Look, he's blind anyway. His life is already going to be hard enough. What good is this education going to do him?"

She groaned, still wondering when her sister would grow up and not be so naive. "Your son really needs a good education to fall back on. He'll need to find a job and support himself when he gets older." She raised her voice, and her heart pounded faster. Tears trickled down her cheeks, so she wiped them away. "If you come here and take this child away, so help me God, I'll take you to court and prove what an unfit mother you are!" Her hands shook as she clutched the phone. A bead of sweat trickled down her brow, and she wondered if she was going to faint.

"Monica—"

"Do you know how much I worry about him, about what'll happen to him when he grows up?" She suddenly stood, leaning against the cool glass window, staring at the frigid beach in the distance. "Gina, don't cross me now because I have God in my corner, and I want what's best for my nephew." She sniffed and walked to her dresser, grabbed a few tissues to blow her nose, and wiped her eyes. She was so upset that she barely noticed Gina was sobbing also.

"Look, Monica. I know I haven't told you this, but I appreciate all you've done for my son. I didn't call you to start an argument."

Monica clutched her soiled tissues in her hand as disbelief settled into her bones. She held the phone tightly, still suspicious of her sneaky sister. "What do you mean?" she asked in a small voice.

"Look, I've had a hard time dealing with Scotty since he came into this world. He was an unplanned pregnancy, plus he was born blind. It's hard for me to deal with his handicap, but I am learning to accept it."

"Your son is just like other kids except he can't see. You just need to treat him the way you would any sighted child."

"I realize that, but it's taken me several months to figure out that you're a better mother than I am. But I should still be a mother to Scotty since he is my child."

Monica still wondered where this conversation was going. "So, what did you want to do? You just said you wanted Scotty to come and live with you. That must mean you want to take him away from me." Thoughts of having Scotty ripped away from her made her heart pound even faster. She lay upon the bed, still holding the phone. "I've worked hard to get Scotty to stop cussing and to start paying attention to his schoolwork. My friend John has also been using his own free time to help him. He doesn't even get paid for doing this."

She heard Gina sniffing, and Monica struggled to calm herself down. Gina spoke. "Look, I wanted to make a proposition to you."

"A proposition?"

"Can I come and live in your house so I can

help raise my son? I promise I'm trying to turn my life around, and I've even started going to church."

Monica stared at the ceiling, still hopeful that Gina would improve her lifestyle. "Are you sincere about this? You want to be here to help Scotty?"

"Yes, I'm finally making some positive changes in my life, and I want to be there for my son. What's wrong with that?"

Monica shook her head, still shocked. Was this an answer to her prayers? "What about working? Are you willing to get a job?" She certainly couldn't afford to support another person on her income. She was already supporting Scotty.

Gina told of her plans to find employment in the Ocean City area. Monica gave her a lengthy list of rules to follow while residing in her home. "You can't smoke in my house. Also, no illegal drugs, and if I find out you're mixing with the wrong kind of people and exposing Scotty to that mess, I'm calling the police," she warned.

Gina took a deep breath. "I know you're right to be leery of me, and I don't blame you. I just want you to give me the opportunity to prove myself while I spend some quality time with my son again."

So many things were twirling through her mind that she didn't know what to do. She rubbed her forehead, sensing an impending headache. "When did you want to move in?"

"How about in two weeks? You have a lot of empty space in the basement. Mom and Dad said I could have the bed and furniture from their guest bedroom. We'll just rent a van and move it in a couple weeks."

She finally said good-bye to her sister, still hesitant about another huge change that was happening in her life. When she finally exited her bedroom, she was stunned to see John standing at the bottom of the stairs. "John?"

He met her halfway up the stairs, taking her hands into his. "I heard you yelling all the way down here."

"Oh!" She covered her mouth. "Did Scotty hear me?" she whispered.

He shook his head. "When I knocked on the door, he let me in then went out back to play with his ball."

"He knows he's not supposed to answer the door unless I tell him it's okay." She looked away from his concerned warm brown eyes. "Did you really hear everything I said while I was upstairs?" She was ashamed of her outburst and wished she'd handled her anger in a more Christian way.

He beckoned her down the stairs and pulled her into his arms. "I didn't hear everything, but I did hear enough to know you were yelling at your sister."

She still felt dazed about her conversation as he led her to the couch. Her tears had left wet trails, and he ran his fingers over them. Her stomach quivered with delight as he kissed each of her tearstained cheeks. "What happened?"

"Actually, it's a good thing."

"Oh?" He gave her a dubious look, obviously not believing her. "You don't look like it's a positive thing."

"There's so much happening right now." She thought about her sister's heartfelt plea. "Gina wants to move in with me to help raise Scotty and to straighten out her life."

"Oh? Well that's better than taking him away from you. Are you sure the two of you will be able to live together?"

She shrugged. "I'm willing to try, for Scotty's sake."

"Are you sure she'll uphold your Christian values while in your home? She won't be smoking, drinking, and acting up as you say she does?"

She shrugged again. "I told her if she does those things, I'll call the police." Dejected, she wondered how long the conversation would bother her.

"What's the matter?"

"I wish I hadn't yelled at her. I was so furious that I thought I was going to pass out. It's been several years since I've been that angry."

He touched her cheek. "I think Jesus understands your frustration. You've been trying to help your sister for years, and now you're trying to help her son. It initially looked like she was stabbing you in the back for taking care of him."

She shook her head, refusing to be comforted by his words. "I still should have acted like a Christian. Don't you see why I'm so upset with myself? I sense Gina may be trying to find her way to God. What kind of example was I, yelling at her when she wasn't out to take Scotty away from me after all?"

"Don't beat yourself up over this. You can apologize to Gina later, and if she forgives you, everything will be all right. When will she be moving in?"

She gave him the details about Gina's arrival.

"I have an idea. How about we rent a van and go down there and help her move?"

"You would do that for me?"

"I'd do anything for you, Monica."

She wondered if that was true. She wanted to tell him to give up his idea of ministering to agnostics and nonbelievers all over the world but held her tongue. She certainly couldn't convince him not to do the Lord's work if that's what he felt he needed to do.

CHAPTER 27

JOHN ENTERED HIS friend Pete's nursery. Pete came from the back and shook his hand. "Hey John. Good to see you again."

"Likewise."

He glanced at the early spring plants that Pete had recently had delivered to his shop. He'd been selling a lot of floral arrangements and had told John that business had been doing well. Well, he'd focus on the different plants later. Right now, he just wanted to talk to his friend. He had so much on his mind that he needed a second opinion.

He followed Pete back to the kitchen. He plopped into a chair. Pete had a box of Chocolate Dreams candy on the table. Well, candy might cheer him up. He helped himself to a piece of candy while Pete made them cups of tea. After his friend had gotten comfortable in his chair, John sniffed. "I smell mint."

Pete nodded. "Got some mint plants delivered recently. You should take some home with you.

That fresh mint tastes mighty nice when you chop it up in fresh fruit salad."

John nodded. "Make sure to remind me to purchase one before I go home."

Pete nodded. "Sure thing." Pete sipped his tea. "You know, I was kind of shocked that you called and said you needed somebody to talk to."

"Yeah, I've had a lot of stuff on my mind lately, but I've only discussed it with two people."

"Well, whatever has been on your mind, I hope one of the people you discussed it with was God."

John nodded, as he sipped his tea. "Jesus was the first one I spoke with. I've been praying about this for a while."

"I'll bet the other person you spoke with is Monica Crawford."

He opened his mouth, amazed Pete was so perceptive. "How'd you guess?"

Chuckling, Pete leaned back in his leather desk chair. "You've mentioned her to me. I know it bothered her that you weren't saved initially, and I'm glad you made the right decision to find Jesus."

He nodded, glad he'd made the right decision also. "I guess I've been feeling kind of guilty."

Pete's smile faded. "Guilty? Why? Guilt is not a feeling that's associated with salvation. Once you accept Christ, you're starting off with a new clean slate, and you're forgiven for all sins. Just try to live your life according to His commands the best that you can, and that's all He asks of you."

John hesitated. "I guess you could say I feel I should be doing more in the ministry. I feel like I should have researched this and accepted Christ earlier in my life. I want to make up for lost time and try to get as many people as possible to come to Jesus."

Pete raised his thick eyebrows. "How do you propose doing that?"

He took a deep breath, explaining the ministry he wanted to join. "I figure if I take a year's hiatus from my job and join this ministry, I could make up for at least some of those years when I was an agnostic."

Pete shook his head. Steepling his hands below his chin, he gave John a shrewd look. "That's not a good reason to go into the ministry. You need to go because you feel called to do it."

"I guess as a new Christian, I'm having a hard time figuring out if I'm called or not."

"Feeling called is when you experience a certain peace and contentment in what you feel the Lord is guiding you to do."

"How would I know if the Lord is guiding me?"

"You'll just *know* by the feeling of peace that settles in your gut and a gentle calm that settles upon you when you've made a decision guided by the Lord. What is your heart telling you to do?" John looked around the office. Surprisingly, Pete's words mirrored what Monica had tried to tell him. "If you feel uncomfortable answering the question. . ."

He shook his head. "My heart is telling me to stay here and be with Monica." He gathered his thoughts. "But my mind is telling me to pursue this ministry. I'm a scientist and a professor, and whenever I've failed in something, I feel I should give more effort to find the right solution."

Pete stood. "John, Christianity doesn't work that way. Just look at the scriptures and use that scientific mind to research what God is telling you to do." He took a deep breath before continuing. "You'd mentioned a men's retreat at your church awhile back. Are you going?"

"Yes."

"Good."

"Why? Are you going?" Pete didn't even attend his church.

"Well, they advertised Mustard Seed's retreat at my church and my pastor told me that, Brian Smith, a former agnostic, will be one of our speakers."

"You're kidding! He's in charge of the ministry I want to join." John shook his head. "There must be some mistake. He wasn't on the list of speakers that I saw printed last week."

Pete grinned. "My pastor told us that it was a last-minute change…today. One of the speakers cancelled, and Mustard Seed found Brian at the last minute. But I think this change was God working behind the scenes as usual. I want you to talk to Brian and see what he thinks about your reasoning." So strange, hearing this from Pete of all people.

His phone buzzed. He removed it and spotted Aiden's number. "Hey Aiden."

"John, Brian Smith is the new keynote speaker at our men's retreat." The excitement in Aiden's voice resonated in John's ear.

"Yes, my friend Pete was just telling me about that."

"Who's Pete?"

"A friend of mine. He said that Mustard Seed advertised our men's retreat at his church."

"You need to talk to him."

"I will, Aiden." He had no choice. Brian may be able to help him with his struggle.

"Also, I wanted to tell you that Beverly is pregnant."

"Congratulations." He smiled, pleased for both of them. After Brian's death, Beverly had hinted that she didn't want more children, but looked like she'd changed her mind. After he said good-bye to Aiden, John stood and shook hands with the Pete. "All right, I'll be sure to snatch Brian Smith for a few minutes at the retreat."

During the next couple of weeks, John struggled with his decision to join the ministry, but he looked forward to talking to Brian Smith at the men's retreat. He wanted to join this ministry to make up for lost time. However, he didn't want to sacrifice a possible future with Monica to fulfill his ministerial needs. He knew if he did take a year off to go away, he would be thinking about her constantly, wondering if another man would make a move on her, romancing her until she fell in love again.

He continued to stroll around campus and pray about the situation, still not sure of what he was going to do. He wanted God to show him a sign, telling him if he should stay in Ocean City with Monica or travel for a year preaching to others.

Finally, on the day they were scheduled to help Gina move, John awakened, the chant of birds beckoning the new day. He looked forward to seeing Monica that day and visiting her parents. He had to wonder what she had told them about their brief breakup and recommitment. He wondered if she'd told them about his desire to go into the ministry.

An hour later, he picked up the moving van from the lot and signed the paperwork. The van was due back the following day. He then drove to Monica's house, eager to get a start on this day.

As he rapped on her door, he recalled the time they'd spent together the last couple of weeks. Amid his choir practice and socializing with his Christian brothers, he'd made sure he found time to spend with her on weekends. They'd spent one Saturday night at the movies, taking Scotty with them. Although the boy could not see the screen, he still enjoyed the songs and the voices in the newest Walt Disney flick.

He'd also continued to tutor Scotty twice a

week. He knew Monica still had doubts about Gina's moving in with her, and he wanted her to know he was there to support her in her decision.

He heard footsteps pounding on the floor. Scotty opened the door. "Mr. John, is that you?"

"Yes, Scotty, it's me."

"Aunt Monica is in the kitchen."

He ran his fingers over the boy's head as he followed him into the kitchen. She looked adorable in her baggy jeans and oversized sweatshirt. He kissed her cheek as she flipped pancakes on the griddle. "Breakfast will be ready in a minute. Scotty is anxious to see his mother."

After they'd said grace and enjoyed their pancakes, they were on their way to her parents' house. The ride was quiet and uneventful. They turned the radio on to a Christian talk station while Scotty listened to his earphones during the drive.

When they were almost at her parents' house, John thought about the van's seating capacity. "Hey, do you think all of us can fit into the front seat of this van on the way back?"

Her warm brown eyes glowed. "Oh, that's right, I haven't told you yet."

"Told me what?" He took an exit off the main highway.

"About what my parents did. They purchased a used car for Gina."

"Really?" He wondered if Gina really deserved a car but decided to keep his thoughts to himself.

"She's going to follow us back in her car. Scotty will ride with her." He was pleased to hear this. He wanted some time alone with Monica on the drive back. "I wish they'd waited. . . . At least until she found a job."

He patted her arm. "Don't worry. Everything is in God's hands."

"I know everything is in God's hands, but I can't help but worry about my sister. I wonder how her presence will affect Scotty."

He tried to be optimistic about the situation. "You say she's been going to church and reading her Bible. That's a good start."

She nodded. "Yes, it is." Then she smiled. "I'm glad you decided to come with me."

He returned her smile. "I'm glad I came, too. I had to miss some church activities today to do this, but I don't mind. I know how hard this is for you, letting your sister move in with you so suddenly, but I just want you to know that I'll be there for you if you need me."

Minutes later, they pulled into her parents' town house complex. After John opened their doors, Scotty scooted out of the cab of the truck. "Be careful, Scotty," she warned.

"I want to see my mom." She led him to the front door.

Gina answered, her long locks covered with a multicolored scarf. As soon as she saw Scotty, she pulled him into her arms. "Hi, baby."

She kissed his cheek before she released him,

leading him into the house. John and Monica followed close behind. John watched Gina as she placed some items into a box. He wondered if she really had made a positive change in her life.

Monica's mother hugged him, beckoning everybody into the living room. "Gina doesn't have a whole lot of stuff to move, besides the furniture. I figured we could sit around and visit for a few hours."

John joined the older couple in the living room while Scotty talked with his mother in the corner, telling her about his school and about the advances he'd made during his tutoring sessions. After their conversation ended, Gina approached Monica and asked if she could speak with her privately. Monica trudged up the stairs, following Gina.

As Mr. Crawford tried to engage him in a discussion about the latest basketball games on TV, John could barely listen. He wondered what in the world Gina was saying to Monica upstairs in the bedroom.

CHAPTER 28

MONICA FOLLOWED HER sister upstairs, wondering if Gina was going to be the bearer of bad news. She tried to calm her racing heart as they entered Gina's bedroom. Boxes were stacked in the corner, and the bed had been stripped. The hardwood floor gleamed under the bright sunlight streaming from the window.

Monica closed her eyes, asking the Lord to guide her and accept whatever her sister had called her into this room to say.

"You're praying, aren't you?" asked Gina.

Monica nodded. "Yes, I am. You know that prayer has always been an important part of my life. I've been praying for you for years."

Gina plopped on the bed, and Monica sat beside her.

Monica gazed at her sister before she spoke. "Look, I wanted to apologize."

Gina's head jerked back so hard, her multicolored scarf fell off. Her dark eyes widened as she picked up the scarf. "You want to apologize to me? That's a switch. Why?"

"For yelling at you when you called me a couple of weeks ago," Monica explained. "I love Scotty so much, and I wanted to protect him from your old lifestyle. Do you realize how much your son means to me?"

"I think I have an idea how much he means to you. I know he loves you, and I'm glad you were able to help me out."

Monica took a deep breath and continued. "When I yelled at you, I didn't act like a Christian. I took my anger out on you before you had a chance to speak. If I'd been patient and listened to you from the beginning, I would have known that you weren't proposing to take Scotty away from me." She squeezed her hands together, still gathering her thoughts. "I know you've been reading your Bible and going to church, and I just didn't want my actions to color your perceptions about the way a Christian should act." She thoughtfully considered her next words. "I also wanted to apologize about the way I've been acting since you've left Scotty in my care."

Gina furrowed her brow. "What do you mean?"

"I kind of feel like I've been wrongly judging you. I've been upset with you for not acting in a Christian manner when maybe you just didn't have it in you to give your son the attention he needed." Monica shrugged. "It's kind of hard for me to explain, but when you dropped Scotty off, I agreed to keep him, and maybe that's what the Lord felt was best for Scotty at the time. It was wrong for me to hold all of this animosity toward you when you went with Randy to the circus." Monica realized it was wrong of her to expect Gina to live as a Christian when she'd never openly professed to accepting Christ as her Savior.

Gina poked out her full lips, gazing at her sister. "Look, I don't blame you for getting mad, but I do want to ask you to do something."

"What?"

"Be patient with me. I know you've pretty much broken Scotty of the habit of cussing over the last few months and he's doing better in school, but I've still got a long way to go."

"What do you mean?"

"I want you to be patient with me if a cuss word slips from my mouth once in a while. I'm not cussing nearly as much as I used to; I've gotten a lot better."

"Well, try to be more careful when you're around Scotty. It's taken some hard work to get him into more positive habits, and I'd hate to see all that work gone to waste."

Gina nodded as she tightened the scarf around her head. "I promise. Also, I am seriously looking to God for answers to a lot of things, and I've been going to church lately. I know I've been sneaky and untruthful sometimes—"

"Sometimes?"

She shook her head. "Okay, most of the time, but I want you to know that these changes I'm making in my life this time are for real. I really want to become a better person for myself and for Scotty."

Monica hoped Gina's words were truthful. If Gina made these changes in her life and believed in the Lord, her burdens would be lighter due to her faith in Him.

Unexpectedly, Gina pulled her sister into her arms. Monica was shocked by the sudden embrace, but returned the hug, trying to recall the last time she'd been hugged by her sibling.

After Monica ended their embrace, she asked Gina what had happened to Randy. Gina blew air through her full lips. "Girl, he never even married me like he promised. I hooked up with a few other people in the circus, and you saw the black eye I had on Thanksgiving." Monica nodded, and Gina continued to explain. "My latest boyfriend was abusive, and he gave me that black eye."

She laid her hand on her sister's shoulder. "You need to trust God to help you in your personal relationships, Gina."

Gina nodded, silently agreeing with her sister.

Minutes later, they returned to the living room. John stood, his dark eyes full of concern. She walked toward him, and he squeezed her hand. "Is everything okay?" he whispered.

She nodded. "Don't worry," she whispered back.

Mrs. Crawford stood, calling everybody into the kitchen. "I made pot roast and potatoes for lunch, and we've got some sodas to drink. Ya'll come in here and eat before you start loading up the van."

They sat at the laden table and joined hands. Mr. Crawford said a prayer of thanksgiving and asked God to watch over his family as they made the trek back down to Ocean City.

As Monica got into the seat beside John, he revved the truck's engine, clearly anxious to get on the road back to Ocean City.

As they passed the Inner Harbor in Baltimore, he gestured toward the dashboard. "Open the glove compartment."

She opened it and removed a folder. "What's this?"

"Read it and see."

She looked at an outline of the ministry program he wanted to join. "So, you've decided to go?"

"I'm still praying about it. I've spoken with my pal Pete." He then told her about the men's retreat he was going to attend and about their new guest speaker.

"So, you're hoping to make a final decision after the men's retreat?"

"Yes, hopefully I will. I'm also hesitant about going into this ministry because of you."

"Me?"

"Yes, I love you so much that I don't know if I

could leave you for a year. I wish you'd wait for me."

"John, I don't know."

"Do you love me?"

She held her breath, remaining silent.

"You're not answering me. I guess that means no."

"There's just so much at stake here."

"What's wrong with telling me how you feel about me?" he argued.

"It's hard for me to tell my true feelings to somebody. Especially a man."

"But I would never hurt you. If you loved me, you wouldn't mind waiting for me."

"How can I be assured you wouldn't be dating anybody else while you're gone?"

"I'm hurt. Of course, I wouldn't date anybody while I'm gone."

She shrugged, still uncomfortable about waiting for him for a year. She also hoped that John was spiritually strong enough to make the decision to join this ministry. Was it really the right avenue for him to pursue?

The following week John took Monica out to celebrate Valentine's Day. She'd gotten Karen to babysit Scotty so they could go to a fancy restaurant. The dinner was romantic and tasty, and it was nice to spend the evening with her. They didn't speak about his ministerial plans.

On the Saturday after Valentine's Day, John found himself looking for Brian Smith at the men's retreat. The posh hotel had reserved their conference rooms and lodging accommodations at half price since it was off-season. When he finally found Brian in the lobby, he stopped and introduced himself, asking if he could spare a minute to talk to him.

Several minutes later, bundled in thick down-filled coats and holding cups of hot coffee, they stood on the frigid beach, watching the waves crash upon the sand. Both men were comfortably silent as they sat on a bench and watched a few winter surfers sporting wet suits ride the cold waves. "It sure is nice out here," said John as he sipped his coffee.

Brian cradled his coffee cup, gesturing toward the ocean. "Yes, it's magnificent." The elderly man focused on John. "But I'm sure you didn't ask me to come out here to stare at the ocean."

"Well, you know that ministry you started awhile back? After I got saved, I found out about it, and I was thinking about joining it. But I've been undecided over the last few weeks." Not wanting to take up too much of Brian's time, John briefly told him more about his problem, and Brian gave his advice.

"Well, John, when I started this ministry, I wasn't looking for new Christians to join it."

"Why not?"

"Because I know new Christians can be eager and zealous, but, also, they might not be spiritually ready to enter a ministry. When we find out a new Christian wants to join, we have to probe and find out if he feels called to do it." Brian sipped his coffee. "John, as a former agnostic, I can tell you one of the hardest things I did was going to God for help. I wanted to do what *I* wanted to do, not what God wanted me to do."

"But I can't help it. Sometimes it just seems like this ministry is the right thing to do."

"But you can't think about what *you* think is the right thing to do. You need to seek God for the answers to your questions. That's what you need to do."

"But I don't want—"

"Don't think about what you want or don't want. You need to seek God for the answer. I'm sure once you opened your heart and sought out God, He revealed Himself to you, right?"

John nodded, still listening. Brian continued, "Well, you need to seek His will about this ministry. We need to seek out God and not lean on our own understanding. Being a scientist, one of the hardest lessons I've learned is that our minds are limited, but God's mind is limitless." He paused before continuing.

"You say you don't want to leave Monica?"

He quickly nodded. "I love her. I've never loved

a woman as much as I love her. It'll make me sick to leave her."

"If your heart is telling you not to leave her, maybe you shouldn't. It sounds like she's going through a lot lately, raising her nephew and dealing with her younger sister. She's got a lot on her plate. Perhaps the Lord is guiding you, through your heart, to stay with her and support her."

Brian invited John to stand, and they walked toward the chilly ocean. As they paced along the shore, John continued to speak. "Since I was an agnostic, I know how other agnostics think. I feel that I could bring more to this ministry than an ordinary non-agnostic person could."

Brian raised his hands. "And?"

"And that's why I feel I should do this. Think about all the good I could do."

Brian placed his hand on his shoulder. "Son, I'll be praying for you. But you've got to remember what the Bible says about Christianity and salvation. Pray about what God is trying to tell you through His Word." He rubbed John's shoulder. "Also, perhaps the Lord placed this ministry on your mind for another reason."

"Such as?"

"Perhaps it's something He wants you to do another time? Maybe when things are more settled between you and Monica, you can reconsider doing this ministry, if you feel you should do it in your heart, and bring her along with you." Brian sighed. "I know what you're going through, and I think that's one of the reasons why the Lord called on me to be here today. I'm glad you talked to me because I went through a similar situation when I was first saved."

John was intrigued. "What happened?"

Brian chuckled. "I know this is a serious subject, but I can't help laughing about how foolish I was back then. I was in college when I got saved, and after I graduated, I went on a mission trip to Sydney, Australia." He shook his head. "I didn't pray about it or ask for any guidance. I was young and hotheaded, and I knew I just wanted to go down under and save as many souls as possible. After I had been there about a month, I realized I'd been able to get only one person to accept Christ. I was mad because I envisioned myself helping others, bringing lots of people to the gospel, getting people saved! I told the pastor I was a failure since I'd helped only one person find Jesus."

"Did the pastor set you straight?"

"He sure did! A month later, it was time to come back to the States, but the pastor told me I should prayerfully seek out what I felt God wanted me to do and to not lean on my own understanding. My thoughts of saving tons of people were skewed. The pastor said if I just helped one person find Christ, that's a blessing. He said I shouldn't be concerned with the number of souls I save, but to just tell people about the gospel. It's up to them if they want to accept Christ."

They strolled along the shore for several minutes as John thought about Brian Smith's words. "Thanks, I'll think about all this."

"Do better than think about it. I want you to pray about it."

Brian touched John's shoulder before draining his coffee cup. "I have to go now, since I'm leading the small group study in the conference room."

John barely waved to Brian as he took his exit. His mind was now consumed with so many conflicting thoughts.

CHAPTER 29

TWO DAYS LATER, John knocked on Monica's door. She answered it, looking professional in her dark business suit. "John, I didn't realize you were coming over tonight." She hugged him. "I have great news. I got the job, the marketing director position! I start the new position in two weeks!"

"That's wonderful, Monica." He kissed her cheek. "I'm taking you out sometime…well sometime soon to celebrate this weekend."

"Thanks, John. I'm so happy that I don't think I'll be able to sleep tonight. Plus, I just finished my last grad school class. I officially have my MBA!"

"Monica, I'm so proud of you." They shared a long deep kiss. "I have to catch my breath from that amazing kiss."

She paused. "I just got home from work and was just about to make dinner for Scotty, Gina, and me." Her mouth was now set in a firm line.

"What's the matter?"

She glanced up the stairs, as if hesitant to

discuss what troubled her lest Gina and Scotty would overhear them, and beckoned him into the kitchen. A package of ground beef thawed on the stove, and a raw onion sat beside the meat. She rubbed her forehead, and he wondered if she was getting a headache. He touched her shoulder. "Are you okay?"

She nodded and composed herself. "Gina is trying to make a change in her life, but it's kind of slow getting that change to take place."

"Really? What happened?"

"Well, when I was in the back of the house yesterday, I saw some cigarette butts in the yard, so I know she's been sneaking outside to smoke."

He took her hand. "Give it some time. I've never smoked before, but I do know several people who do, and I know what a struggle it is for them to quit. It's an addiction. Perhaps she can see a doctor. I do know there are things out there for people to use if they want to quit smoking."

She nodded. "Okay."

"Is that all that's bothering you?"

"No, I smelled alcohol on her breath last night. She knows she can't drink while she's in my home."

"Honey, I know she's still struggling with these things. Has it been really bad? Is she at least attempting to make the changes in her life?"

She nodded. "She doesn't cuss, and she does seem to take comfort in the scriptures."

"Has she been looking for a job?"

"Yes, she's online everyday job searching. I helped her get a résumé together, too."

"Well, that's good. Maybe she'll be ready to accept Christ soon."

Monica squeezed his hand. "Yeah, maybe." She looked into his eyes. "I sense you didn't come over here tonight to talk about Gina. You look like something is on your mind. Is everything going okay with all of your church duties? How are things going in the men's choir?"

He squeezed her hand, softening his voice. "The men's choir and Bible studies are going well. I wanted to talk about us."

"Have you decided to join that ministry?"

"Baby, I haven't decided that yet." He told her about his conversation with Brian Smith. "He said some things that made me think."

"And?"

"And I'm still not sure about my decision to go, but I need some space for a couple of weeks to think and pray about it. I'll probably see you in church and stuff, but I wanted to know if you would give me two weeks of privacy while I pray and make my decision."

"Okay, I'll give you your two weeks of privacy as long as you tell me the truth about your decision as soon as this hiatus is over."

He squeezed her shoulder. "I promise." He kissed her before he left.

Monica placed her head in her hands, praying, hoping He would place the right decision on John's heart. As she whispered an amen, her phone rang. She was glad to hear Karen on the line. After they spoke for a few moments, Karen said, "Monica, I can tell something is on your mind. What's wrong? Does it have anything to do with John?"

"Yes. He needs to give our relationship a two-week break." "Why?"

Monica explained the situation to her, and Karen stated her opinion. "I can understand why he would need this time alone with God. He just wants to make sure he makes the right decision, and he still feels as if he should straighten out his life."

"His life is straightened out. He just wants to make sure that if he decides to go into this ministry it's what God wants him to do."

Karen sighed. "Monica, he must still feel like his life is in shambles since he wants to make up for lost time by saving souls for God. That's not the way salvation works."

"I hope he decides to stay. He doesn't seem to feel the calling of this ministry in his heart, and until he does, I think he should stay in Ocean City until he finds his true calling."

"Monica," Karen said gently, "maybe this is his

true calling. If he does decide to go, you can't get angry. You'll need to be behind him 100 percent. Don't be so selfish, thinking about the happiness you'll give up when he leaves. If he's doing this for the glory of God, there's nothing you can do about it. This is between him and the Lord."

Karen's spiritual perception stayed on Monica's mind the entire evening. Even after she had cooked their spaghetti dinner and made sure Scotty had done his homework, she still thought about Karen's words. As she prepared herself for bed that night, she asked God to give her the strength to accept John's decision gracefully.

During the next two weeks, John was grateful for time alone with God. He attended his Sunday church services but spent most of his spare time in ear- nest prayer and studying God's Word. He had highlighted the scriptures Pastor Martin and Brian Smith had given him. He read those key verses numerous times and decided his heart was telling him not to join this ministry right now. As he thought about his ministerial endeavors, he recalled the college students he taught at the university every day. He recalled the Christian organizations on campus and how the students would sometimes invite professors to attend these events. He could tell the students about his quest for God and about how he'd finally found Him. The university was the best mission field for him right now. He knew he should stay here to make a difference in the lives of these students.

Once he finally made his decision, he fell on his knees, thanking God for giving him the wisdom he craved. *Lord, I know I don't feel the desire to go into this ministry in my heart. I know You're telling me to stay right here in Ocean City, and within this church, and reach out to the community and the college campus right here. I know I want to stay here, near Monica, so that, if she'll have me, we can be together in a way that is acceptable in Your eyes. In Jesus' name, amen.*

Monica tried to hum as she worked, but found her heart just wasn't in it. Gina had taken Scotty to lunch and a Saturday afternoon movie. Instead of taking this time alone to sit and lament about John, she'd decided to use her energy cleaning her messy house. She turned her vacuum cleaner off and admired her freshly cleaned living room. She'd missed John for the last two weeks but knew she needed to give him his space so he could talk to God and make his decision.

She got a glass of ice water and sat on the couch. Her relationship with Gina was improving, and she had to admit her sister did have some common sense. Gina chastised her about not being truthful with John about her feelings. "If you love the guy, let him know," she'd advised.

So, Monica promised herself that when she saw John again, she would let him know she loved him. Even if he did decide to leave for a year, she would take Karen's advice and learn to accept it, and she would indeed wait for him.

A hard knock sounded at her door, disturbing her thoughts. She wondered if it was one of the neighborhood kids selling something for school. She opened it and faced John. He looked handsome in his sweatshirt and jeans. Trying desperately to calm her racing heart, she opened the door. "John. . .hi."

She led him into her home. Before she had a chance to speak, he took her into his arms. She relished the scent of his aftershave as he kissed her. He remained silent, but love and adoration sparkled in his eyes. She swallowed, trying to moisten her suddenly dry throat. "John, before you say a word, I just want to be honest with you about something." He opened his mouth to speak, but she placed two fingers over his beautiful lips. "I love you. I've been in love with you for a while, but I was too scared and insecure to let you know. It was wrong of me not to be honest about my feelings for you, and I'm sorry I didn't tell you sooner."

"Monica Crawford, that's the sweetest thing you could ever say to me." He enfolded her in his arms again before releasing her. "And I want to let you know that I'm not ready to go into the ministry now. I was pursuing it for the wrong reasons, and I want to stay here, with you, right here in Ocean City." He kissed her and took her hand. "Do you think you can find a babysitter for Scotty tonight?"

"I'm pretty sure I can recruit somebody."

He smiled. "Good, because I want to take you out to dinner. Be sure you're wearing a nice dress. I'll be by to pick you up at six o'clock."

Monica continued to smile after John left, eagerly looking forward to their dinner that evening.

That night after Monica had changed into her favorite red dress and Scotty was happily eating popcorn and spending time with Gina, John picked her up. Though he appeared nervous, he was handsome in a very appealing dark gray suit with a royal blue necktie. As they drove to their destination, soft jazz music played from his stereo. He seemed very preoccupied. Every time Monica said something to him, she had to repeat herself.

A short time later, they arrived at Fager's Island Restaurant. The lighting in the fancy dining room was dim, and candles winked at the white-cloth-covered tables. A waiter approached and introduced himself. "Hi, my name is Alex, and I'll be your waiter this evening." He glanced at John for a few seconds before continuing. "Your table is right over here."

Monica gasped when she noted the large

floral display of bright red roses gracing their table. There was also a crystal bowl filled with cocktail sauce and large shrimp tapered at the sides. Shrimp cocktail was one of her favorite appetizers, and she was ecstatic that John had planned this wonderful night out to celebrate his decision to stay in Ocean City. Perhaps since he'd decided to stay, their relationship could deepen and turn into something permanent. "Do you like the flowers?" John asked softly.

Her heart pounded as she pulled him into a hug. "Yes, I love them. Thank you."

They walked to the table, and he pulled her chair out for her. She was so excited that she didn't think she could even eat the shrimp. John took her hand. "Before we start eating our appetizer—"

Alex approached carrying a bottle of sparkling cider and two wine glasses. "I'm so sorry. We forgot to leave this on the table as you requested."

John waved the man away as if anxious for him to leave. After their waiter had taken his exit, John pulled a velvet box out of his pocket and pressed it into her hand. Monica opened the box and gasped, staring at the most exquisite diamond solitaire ring she'd ever seen.

"Monica, will you marry me?"

Tears slid down her cheeks as she clutched the box and stared into John's warm brown eyes. "Yes, John, I will marry you." He then leaned toward her and his mouth joined with hers.

As they kissed, she silently thanked the Lord for placing John French into her life.

EPILOGUE

Six months later

MONICA SMILED AS she walked down the sandy shore of the predawn beach, her cream-colored wedding dress flowing like liquid satin.

As the waves tumbled onto the shore, a gentle warm breeze caressed her skin. Her father squeezed her elbow as he marched beside her, murmuring words of encouragement on this important day.

The enchanting event was so unreal, and her happiness piled up in her so high she thought she would burst. As birds swooped from the sky, a woodwind quartet played "The Wedding March," creating a sense of euphoria in the small crowd of wedding guests. Monica's smile brightened further as she approached her wedding party.

Anna, Karen, and Gina made striking bridesmaids in their royal blue dresses. The silky material of their gowns billowed in the wind as they awaited Monica several feet ahead on the stretch of Ocean City beach.

Monica happily thought about the arrangements she'd made for Gina and Scotty. Since Monica was going to be living with her new husband, Gina had agreed to stay in Monica's house and take over the house payments, eventually purchasing the house from her. Gina had been working for five months now, and she was attending church regularly. Monica was glad she was still going to be nearby if Gina needed help with raising Scotty.

Monica saw Anna glance at Dean Love periodically, and she was pleased that Anna appeared to have found the man of her dreams. Dean had recently proclaimed his love for Anna, and Monica hoped their relationship would lead to marriage.

John's friend Pete, as well as Aiden, wore tuxes as they stood opposite the bridesmaids. Scotty clutched his ring-bearer pillow, impatiently waiting for Monica. Beverly had also attended the wedding. Beverly was due to deliver the baby any day now, and Monica was glad that she could come to the wedding.

Monica thought John looked the finest of all. When she was finally standing in front of him, he kissed her before the wedding ceremony began.

Their pastor beamed at the couple as he performed the wedding service. After the short sermon was over, and their vows and rings had been exchanged, John kissed his bride again.

If you enjoyed Chocolate Dreams, then I'd appreciate it if you left a sweet one or two-sentence review on one of these Amazon links: Amazon US or Amazon UK! Reviews are often used by readers to find wonderful books. Thank you!

EXCERPT

CHAPTER 1

FRANKLIN REESE BANGED on the battered screen door. Where was everybody? As he pulled out his phone to check the time, he recalled the conversation he'd had with his boss that morning.

If the opening of the farm and ranch branch of their accounting firm proved successful…well… this could mean a partnership for him. Well, his boss didn't really *say* that but, he'd hinted. A partnership meant more money that he could use donate to a cause worthy of—

The loud bellow of a cow pierced the rancid air. He swallowed as he eyed the time. Nine o'clock. So, he wasn't late. He slid his phone back into his pocket. His stomach soured like curdled milk and his head pounded with pain. He needed to find the farmer and it appeared his new client may be in the barn with the bellowing cow. He might as well go find her. Taking a deep breath, he walked as fast as he could toward the barn. Another loud bellow pierced the air.

He approached the faded red barn and then stopped as soon as he spotted the big black and white cow suffering through a breach birth. Dumbfounded, he dropped his briefcase as he peered at the feet of the baby sticking out of the mother's bloody birth canal. A rope was looped around the legs of the young animal. A light brown woman pulled the rope so hard that the muscles in her slender arms flexed. Her eyes squeezed shut while she grunted, reminding him of the noises people made when they bench-pressed weights. She opened her eyes. "Casey, hold on," she cooed. As he watched the birth, his sour stomach worsened, and the bagel and cream cheese he'd managed to eat for breakfast felt like a dead weight in his belly.

Her tears mingled with the sweat rolling down her face. She continued to pull and glanced in his direction. "Oh, thank God you came. Come and help me."

Her light brown eyes pleaded with him. A plethora of unfamiliar scents tingled his nose. He swallowed, losing his voice. What was he supposed to do?

She continued to look at him, pulling on the rope periodically. "I already left a message on your answering service that it was coming out backward." Looked like he didn't have a choice. He may as well try to help her. This pretty farmer obviously had him confused with someone else, but, he couldn't focus on that right now. Pushing the door open, he entered the room adjoining the barn. His stomach clenched again. Hopefully, he wouldn't throw up. She nodded toward the rope, still tugging. "With both of us pulling, maybe we'll be able to get the calf out."

"Okay." He swallowed his nausea and pulled, mimicking the way he used to grunt when bench-pressing heavy weights. He followed her example, keeping tension on the rope and pulling each time the cow had a contraction. She grunted also, and their noises continued until the bloody calf slid out of the birth canal minutes later. She dropped the rope, and he rushed behind her to look at the young animal. He touched the newborn, awed by the birth. She glanced at him as she cleaned gunk off the calf's nose and mouth.

Her sigh filled the space when she noticed the animal was breathing. "Aren't you going to examine the cow and calf?"

Before he could respond, a young man holding a large black plastic tote entered the pen. "This the Cooper farm?"

She frowned and bit her lip as she glanced at him. She folded her arms in front of her chest as she quickly eyed Frank and the newcomer. The newcomer rushed to the baby cow and began examining it. "I'm Dr. Lindsey's son. I'm taking over my daddy's practice this week since he's on vacation. He told you that, didn't he?"

She nodded, still looking confused. "I left a message on your answering service earlier."

The vet grunted. "I was down the street at the horse farm helping out with another birth, so I couldn't leave."

"Are the cow and calf okay?"

"They both look fine." He stopped his examination and looked at them. "I'm glad you had somebody helping you. You might not have gotten him out in time if you'd been pulling him on your own." He pulled a tool out of his bag. "You have antibiotic on hand for the calf, right? If not, I've got some."

The attractive woman nodded, her dark hair clinging to her sweaty neck as she promised the vet she would give the new calf the medicine. Frank watched, mesmerized by the whole process. A short time later, the newborn nursed from the mother. "Thank you, doctor," said the woman, patting the man on the shoulder.

The doctor shook his head, placing his tools back into his bag. "Don't thank me. You two got him out in time." He hoisted his back. "Well, I've got another appointment. I'll send you your bill." Seconds later, the vet revved the engine of his battered pickup truck before speeding away.

She eyed Frank slowly, starting from his casual tan shoes, then to his khaki slacks and oxford shirt. She looked as if she'd never seen such clothing before. What was wrong with her? He supposed she'd been so busy birthing the cow that she'd not noticed that he wasn't dressed like a vet.

Noticing his bloody hands, she beckoned him

over to a room containing a sink and a large steel tank. After ripping off the long plastic gloves covering her hands and forearms and dropping them into the trash can, she turned the water on, pumped out several squirts of soap, and washed. "I thought you were the vet," she said, continuing to scrub her hands and forearms. "I've never met Dr. Lindsey's son, so that's why I assumed you were him." After rinsing, she pulled paper towels from a dispenser and gestured for Frank to use the sink.

Frank shrugged and walked to the sink, placing his hands under the running water. "Sorry. I helped you out, but I didn't have any idea if I was doing it right. It's probably good I showed up when I did. It looked like you'd been trying to help that cow for a long time."

She shook her head. "Cows are tough. They can be in labor for hours before giving birth. When you came, I'd just started pulling the calf out with the rope." She continued to stare, frowning. "Well, if you're not Dr. Lindsey's son, then who are you?" Good grief, it was downright ridiculous that she didn't seem to remember that she'd booked an appointment with his accounting firm. Maybe birthing that cow was making her forget about her financial affairs.

He offered his recently washed hand. He mentally sighed with relief. Good thing the nauseous feeling had evaporated from his stomach. He certainly didn't want to vomit on his attractive new client. "I'm Franklin Reese, Certified Public Accountant."

ORDER NOW

https://ceceliadowdy.com/milk-chocolate-kisseslp/

OTHER TITLES BY CECELIA DOWDY

THE BAKERY ROMANCE SERIES

Loving Luke *(Book 0)*
Raspberry Kisses *(Book 1)*
Shades of Chocolate *(Book 2)*
Sweet Dreams *(Book 3)*
Sugar and Spice *(Book 4)*
Southern Comfort *(Book 5)*
Sweet Delights *(Book 6)*
Cinnamon Kisses *(Book 7)*

THE CANDY BEACH SERIES

Caramel Kisses *(Book 0)*
Chocolate Dreams *(Book 1)*
Milk Chocolate Kisses *(Book 2)*
Bittersweet Dreams *(Book 3)*
Coffee and Kisses *(Book 4)*
Rocky Road Dreams *(Book 5)*

STANDALONE TITLES

The Bakery Bride
The Underground Railroad Brides Collection –
a historical romance novella collection

Courting the Doctor
A Teachers Heart –
a historical romance novella collection

Contact Cecelia Dowdy

Sign up for my newsletter:
https://ceceliadowdy.com/sign-up-for-my-email-list/

My website:
https://ceceliadowdy.com/

Social Media:
Facebook: *https://www.facebook.com/CeceliaDowdyAuthor/*
Twitter: *https://twitter.com/cdnovelist*

Let's discuss the Bible – visit my Sunday Brunch biblical discussions on my blog:
http://ceceliadowdy.com/blog/category/sunday-brunch

About Cecelia Dowdy

CECELIA DOWDY is a world traveler who has been an avid reader for as long as she can remember. When she first read Christian fiction, she felt called to write for the genre. She currently has several romance novels published in the Christian market. She loves to read, write, and bake desserts in her spare time. Cecelia currently resides with her husband and son in Maryland.